Instinct and the Unconscious

W.H.R.Rivers

Table of contents

Appendix

This book has two parts. The first gives the substance of lectures delivered in the Psychological Laboratory at Cambridge in the summer of 1919, and repeated in the spring of the present year at the Phipps Clinic of the Johns Hopkins Medical School, Baltimore, under the direction of Professor Adolf Meyer. The second part consists of appendices in which are republished occasional papers written as the result of clinical experience gained during the war. A few alterations have been made in these, chiefly in order to bring the terminology into line with that adopted in the body of the book, and in the second Appendix the original paper has been amplified. A few of the opinions expressed in these appendices differ in some respects from those of the lectures, but have been left as originally stated because they present alternative points of view which may possibly be nearer the truth than those adopted as the result of later deliberation.

The general aim of the book is to put into a biological setting the system of psycho-therapy which came to be generally adopted in Great Britain in the treatment of the psycho-neuroses of war. This system was developed in the main at the Maghull Military Hospital under the direction of Dr. R.G. Rows, to whom I owe my introduction to this branch of medicine and my thanks for much help and guidance when serving under him as medical officer.

My thanks are also due in especial measure to Dr. W. H. Bryce, who was in charge of Craiglockhart War Hospital while I was working there. That hospital gave an unrivalled opportunity for gaining experience of the psycho-neuroses of war, and any use that I was able to make of that opportunity, [p. vi] in spite of serious difficulties, is due to the never-failing help a~td encouragement of Dr. Bryce.

I am greatly indebted to the Medical Research Committee (now the Medical Research Council) for the assistance which made it possible for me to work at Maghull and with the Royal Air Force. I am glad also to express my thanks to the Medical Department of the R.A.F. for the opportunity of acquiring experience in the varied psychological problems presented by Aviation in time of war, and to my colleagues in that Force for their help in making use of this experience.

I am indebted for permission to publish the appendices to the editors of the Lancet and Psychoanalytic Review, to the Royal Society of Medicine, the National Committee of Mental Hygiene of the United States, the Medical Research Council, and the Medical Department of the Royal Air Force.

W.H.R. RIVERS.
St. John's College, Cambridge, July 15, 1920.

In the secondary title of this book I have indicated that one of its main aims is to give a biological view of the psycho-neuroses. My purpose is to bring functional disorders of the mind and nervous system into relation with the concepts concerning their normal mode of working, which are held by the biologist and the physiologist. It will, I hope, help my readers to understand this purpose if I sketch briefly the conditions out of which this aim arose, and the general lines of the process by which the study of a certain group of the psycho-neuroses has led me to the views here set forth.

One of the most striking features of the war from which we have recently emerged -- perhaps its most important feature from the medical point of view -- has been the enormous scale on which it produced those disturbances of nervous and mental function which are grouped together by the physician under the heading of psycho-neurosis. The striking success in coping with the infectious diseases, which in all other recent wars have been far more deadly than the weapons of the enemy, shows that modern medicine war prepared for this aspect of the war, and had ready for use the main lines of treatment which would take the sting from these scourges of warfare. Surgery also was forewarned and forearmed for its task of dealing with the wounds inflicted by modern weapons. Any increase in the deadly power of these weapons is due to the greater number they can reach rather than to the greater deadliness of the injuries they inflict upon the individual. Though surgery has made great advances during [p. 2] the war, these are only developments for which the surgeon was prepared and involved no radical alteration in his outlook.

The case is very different when we turn to the field presented by psycho-neurosis. Though the Russo-Japanese war might have led physicians to expect psycho-neurosis on an extensive scale, the medical administration of our own and other armies was wholly unprepared for the vast extent and varied forms in which modern warfare is able to upset the higher functions of the nervous system and the mental activity of those called upon to take part in it. Moreover, before the war, the psycho-neuroses had interested few practitioners of medicine. Common as these disorders are in civil life, they are left almost without notice in medical education, while those who had paid special attention to the subject were torn asunder by fierce differences of opinion, not only concerning the nature of these disturbances of nervous and mental function, but also in regard to the practical measures by which they might be treated or prevented. The outbreak of the war found the medical profession with no such common body of principles and measures as those which enabled Medicine and Surgery to deal so successfully with the more material effects of warfare upon the human organism.

In accordance with the general materialistic tendency of medicine the first stage of this branch of the medical history of the war was to ascribe the psycho-neuroses of warfare to the concussions of shell-explosion, an attitude crystallised in the unfortunate and misleading term "shell-shock" which the general public have now come to use for the nervous disturbances of warfare. It soon became clear, however, that the great majority of the functional nervous disorders of warfare are not traumatic in the strict sense, but occur in pronounced forms either in the complete absence of any physical shock, or after exposure to shell explosions of a kind very unlikely to have caused physical injury. It became evident that the shell-explosion or other event which forms the immediate antecedent of the illness is only the spark which sets into activity a morbid process for which the mental stresses and strains of warfare have long prepared the ground. Once it is recognised that the essential [p. 3] causes of the psycho-neuroses of warfare are mental, and not physical, it becomes the task of the physician to discover the exact nature of the mental processes involved, and the mechanisms by which these processes are so disordered as to produce the vast diversity of forms in which the morbid state appears.

In civilian practice cases of psycho-neurosis fall into two chief groups set up by very different conditions. One of these groups, usually called traumatic neurasthenia, is especially known as the sequel of railway accidents, and since this form of neurosis closely resembles that due to warfare, our knowledge of war-neurosis might have advanced more rapidly if this had been taken as a guide. Owing, however, to its comparative rarity, the traumatic form of psycho-neurosis was less known than that arising out of the stresses and strains of ordinary life. Progress in our knowledge of this second group was hindered by wide differences of opinion concerning the nature of the factors to which its various forms are due. Many failed to recognise that, though the essential pathology of war-neurosis must be the same as that of civil practice, the factors concerned in this pathology might be very different.

The situation was especially complicated by the existence of a definite theory of psycho-neurosis which, though it succeeded in bringing into a co-ordinated scheme the vast diversity of form in which functional nervous and mental disorders become manifest, had yet not merely failed to meet with general acceptance, but was the subject of hostility exceptional even in the history of medicine. This hostility was almost entirely due to the fact that the author of the theory, Sigmund Freud of Vienna, found the essential cause of every psycho-neurosis in some disturbance of sexual function. Further, the process of psycho-analysis, which formed Freud's chief instrument, of inquiry, led him to the view that these disturbances of sexual function often went back to the first few years of life and implied a sexuality of the infant which became an especial ground for the hostility and ridicule of his opponents. At the beginning of the war the medical profession of this and other countries [p. 4] was divided into two sharply opposed groups; one, small in size, which accepted the general principles of Freud, either in their original form or as modified by Jung and other disciples; the other, comprising the vast majority of the profession, who not merely rejected the stress laid upon the sexual, but in setting this aside refused to attend to many features of Freud's scheme which could hardly have failed to appeal to them if they had been able dispassionately to face the situation.

Among the laity Freud's views met with a greater interest and a wider acceptance. In some cases this acceptance was founded on observations furnished by the study of dreams or of such, occurrence of everyday life, as had been so ably used by Freud to support his scheme, but inability to study the main line of evidence upon which the Freudian system was based prevented the interest of these students from being more than that of the amateur.

The frequency of the psycho-neuroses of war brought the subject within the reach of many who had hitherto taken no special interest in this branch of medicine, while in other cases, those whose interest had hitherto been of an amateur kind were now brought into contact with clinical material by which they were enabled to test in detail the Freudian doctrine of psycho-neurosis. The opportunity thus afforded to independent and unbiassed [sic] workers had certain definite results. Freud's work, in so far as it deals with psycho-neurosis, has two main aspects. As in every scheme of a pathological kind we can distinguish between the conditions or causes of the morbid process and the mechanisms by which these conditions produce the manifestations or symptoms of disease. In the heat engendered by differences of opinion concerning the conditions of psycho-neurosis, the pathological mechanisms had been neglected and had aroused little interest, a neglect which is readily intelligible, for few will find it worth while to study the details of a structure resting on foundations they reject.

The first result of the dispassionate study of the psycho-neuroses of warfare, in relation to Freud's scheme, was to show that in the vast majority of cases there is no reason to suppose [p. 5] that factors derived from the sexual life played any essential part in causation, but that these disorders became explicable as the result of disturbance of another instinct, one even more fundamental than that of sex-the instinct of self-preservation especially those forms of it which are adapted to protect the animal from danger. Warfare makes fierce onslaughts on an instinct or group of instincts which is rarely touched by the ordinary life of the member of a modern civilised community. War calls into activity processes and tendencies which in its absence would have lain wholly dormant.

The danger-instincts, as they may be called, are not only fundamental, but they are far simpler both in their nature and their effect than the instincts which are concerned in continuing the species or maintaining the harmony of society. The awakening of the danger-instincts by warfare produces forms of psycho-neurosis far simpler than those of civil life, which depend in the main on disturbance of the other two great groups of instinct. The simplicity of the conditions upon which the psycho-neuroses of war depend makes it easier to discern the mechanisms by which these conditions produce their effects. Those who were able to approach the subject without prejudice could not fail to see how admirably adapted are many of the mechanisms put forward by Freud to explain how the conditions underlying a morbid state produce the symptoms through which the state becomes manifest. It seemed as if Freud's mechanisms might have been obvious to all, or at least might have met with far earlier acceptance, if war-neurosis had been of habitual occurrence and civil neurosis had occurred only as the result of occasional catastrophes. The aim of this book is to consider these mechanisms in their relation to the more normal processes of the animal organism, and especially to the mechanism by which certain parts of experience become so separated from the rest that they are no longer capable of recall to consciousness by the ordinary processes of memory. Psycho-neurosis depends essentially upon the abnormal activity of processes which do not ordinarily enter into consciousness, and the special aim of this book is to consider the general biological function of the process [p. 6] by which experience passes into the region of the unconscious. I shall attempt to show that the main function of psycho-neurosis is the solution of a conflict between opposed and incompatible principles of mental activity. Instinctive processes and tendencies, and experience associated therewith, pass into the unconscious whenever the incompatibility passes certain limits. As indicated in the title, the special aim of the book is to study the relation between instinct and that body of experience we are accustomed to speak of collectively as "the unconscious." In this study the first task is to make as clear as possible the senses in which these terms will be used and this will be the aim of the following chapters.

The concept of "the unconscious" in psychology is one which has aroused the liveliest differences of opinion and has been met by bitter opposition. Even those who are ready to accept the vast influence of unconscious factors in psychology may well be appalled by the difficulties of treating the unconscious in a scientific manner and fitting so necessarily hypothetical a factor into the explanation of behaviour. One line of opposition has come from advocates of the older introspective school of psychologists who have found it difficult to fit an unconscious region of the mind into their schemes of description and explanation. The aim of the older psychology was to furnish a rational explanation of human behaviour and endeavour. As the material for such explanation they used almost exclusively the happenings in their own minds, which could be directly, though really only retrospectively, observed, and made this material the basis of constructions whereby they fitted into coherent schemes the infinitely varied experience of the human mind. When their introspective method failed them, and they were driven to assume the existence of factors lying outside those accessible to introspection, they were accustomed to assume subconscious processes, or to speak of psychological dispositions and tendencies, or they would even throw psychology wholly aside, bringing into their schemes of explanation factors belonging to the wholly different order of the material world, and used physiological processes as links in the chain whereby they connected one psychological happening with another.

Those who adopted subconscious processes as elements of their constructions, viz., processes which only differed from other [p. 8] mental processes in the lesser degree of distinctness and clearness with which they could be observed, paid in this way lip-service to the supposed essential character of consciousness in psychology, but failed to recognise that they were only evading a difficulty by clinging to a simulacrum of the conscious, the existence of which was just as hypothetical as any of the constructions of the thoroughgoing advocates of the unconscious.

Those who spoke of psychological dispositions, or going still further, adopted physiological dispositions in their place, were also positing purely hypothetical factors where those open to direct observation failed them. These measures were only means by which these psychologists and psycho-physiologists escaped from the necessity of facing the difficulties presented by many aspects of animal and human behaviour, and especially those presented in Man by the phenomena of disease.

It is noteworthy that the due recognition of the importance of the unconscious and the first comprehensive attempt to formulate a scheme of its organisation and of the mechanisms by which it is brought into relation with the conscious should have come from those whose business it is to deal with the morbid aspect of the human mind. The necessity for the use of unconscious factors continually arises when dealing with the experience of health, but the opportunities afforded by such experience are usually so fleeting, and the experience itself often so apparently trivial, that they failed to force the psychologist of the normal to face the situation. It was only when unconscious experience had contributed to wreck a life or produce a state with which the physician had to struggle, and then often ineffectually, for months or years that it became impossible to push such experience aside or take any other line than that involved in the full recognition of its existence. It is only the urgent and inevitable needs of the sick that have driven the physician into the full recognition of the unconscious, while it has needed the vast scale on which nervous and mental disorders have been produced in the war to force this recognition upon more than the few specialists to whom it had been previously confined. [p. 9]

 In entering upon an attempt to make clear the sense in which the term "unconscious" will be used in this book, I will begin by pointing out one sense in which it will not be used. At any given moment we are only clearly conscious of the experience which is in the focus of attention. This forms only an infinitesimal proportion of the experience which is capable, by being brought into the focus of attention, of becoming conscious with an equal degree of clearness. Again, at any one moment a much larger amount of experience is within the region of the conscious though less clearly, but even the largest amount which can thus I be brought within the outermost fringe of consciousness at any instant or even within any brief space of time, forms but a very small proportion of that which, with other directions of the attention, could come into the field of consciousness. At any given instant there is a vast body of experience which is not in consciousness because at that instant it is neither the object of attention nor so connected therewith as to occupy consciousness with more or less clearness at the same time. Experience of this kind will not be included within "the unconscious" as the term is used in this book. In so far as the term "the unconscious" applies to experience, it will be limited to such as is not capable of being brought into the field of consciousness by any of the ordinary processes of memory or association, but can only be recalled under certain special conditions, such as sleep, hypnotism, the method of free association, and certain pathological states.

 The kind of experience which will form the main subject-matter of this book may best be illustrated by some examples.

 A good instance of the unconscious is afforded by the conditions underlying the claustrophobia of a sufferer from war-neurosis, whose case is described in full in Appendix II. as long as he could remember, this patient had been subject to a dread of confined spaces so severe, and producing states so painful and unendurable, that he was debarred from taking part in many of the ordinary occupations of life, or could do so only at the risk of suffering and discomfort. When his profession as a doctor took him at the age of thirty to the front his specific [p. 10] dread was brought into pronounced activity by the necessity of working in dug-outs, and the strain so produced formed a most important factor in producing a state of anxiety-neurosis. During a course of treatment to discover the origin of his claustrophobia, there came to the patient's consciousness an experience at the age of four in which he had been confined in a narrow passage with no means of escape from a dog by which he was terrified. In spite of attempts, continued over several years, to discover some experience of childhood which could explain his symptoms, this memory of the dog in a passage had wholly failed to appear in consciousness, and was only brought to memory by a special procedure. We have no direct evidence that the incident had been wholly unconscious during childhood, but owing to his prolonged search for such experience at a later period of life, and its total failure to appear in consciousness, we have the most decisive evidence that an arresting experience, one accompanied by an emotional state of the most poignant kind, can lie dormant and evade the most searching attempts to bring it into the field of consciousness. When it was at last recalled, this did not happen through any association of waking life but came in the semi-waking state following a dream. Its coming to consciousness occurred in definite connection with an experience of sleep which we know to furnish conditions especially favourable to emergence from the unconscious.

This patient not only affords conclusive evidence for the existence of experience shut off from consciousness under ordinary conditions, but his case shows that this experience, though inaccessible to consciousness directly, may yet be capable of affecting it indirectly. His dread of confined spaces had so definite a relation to the early experience that the two were undoubtedly connected, while the complete disappearance of his claustrophobia, after bringing the long dormant experience to the surface, affords further, though standing alone, not necessarily conclusive, evidence in the same direction.

Psychological literature contains many similar histories. I take this case of claustrophobia as an example, partly because, having come under my own notice, I am able to estimate its [p. 11] trustworthiness. Still more important is the fact that it was possible to obtain conclusive evidence that the infantile experience had really occurred, and was neither the fancy of the patient nor the result of suggestion on the part of the physician, the latter possibility being especially present when a supposed experience of childhood is discovered by means of hypnotism.

The records of others can never, however, carry the conviction which comes from one's own experience, even though such experience can rarely have the dramatic and conclusive character of my case of claustrophobia. One who wishes to satisfy himself whether or no unconscious experience exists should subject his own life-history to the severest scrutiny, either aided by another in a course of psycho-analysis or, though less satisfactory and less likely to convince, by a process of self-analysis. It will perhaps be instructive if I give a result of my own self-analysis, which though at present incomplete, has done much to convince me of the reality of the unconscious.

I am one of those persons whose normal waking life is almost wholly free from sensory imagery, either visual, auditory, tactile or of any other kind. Through the experience of dreams, of the half-waking, half-sleeping state, and of slight delirium in fever, I am quite familiar with imagery, especially of a visual kind, which, so far as I can tell, corresponds with that of the normal experience of others. I am able to recognise also that in the fully waking state I have imagery of the same order, but in general it is so faint and fragmentary that the closest scrutiny is required for its detection. It is clear to me that if it were not for my special knowledge and interest I should be wholly ignorant of its existence. On looking back in my life I am aware that my mental imagery was more definite in youth, and I can remember the presence at that period of fairly vivid visual imagery in connection with certain kinds of experience, especially of an emotional kind.

Some years ago, as part of an examination into my memories of childhood, I discovered that I had a more definite knowledge of the topography of the house I left at the age of five than of [p. 12] any of the many houses I have lived in since. I can make a plan of that house far more detailed, based on memories clearer to myself, than I can make of houses in which I have lived far longer and at times of life when one might expect more permanent and vivid memories. Moreover, I can even now obtain visual images of the early house more clear and definite than any I usually experience, while other memories of my first five years bring with them imagery more definite than accompany the memories of later life. I have concluded, and I think I am justified in doing so, that before the age of five my visual imagery was far more definite than it became later and was perhaps as good as that of the average child.

 For some time I explained the loss of imagery of which I am the subject as part of a process by which I had become especially interested in the abstract. I supposed that my imagery had faded for lack of the attention and interest which would have kept it active, even if they had not promoted its development into the instrument which imagery has become in the mental life of the majority of human beings. It is only during the last year or two that I have discovered an aspect of my early experience which has led me to revise this earlier opinion. This discovery is that my knowledge of the house I left when five years old is strictly limited to certain parts of it, and that the rest of the building is even more inaccessible to memory than any of the houses in which I have lived since. So far as I remember the house had three floors. I can remember, and even now image fairly vividly, every room, passage and doorway of the ground-floor. I can in imagination go downstairs into a kitchen in a basement and I can go upstairs towards the upper door, but when I reach the top of the stairs I come to the absolutely unknown, an unknown far more complete than is the case with any house occupied more recently, where I have some idea of the topography, though this is inexact and vague. For more than two years I have been attempting, by means which have succeeded in evoking other early experience, to penetrate into the mysterious unknown of the upper storey. Though I have recalled many incidents of my early life which took place on the [p. 13] ground-floor, in the basement, in the regions before and behind the house, no event of any kind which happened in the upper storey has ever come to my consciousness. Now and then, when in the half-waking, half-sleeping state, peculiarly favourable in my experience to the recovery of long-forgotten events, I have had the sense that something is there, lying very near emergence into consciousness. But I have not yet succeeded in penetrating the veil which separates me from all knowledge of my life in that upper storey.

 The evidence for the existence of unconscious experience which is provided by these memories of my infancy is, of course, incomplete, in that I have not yet discovered the nature of the unconscious experience and have even no certain guarantee that it exists. The feature of the experience which impresses me -- I cannot expect it to have an equal influence on others -- is the completeness of the blank in my mind in connection with that upper storey. I fail to explain that blank by any mechanism provided by differences in the effect of interest on memory. A psychologist of the old school would probably say that we tend especially to remember the striking and unusual, and that it is therefore natural that my memories of the upper storey, where I probably passed most of my life at that time, should be less vivid than those of the lower parts of the house, which I visited less often. This might well explain a different degree of distinctness of memory, but it cannot explain the completeness of the blank left by the memories of the upper storey. Another line which might be taken is that, at any rate during the year before I left the house, I lived on the ground-floor during the day and only visited the upper floor at night when tired. But even if such a reason were valid, it cannot explain the completeness of the blank. Moreover, such explanations seem to be put out of court by the fact that when I recall memories of houses lived in later, I find no such difference between upper and lower storeys. Though my memories of later houses are more vague than the early memory, they are quite as definite for the upper as for the lower parts of the buildings.

 The two cases I have given are examples of the experience of [p. 14] early life which has become inaccessible to consciousness. This period of life is especially apt to afford occasions for experiences to become unconscious, but the passing of experience into the unconscious may happen at any age, and its occurrence has been brought to notice very widely by the experience of war. One of the most frequent features of the nervous disturbances of war has been the complete blotting out of the memories of certain events, the obliteration usually extending considerably beyond the event which furnished its special occasion. In some cases, where the loss of memory for a period of the soldier's life has been produced by physical shock accompanied by complete unconsciousness, as in cerebral concussion, the obliteration has been complete, and the case does not come within the scope of this book, for there is no evidence that any experience exists capable of being again brought to consciousness. In many cases, however, in which the obliteration is due to mental shock or other physical factors, the experience which is inaccessible to the consciousness of the subject under the usual conditions of memory has been recovered in the hypnotic state or by the method of free association or has expressed itself, usually in a distorted form, in dreams. In such cases soldiers have lost the entire memory of their lives from some moment preceding a shock or severe strain until they have found themselves in hospital, perhaps weeks later, although during at least part of the intervening time they may have been to all appearance fully conscious and may even have distinguished themselves by actions on the field of which they have no recollection. Although these memories may remain for months or years quite inaccessible to memory when approached by the ordinary channels, they may be brought to the surface by means of hypnotism or by the method of free association.

In a case of a somewhat different kind under my care a soldier had lost all memory of his life from a day in July when he was training in England until the following January when he found himself in hospital in Egypt, having no recollection whatever of his service in various parts of England, of the voyage to Egypt, or of his life in Egypt before going to hospital. The memory [p. 15] of this period was not recovered until more than a year later following the disclosure of a painful experience in his life which had a definite connection with his amnesia.

In cases such as these the loss of memory forms part of the complex group of changes which make up the state we call psycho-neurosis. There is reason to believe that many of the manifestations or symptoms of this state are due to the activity of the experience which has become unconscious, just as the dread of my claustrophobic patient has been ascribed to the unconscious experience of which he was the subject at the age of four. The effects which can be thus ascribed, at any rate in part, to the unconscious experience of war, fall into two main groups. There are, on the one hand, general changes in personality, and changes in tastes, in likes and dislikes, in preferences and prejudices, while on the other hand, there are specific dreads or other morbid experiences of waking or sleeping life, such as nightmares, hallucinations or morbid impulses, which can be more or less directly ascribed to the activity of the unconscious experience. In such cases we have definite evidence, not merely for the existence of unconscious experience, but for its activity, or capacity for activity, in this unconscious state.

I will conclude this chapter by considering a way in which the term "unconscious" is often used which I shall endeavour to avoid. If an idea springs spontaneously into the mind without obvious antecedents in consciousness we are accustomed to speak of this mode of appearance as unconscious. Again, when a person behaves in a manner which corresponds to something taking place in the mind of another person, but is not wholly, or perhaps not at all, determined by anything in the mind of the behaver, we regard the behaviour as due to the suggestion of the second person and we are accustomed to speak of this process of suggestion as unconscious. In these instances the antecedent of the thought or behaviour may, and probably does, come from the unconscious, in the sense already proposed, either of the person who experiences the thought or of the person by whom the behaviour is suggested, but it is a question whether it is convenient to use the term "unconscious " for the [p. 16] process by which the thought or the behaviour is promoted. It is only necessary to point out that in such a case we are speaking of a change being set up in consciousness unconsciously to see how unsatisfactory is this usage and how little relation there is between the use of the word "unconscious" in this sense and that in which I propose that it shall be used. I shall not, therefore, call such processes as I have mentioned unconscious, but shall make use of a special term to denote them and shall speak of them as "unwitting." When a thought or feeling comes into the mind without antecedents in consciousness so that we suppose it to have come from the unconscious, I shall not speak of the thought as having arisen unconsciously but unwittingly. Similarly, I shall speak of the process of suggestion as taking place unwittingly and not unconsciously, leaving open how far the source of the suggested thought or behaviour is in the "unconscious" as the term will be used in this book.

In the last chapter I have attempted to make clear the sense in which I shall speak of "the unconscious" in this book. I have illustrated its nature by three kinds of example; one taken from a definitely pathological state dependent on an experience of early life; the second derived from my own history, also derived from the unconscious experience of early life, but one which may be regarded as coming within the limits of normal psychology; while the others are taken from cases of psycho-neurosis in which the experience which has become unconscious is made up of the events and memories of warfare. I have now to consider how such experience becomes and remains unconscious.

The first process to be considered is that by which experience becomes unconscious. I shall speak of this process as suppression. Writers on the unconscious often use "repression" for the process in question, but I propose to reserve this term for the process by which we wittingly endeavour to banish experience from consciousness. It seems that this process of witting repression may be one means of producing suppression, that experience wittingly repressed may, at any rate under certain conditions, succeed in becoming suppressed and inaccessible to the general body of consciousness. But there is little doubt that this is only one of the ways in which suppression occurs, and that more often it takes place wholly without the intervention of volition, especially when it occurs as the result of some physical or mental shock. We are still in much uncertainty concerning the exact mechanism by which suppression occurs, but there is reason to believe that in the majority of [p. 18] cases it takes place without conscious effort, or according to the terminology I propose to use, unwittingly. There is even some reason to believe that suppression only follows witting repression, when conditions of some other kind favourable to suppression are present. One of the chief aims of this book is to discover the nature and biological significance of the mechanism of suppression.

One line of inquiry which may be used to this end is the comparison of suppression with the ordinary process of forgetting. Suppression is only one form of forgetting -- a form in which the forgetting is especially complete -- and light should be thrown upon the nature of suppression by a general study of the process by which we forget. Formerly psychologists were especially concerned with the process by which we remember, but they have gradually been coming to recognise that the more important problem is to discover how and why we forget. It is one of the many merits of Freud[1] that he has thrown much light on this problem and with a wealth of examples has illustrated the complex nature of forgetting in the ordinary course of daily life. According to him forgetting is not a passive process, dependent on lack of interest and meaning, or varying with the intensity of an impression, but is an active process in which some part of the mental content is suppressed. The content which is thus suppressed does not disappear because it is uninteresting or unimportant; on the contrary, it is usually of very special interest and has a very definite meaning. It is suppressed because the interest and meaning are of a kind which arouse pain or discomfort and, if present in consciousness, would set up activities which would be painful or uncomfortable. Active forgetting is thus a protective process or mechanism, one by which consciousness is protected from influences which would interfere with the harmony essential to pleasure or comfort. The examples of the unconscious which were recorded in the last chapter are only pronounced examples of a similar process. Just as we tend to forget an appointment which seems likely to be the occasion of a quarrel or forget to write a letter [p. 19] which involves the undertaking of an unpleasant responsibility, so we may suppose that the painful experience of my claustrophobic patient was forgotten because the memories of the passage and the dog were so painful as to interfere with his happiness. The completeness of the suppression may have been due to the fact that the interference with the comfort of the child was so great as seriously to disturb his health. In the case of my own experience it is not possible to say why the memory of the upper floor has been forgotten, since I do not yet know the nature of the suppressed experience, but we can be fairly confident that it was of an unpleasant kind and was forgotten because the memory of it interfered with my comfort and happiness. The memories which disappear in war-neurosis are always of happenings so distressing that the most painful emotions arise when the happenings are recalled. The conclusion to which we are led both by the experience of everyday life and by the analysis of pathological and semi-pathological states is that there is no difference in nature between the forgetting of he [sic] unpleasant experience of ordinary life, often quite trivial in character, and such examples of complete and life-long suppression as those which I have chosen to illustrate the nature of the unconscious.

 If these two kinds of forgetting are essentially alike, if they furnish the two ends of a continuous series, a study of the forgetting of everyday life should provide a means of understanding the suppression which occurs in pathological states. If we attempt such a study the first point which may be noticed is that the active forgetting of everyday life is not voluntary and intentional, but is essentially a process which takes place unwittingly. If we try to forget an appointment which we expect to lead to a quarrel, or try to forget a letter undertaking an unpleasant responsibility, we should not succeed. We should probably only fix these duties the more firmly in our memories. It is characteristic of the active forgetting of which Freud has provided such a wealth of examples[2] that it occurs spontaneously. In such instances as I have given, we do not know that [p. 20] we have forgotten. It is only when we are reminded of the missed appointment, or the overdue letter, that we become aware of the lapse. In other cases, as when we forget the name or address of a correspondent to whom we should write, we know that we have forgotten, but the act of forgetting has still been involuntary and unwitting.

 The pathological suppression taking place in adult life seems in most cases to be clearly involuntary and unwitting. The most complete cases of suppression do not occur in people who have tried consciously to repress painful experience, but have come about without any conscious activity on the part of the sufferer, especially as the result of shock or illness. Hypnotism furnishes a striking example of the process by which experience is suppressed. By means of suggestion given in the hypnotic state any experience, pleasant or painful, which occurs during this state may be banished from the memory. When this has been done the hypnotised person is quite unable to recall the experience, and it will remain unconscious until he is again hypnotised or until the experience is recalled under some other condition in which unconscious suppressed experience comes to the surface. In this case the suppression takes place independently of the will of the hypnotised person, but there is reason to believe that the suggestion to forget is more likely to be successful, the more the forgetting is in consonance with the conscious wishes of the subject. This probably gives the clue to the fact that conscious repression seems often to lead to suppression. The suppression itself is unwitting, but the wish of the sufferer for suppression assists the process, or at least helps in its maintenance and completeness.

 I have now to consider a characteristic of active forgetting and suppression which is of great importance in understanding its nature. The experience which tends to be forgotten or repressed is the immediately painful. If we forget an appointment or a letter in connection with which we anticipate unpleasant emotions, the ultimate consequences may be even more unpleasant than the immediate experience from which we escape by the act of forgetting. If we were able to consider rationally the consequences [p. 21] of the lapse, we should find that in most cases the I course which would give us least trouble and inconvenience is the long run would be to keep the appointment or write the letter. The process of active forgetting, however, takes no account of these ultimate consequences, but is directed exclusively towards the avoidance of the more immediate pains and discomforts. The same seems to be true of cases of pathological suppression. If, as I suppose, the claustrophobia of my patient was the result of the suppression of his four-year-old experience, there can be little doubt that the sum-total of unhappiness due to his dreads was far greater than that which would have resulted from the immediate memories of his terror when in the passage with the dog. The memory was suppressed because of its immediately painful character, and in following this course Nature took no account of the effects of the suppression which were to torment the child and man for thirty years. The suppressions which form so large an element in the neuroses of war we also directed to allow escape from the immediately unpleasant, regardless of future consequences. Suppression is a process of reaction to the pleasures and pains which are immediately present, and takes no account of the more extended experience with which it is the function of intelligence to deal.

Footnotes

[1] See Appendix I.
[2] The Psychopathology of Everyday Life.

The examples of the unconscious and of its instrument, suppression, which have been given in the last two chapters, have been taken from aspects of experience which belong clearly to the domain of psychology, and involve mental processes of a relatively high order. I propose now to consider the relation between the suppression of psychological experience and certain physiological processes. I will begin with an example drawn from the borderland between the psychological and the physiological, one dealing with the sensory concomitants of nervous process in a case of experimental interference with the integrity of the nervous system.

Observations on the sensory changes which accompany the regeneration of a divided and reunited nerve have led Head and his colleagues to distinguish two different kinds of mechanism on the afferent side of the nervous system.[1] Prolonged observations after the division of nerves in Head's own arm brought out clearly the existence of two definite stages in the return of sensibility. In one of these, the protopathic stage, the sensations are vague and crude in character, with absence of any exactness in discrimination or localisation and with a pronounced feeling-tone, usually on the unpleasant side, tending to lead immediately, as if reflexly, to such movements as would withdraw the stimulated part from contact with any object to which the sensory changes are due. At this stage of the healing of the reunited nerve there are present none of those characters of sensation by which we recognise the nature of an object in contact with the body. The sensations are such as would enable one to know [p. 23] that something is there and that it is pleasant or unpleasant. It is also possible to distinguish between mere contact or pressure and stimulation by heat or cold, but within each of these modes of sensation there is no power of distinguishing differences in intensity nor of telling with any exactness the spot where the processes underlying the sensory changes are in action.

The second stage of the process of regeneration is characterised by the return of those features of normal cutaneous sensibility, such as exact discrimination and localisation, by means of which it becomes possible to perceive the nature of an object in contact with the skin and adjust behaviour according to this perception. The modes of reaction which make this exactness of discrimination and power of external projection possible are grouped together under the heading of epicritic sensibility. In interpreting these observations two chief possibilities are open. Epicritic sensibility may be only a greater perfection of protopathic sensibility, experience gradually enabling an exactness of discrimination and localisation which were not at first possible. The other alternative is that the two kinds of sensibility represent two distinct stages in the development of the afferent nervous system. According to this second view the special conditions of the experiment revealed in the individual two widely different stages in the evolution of cutaneous sensibility. Many features of the experiment point strongly to the truth of the second of these alternatives. The way in which epicritic sensibility returns and the fact that it is possible to annul it by treatment affecting only the peripheral factors, without influence on such central processes as would be set up by experience,[2] go far to show that the two modes of sensibility represent two stages in phylogenetic development.

All that we know of the protopathic stage is consistent with its being the representative of the sensibility of an animal which possesses only the power of becoming aware of changes of a crude kind and, according as these changes are pleasant or unpleasant, of reacting at once by such mass-movements as would take it nearer to, or remove it from, the source of the stimulation. If [p. 24] there is only capacity for such mass-movements, there will be no necessity for the discrimination which would enable the exact perception of the nature of the object. There would be a definite correlation between the crude nature of the sensibility and the limited capacity for behaviour possessed by the animal.

Epicritic sensibility, on the other hand, is adapted to behaviour of a far more complex and delicate kind. The sensations do not merely tell the animal or man that something is there and set up the crude mass-movements of approach or withdrawal, but they enable the many forms of reaction which become possible when the exact nature of the stimulating object is recognised.

It is not necessary for my present purpose to consider these two possibilities fully. Whatever be the interpretation of the two stages, there is no doubt as to their existence, and my present object is to point out certain special features of the relation between the two. When epicritic sensibility returns, the earlier protopathic sensibility does not persist unaltered side by side with the later development, but undergoes certain definite modifications. Some of its elements persist and combine with elements of the epicritic stage to form features of normal cutaneous sensibility. Thus, the cold and heat of the protopathic stage blend with the modes of temperature sensibility proper to the epicritic stage, and form the graded series of temperature sensations which we are normally able to discriminate. The crude touch of the protopathic system blends with the more delicate epicritic sensibility of this kind, while protopathic pain, with its peculiarly uncomfortable rather than acute quality, forms a much larger element in the normal sensibility to pain. In this process of blending or fusion certain aspects of the earlier forms of sensibility are modified to a greater or less extent, and in some cases this modification involves the disappearance of certain characters. This disappearance is especially striking and complete in the case of the spatial attributes of protopathic sensibility. In the protopathic stage (when the sensibility of deeper structures is excluded) there is no power of exact localisation. When a point of the skin is stimulated the sensation radiates widely and is often localised at a [p. 25] considerable distance from the actual place of stimulation. These two characters of radiation and distant reference disappear with the return of epicritic sensibility, and afford examples of a process of suppression comparable with that considered in the last chapter. Moreover, these spatial features of protopathic sensibility do not disappear entirely, but persist in a latent form ready to come again into consciousness if the appropriate conditions are present. This was well illustrated by certain experiments made shortly after the return of epicritic sensibility.[3] At this time, when radiation and reference were completely absent at the ordinary temperature of the room, they could be again brought into existence by cooling the limb. Characters of sensibility which a few minutes before had so disappeared from consciousness so they could not be elicited by any kind of stimulus, were again brought to consciousness when the controlling epicritic system, but lately returned and not having yet attained its normal stability, was put out of action by the application of cold. When the limb was warmed the radiation and reference disappeared, but were again made manifest when the limb was once more cooled. In this state of enhanced vulnerability of the lately recovered epicritic sensibility, it was possible to produce suppression experimentally. Moreover, if the whole process of regeneration is interpreted as the manifestation of an early stage of the development of the nervous system, it will follow that the potentiality for the radiation and reference of localisation had been present throughout the life of the subject, but in so complete a state of suppression that we only became aware of their existence through a special experimental procedure. The experiment revealed a feature of primitive sensibility which had been so successfully suppressed that its existence had not been suspected until the beginning of the twentieth century, though radiation and reference in other parts of the body, where they have not been so completely suppressed, might have led students to its recognition.[4]

Another interesting and rather more complex example of suppression became evident in Head's experiment.[5] On the normal skin stimulation by a temperature of 40°C.-44°C. produces a pleasant sensation of heat free from any element of pain, and this effect was present on the dorsum of Head's thumb after epicritic sensibility had returned. The index knuckle lingered in its recovery behind the thumb, so that at one stage of the experiment when epicritic sensibility was present on the thumb, it was still absent on the index knuckle. At this time stimulation of the knuckle by cold produced a referred sensation of cold on the dorsum of the thumb. When the two regions were stimulated simultaneously, the thumb by a stimulus of 40°C.-44°C. and the index knuckle by cold, the two temperature sensations on the thumb neutralised one another and a third mode of sensation, one of pain, appeared. The observation is most naturally interpreted by the supposition that when a temperature sensation is present, any painful element is suppressed. Though the pain was localised on the thumb, it may have belonged either to the heat sensation due to direct stimulation of this region or to the referred cold, and observations on another part of the body point to the former alternative. When a part of the glans penis which is free from heat-spots is stimulated by a temperature of 40°C.-44°C. there is no sensation of heat, but only one of pain. This part of the body is normally devoid of epicritic sensibility, and the occurrence of pain on the glans, as the result of stimulation by heat, points to the pain on the thumb having been the result of the direct stimulation of that region by heat rather than an element of the referred cold. In either case the special conditions of the experiment allowed the emergence of a mode of sensation which in the normal state is kept in a state of suppression, though it is manifest on the glans penis in the absence of heat-spots and of epicritic sensibility.

The special interest of the case is that there is no such suppression for temperatures of 45°C. and upwards, where pain is the normal result of stimulation. It is only in the case of [p. 27] temperatures less than 45°C., where the presence of pain would conflict with the pleasurable character of the heat sensation, that suppression has taken place.

These examples of suppression have been taken from the physiology of the nervous system. Though they became manifest through the changes in consciousness we call sensations, they are nevertheless the expression of purely physiological processes in the peripheral nervous system.

There is reason to believe that the two forms of cutaneous sensibility, which I have described, represent two different stages in the evolution of the nervous system with their associated varieties of consciousness. The facts seem best to fit with the hypothesis that the manifestations of protopathic sensibility which are suppressed belong to a crude form of nervous system which has been superseded by a later and more efficient mechanism. If now we pass to the central end of the nervous path by which the impulses subserving cutaneous sensibility reach the brain, Head working in conjunction with Holmes[6] has discovered a relation between the cerebral cortex and the optic thalamus very similar to that existing between protopathic and epicritic sensibility. In this case the special modes of activity they have studied are associated with structures which belong to widely separated stages of the development of the nervous system. The optic thalamus represents the dominant part of the brain of lower vertebrates, while the cerebral cortex or neo-pallium developed far later. When by injury, disease, or operative procedure, the cortex cerebri has been put out of action, stimulation of the skin produces sensations characterised by a peculiar quality such as would be produced by over-weight of the affective aspect of sensation, very similar to that shown by protopathic sensibility. Moreover, there is an absence of objective character very similar to that of this form of sensibility. When the cortex is in action the affective over-response of the thalamus is largely suppressed under ordinary conditions, but the process of suppression does not come out so strongly as in the case of the peripheral nervous system because some of the [p. 28] primitive features which most need suppression have already suffered this fate. Thus, removal of cortical activity does not produce radiation and reference of localisation because the suppression of these characters is still being maintained at the periphery.

Similar examples of suppression have been observed in the reflexes. In reflex action a movement takes place in response to stimulation which depends on a highly-organised and strictly-determined physiological mechanism. The whole process is immediate and incapable of modification. With a given stimulus and an intact nervous system, the effect follows the cause with a simplicity and definiteness far more obvious than in the case of activity which is accompanied by consciousness. In the normal state most of the reflexes, at any rate those in which the limbs and exterior of the body are concerned, are of a kind which, were they accompanied by consciousness, would imply accuracy of localisation and other forms of discrimination.

Experiments on animals, in which there has been interference with the integrity of the nervous system, have shown the exaggeration of certain forms of reflex action, pointing to the existence of some degree of suppression, but it has been reserved for injury of the nervous system in Man to show this process in its most characteristic forms.

Head and Riddoch[7] have observed a number of patients in whom the spinal cord has been completely divided, and in these cases have been able to study the functions of the lower end of the spinal cord when isolated from the rest of the nervous system. In such cases they find a peculiar form of reflex with characters unknown when the nervous system is intact. The reflex shows itself in movements, chiefly of flexion, involving mainly the stimulated side of the body, but far more widespread than is the case with the reflexes of health. The reflex can be produced by stimulating almost any part of the limbs or trunk below the site of the injury. The nature and extent of the movements does not vary with the locality of the stimulus as in [p. 29] normal reflexes, but is of much the same nature whatever the stimulated part. Moreover, the movements of the limbs and trunk muscles are accompanied by sweating and contraction of the bladder. This form of reflex has been called by Head and Riddoch the "mass-reflex." They note that such a mass-reflex would form an excellent answer to noxious stimuli in the lower animals. Owing to the necessary conditions of their observations the movements are limited to part of the body, but similar movements of the whole body would tend to remove an animal from noxious stimulation. They point out that this kind of reflex would be useless for the purpose of discrimination. The "mass-reflex " has a generalised character and shows an absence of discrimination and localisation which reminds us at once of the characters of protopathic sensibility. The special feature of interest from our present point of view is that this diffused and generalised reflex is wholly suppressed in the normal human being, the suppression having taken place in favour of reflexes delicately regulated according to the locality and, to some extent, according to the nature of the stimulus. Here, as in the case of protopathic sensibility, the suppression has been so complete that the presence of the mass-reflex is only revealed by disease or injury. It has been so successful that it needed the vast scale on which injuries of the central nervous system have been produced during the war to enable Head and Riddoch to discover the presence in Man of these old and long-suppressed processes.

In this case, and in the case of protopathic sensibility, we are not dealing with the suppression of individual experience, but with the suppression in the race of experience belonging to the earlier phases of its history. Through a special experimental procedure, or through the accidents of war, it has been possible to follow the suppression of this experience in the individual. The fact that this is possible suggests that the racial suppression is repeated in every individual as part of the recapitulation of the racial history. If this be so, however, the suppression takes place at so early an age that its detection is impossible. It would never have been suspected if the experiment and the [p. 30] clinical observations of Head had not pointed to the way thereto.

The special importance of suppression on the reflex and sensori-motor levels is that it reveals clearly the biological significance of the process. The exact localisation of fully developed cutaneous sensibility would be impossible if the early radiation and distant reference of the protopathic stage persisted. These features would furnish elements of vagueness and confusion wholly incompatible with the exact power of localisation which developed later and enabled the animal to modify its behaviour according to the nature of the external object by which the sensations were being produced. It is essential that reactions founded on the exact discrimination and localisation rendered possible by the epicritic system shall be prompt and definite. This would not be possible if the properties of the new order of sensibility were continually being complicated by sensations characterised by the old vagueness and the old inexactness of spatial reference.

Similarly, the uncomfortable feeling-tone of protopathic sensibility and the strongly affective aspect of the reactions of the thalamus need suppression when it is necessary to discriminate with exactness and to adjust behaviour to the more complicated conditions of life, made possible by the development of epicritic and cortical activity. In these cases, however, the suppression is less complete and only occurs when the affective accompaniments would interfere with the perfect adjustment of behaviour to the needs of the situation which the animal has to meet. The affective reactions lie ready to spring into activity whenever the situation calls for an emotional rather than an intellectual response.

In the case of the reflexes the need for suppression is imperative. The essence of reflex action is its immediacy and perfection based on the thorough organisation of the physiological mechanisms. The perfection of one of the higher reflexes would be hopelessly prejudiced if there were even a trace of the activity of the older mass-reflex with its diffuse character and implication of visceral processes. The movements of the [p. 31] localised reflex could not perform their task properly if at the same time they were involved in mass-movements of a wholly different kind. Suppression is here even more essential than in the case of conscious activity.

The argument of this chapter has been directed to show that the process of suppression by which elements of conscious experience pass into the "unconscious" is of the same order as the suppression which takes place on the sensori-motor and reflex levels. A number of processes have been found which form intermediate links connecting the suppression of highly complicated mental process at one end of the series with the suppression necessary for the perfection of reflex action at the other end of the series. In all cases we have to do with the means by which behaviour, whether of human being or animal, is adjusted to the needs with which man or animal is confronted. The suppression of conscious experience is only one example of a process which applies throughout the whole of the animal kingdom and is essential to the proper regulation of every form of human or animal activity. This suppression is only an example of processes even more fundamental in the animal economy. Every living process of the animal involves, not only activity devoted to the special end the animal has to meet, but also the inhibition of tendencies to activity of other kinds. The suppression which I have been considering in the last two chapters is only one aspect of the universal physiological property of inhibition. It is now recognised that the activity of every functional unit of the nervous system is of two kinds. Every unit forms part of a hierarchy in which it controls lower, and is itself controlled by higher, elements of the hierarchy. Control or inhibition belongs to the essence of nervous activity, and the lesson suggested by the study of sensation and reflex action is that the suppression by which experience becomes unconscious is only a special variety of the process of inhibition, common to every phase of animal activity.

There is one aspect of the psychological processes I have been considering which I should like especially to emphasise. If I am right in my interpretation of the facts revealed by the [p. 32] observation of cutaneous sensibility during the regeneration of a divided and re-united nerve, the earlier and cruder kind of sensibility undergoes two different kinds of fate. Such elements as are serviceable are utilised when the later and higher forms of sensibility come into existence. These useful elements of protopathic sensibility become fused with epicritic elements to form the fully developed sensibility which is possessed by the normal skin. Utilisation by means of the process of fusion is the fate of the greater part of the complex body of processes which make up protopathic sensibility. It is only the smaller part which undergoes the other fate of suppression. It is only those features of early sensibility which are incompatible with later developments which are suppressed. Thus, the wide diffusion and distant reference of protopathic spatial sensibility are suppressed because, if they persisted, they would prejudice in the most serious manner the exact localisation and spatial discrimination of fully developed cutaneous sensibility. Again, the suppression of the painful element when the normal skin is stimulated with an object at 40° C.-44°C. takes place because this painful quality would interfere with the pleasant character of the normal heat sensation and with the discrimination which is normally possible at that temperature. In the case of cutaneous sensibility there has taken place a differentiation of treatment according as the earlier material could or could not be utilised in the interests of the higher purpose offered by the possibility of discrimination and graduation. Corresponding with this distinction two kinds of elements in the unconscious might be recognised -- those which have only disappeared from consciousness in their original form, but continue to exist in the different form they have assumed through the process of fusion, and those whose disappearance has been more complete so that they do not enter into consciousness even in an altered form under normal conditions, though their continued existence is shown by their reappearance under peculiar conditions such as those which accompany the regeneration of a divided and reunited nerve.

There is little doubt that a similar twofold possibility is also [p. 33] open in the case of other kinds of early experience. There is reason to believe that al kinds of early experience undergo transformations similar to those undergone by protopathic sensibility. According to this view certain elements of early experience are utilised and form, by fusion with other elements, the products which make up the experience of any later period of life. It is only elements of experience and modes of behaviour which are incompatible with these later developments which are suppressed.

It now becomes necessary to reconsider the sense in which we shall use the term "the unconscious." It would be possible to use it to include not only the fully suppressed elements, but also those which might be regarded as unconscious because they no longer exist in their original form but in the form they have assumed through their fusion with later products of mental development. It will, I believe, be convenient to limit the use of the term "the unconscious" to the former category, to those earlier forms of mental activity and mental experience which have not been capable of utilisation by the process of fusion, but have required the more drastic measure of suppression.

Footnotes

[1] H. Head, W. H. R. Rivers, and J. Sherren, Brain, vol. xxviii. (1905), p. 99; H. Head and J. Sherren, ibid., vol. xxviii. (1905), p. 116; W. H. R. Rivers and H. Head, ibid., vol. xxxi. (1908), p. 323.

[2] Brain, vol. xxxi. (1908), p. 396.

[3] Brain, vol. xxxi. (1908), p. 396.

[4] H. Head, "On disturbances of sensation with especial reference to the pain of visceral disease," Brain, vol. xvi. (1893), p. 1; vol. xvii. (1894), p. 339; vol. xix. (1896), p. 153.

[5] Brain, vol. xxxi. (1908), p. 445.

[6] H. Head and Gordon Holmes, Brain, vol. xxxiv. (1911-12), p. 102.

[7] H. Head and G. Riddoch, Brain, vol. xl. (1918), p. 188; G. Riddoch, ibid., p. 264.

The last three chapters have been devoted to the definition of the unconscious and the consideration of the mechanism by which experience becomes unconscious and exerts activity in the unconscious state. I have now to consider the nature of the experience which forms the content of the unconscious.

In the examples which I have given the suppressed experience covers a very wide ground. In the case of my claustrophobic patient it included all the memories, memories involving very impressive emotional experience, of a series of activities of unusual complexity in the life of a four-year-old child. In the case from my own life we have the suppression of all the events which took place in part of my infantile environment where much must have happened, equalling, if not surpassing, in interest the many events in other parts of the environment of that early age which I have remembered. The suppression of war-neurosis involves the disappearance from consciousness of both intellectual and emotional experience of the most impressive and varied kind.

If now we turn to the nature of the experience suppressed on the sensori-motor and reflex levels, we find that it includes sensations which, in spite of their crudeness, can be regarded as belonging both to the affective and intellectual aspects of mind. The diffusion and faulty localisation of protopathic sensibility, which I have specially chosen to illustrate suppression on the sensori-motor level, must, in spite of its imperfection, be classed with the intellectual activities of more highly developed mental process. In general, however, the elements which produce this need for suppression belong rather to the affective aspect of [p. 35] mind, while the mass-reflex which furnishes so good an example of the need for suppression on the purely physiological level of reflex action seems also to be associated with experience of an affective kind. The lesson suggested by the study of suppression in the domain of sensation is that it is emotional or affective experience, or intellectual experience with a strong affective tone, which is especially liable to be suppressed.

If we consider the experience from which I have drawn my examples of suppression in the domain of the higher mental processes, we find that the process of suppression is especially likely to occur -- there is even reason to suppose that it only occurs -- when the emotions have been strongly aroused. It is certainly more likely to occur the more strongly this stirring up of the emotional aspect of mind has taken place. The experience which was suppressed in my claustrophobic patient was accompanied by emotion of a most intense and poignant kind; and this is also universally true of the experience which is suppressed in war-neurosis. Suppression is especially apt to occur as a means of getting rid of painful experience, the memory of which would interfere with comfort and happiness, or as its immediate effect would prejudice health.

It is necessary, however, to distinguish between the primary motives for suppression and others which take part in determining the nature of the content of the unconscious. My own infantile experience suggests that if for any reason some part of the mental content is suppressed it tends to carry with it into unconscious a vast amount of other experience of a neutral kind. We do not yet know the nature of the experience which to the suppression of all memories of the upper floor in which I passed so much of my infancy, but if suppression took place on account of some especially unpleasant event; this suppressed unpleasant experience took with it into the unconscious a vast mass of neutral experience, for it would be absurd to suppose that the whole of my life in that upper storey was accompanied by an unpleasant affective tone. Ignorance concerning nature of the experience which led to suppression makes this case inconclusive, but all the knowledge gained by [p. 36] the process of psycho-analysis points definitely in the same direction. We can be confident that when an experience is suppressed on account of its unpleasant nature, it may take with it into the unconscious a vast mass of neutral experience which would have remained accessible to consciousness if it had not been associated with experience needing suppression. There is a large body of evidence pointing to the presence of experience of this neutral kind in the unconscious region of the mind. The investigation of cases of multiple personality, and the exploration of the unconscious by means of hypnotism in healthy persons, point to the presence of much experience for the suppression of which it would be difficult or impossible to find any adequate motive. It is at least a legitimate hypothesis that this experience has come to form part of the content of the unconscious on account of its association with experience which needed suppression on account of its painful character.

It is necessary now to consider how far we are justified in supposing that affects and conative tendencies can be regarded as entering into the content of the unconscious. The nature of the suppressed experience, both on the sensori-motor and fully conscious levels, points to the great importance of feeling and affect as furnishing the immediate motives for suppression, while the experience which is suppressed, especially on the sensori-motor level, is predominantly of an affective kind. This would suggest that the content of the unconscious is made up of affective elements and conative tendencies together with sensory and intellectual experience associated therewith. There is little difficulty in conceiving that affective states and conative tendencies should be suppressed, and that they should nevertheless be ready to reappear and manifest themselves when the suitable occasion arises. It is more difficult to conceive them as parts of the content of the unconscious. It seems to be easier for us, or at any rate for most of us, to conceive the content of the unconscious in terms of intellectual elements such as the memories of my claustrophobic patient or of my own life [in] the upper storey. It is a question, however, whether it is not best to go the whole way and acknowledge that affective states and the [p. 37] impulses associated therewith may be elements in the content of the unconscious, and there is much in the more pathological aspects of suppression which can be most adequately expressed if it be assumed that affective processes are actively present in the unconscious.

This subject is of great interest in that it brings us face to face with the unconscious "wish" of Freud. Many of those[1] who accept the main teachings of this writer are troubled by his use of the term "wish" as the basic element of his system of the unconscious. This term is definitely derived from the psychology of the conscious and it tends to convey much which is very doubtfully to be ascribed to those elements of the unconscious to which so potent a rôle is assigned in the Freudian psychology. It is of the utmost importance that we shall attain clear ideas concerning this fundamental aspect of the psychology of the unconscious. In attempting to deal with this matter it is an obvious task to consider the general character, of affective experience and of the conative trends associated with it.

Through the work of modern psychologists, and especially through that of Shand and McDougall, we have come to see the close relation between affect and instinct. Each of the emotions can be regarded as an affective aspect of an instinctive reaction. Thus, fear is especially connected with the instinctive reaction to danger by flight; anger with the reaction to danger or injury by aggression; love with the parental and sexual instincts, etc., while the primary states of pleasure and pain are the psychical accompaniments of the fundamental reactions of attraction towards the useful and repulsion from the harmful. The primary feelings of pleasure and pain and all emotions, whether simple or complex, can be regarded as aspects of consciousness especially associated with instinct. This close relation between emotion and instinct leads us to a definite theory concerning suppression and the unconscious. It has been found that experience which becomes unconscious through the agency of suppression either belongs definitely to the affective aspect of mind or, when intellectual in character, has [p. 38] been suppressed on account of its association with affective elements. The relation of affect to instinct suggests that the special function of the unconscious is to act as a storehouse of instinctive reactions and tendencies, together with the experience associated with them, when they are out of harmony with the prevailing constituents of consciousness so that, when present, they produce pain and discomfort.

If, now, we study our examples of suppression on the sensori-motor level, we find that they lead us in the same direction. The crude, immediate, and, as it were, unreflecting reactions of protopathic sensibility, which need suppression in the interests of the later and more delicate reactions of epicritic sensibility, are just such as we associate with instinct. According to the view put forward in the last chapter they are reactions belonging to an older order which have been suppressed because they are out of harmony with later and more exact modes of behaviour. We are in similar case when we turn' to the reflexes. Reflex action is generally acknowledged to be clearly related to instinct. Reflex acts are products of evolution even more highly organised than the instincts. It is therefore quite in accordance with the function of suppression in relation to instinct that this process should come into action in connection with the reflexes.

If, therefore, we accept the close relation between emotion and instinct, all branches of our inquiry lead us to the view that the content of the unconscious is made up, in the first place, of the feelings and affects which normally form the conscious aspect of instinctive reactions and tendencies, and in the second place of sensory and intellectual elements which have been associated with these instinctive and affective reactions and tendencies. It is thus suggested that there is the closest relation between the unconscious and instinct, that the unconscious is a storehouse of experience associated with instinctive reactions. Moreover, I have shown that suppression, the process by which the conscious becomes unconscious, itself takes place unwittingly. The question arises how far the unwitting character of a process is a mark of instinct and is associated with instinctive reactions.

The argument of this book has now brought into connection [p. 39] with one another the two concepts which form its title. Up to this point I have been chiefly occupied in making clear what I mean by the unconscious and describing its mechanisms and its content. It is now necessary that we shall become equally clear concerning the meaning to be attached to instinct, and I shall enter upon this task in the next chapter.

Footnotes

[1] See, for instance, E. B. Holt, The Freudian Wish, London (1915)

It is not long since it was regarded as a sufficient definition of instinct that it is the mode of mental activity proper to animals as distinguished from the intelligence which was believed to be the chief, or even the only, factor of any importance in regulating Man's behaviour. All recent work in psychology 'has shown this distinction to be of little value. On the one hand, it has been found that the behaviour of animals, even such animals as the insects which are regarded as pre-eminent patterns of the instinctive, shows many features, such as adaptability to unusual conditions, which can only be explained by qualities of the same order as those belonging to intelligence.[1] Exact observation on animals has shown that their reactions to their surroundings have not the rigid and mechanical character which was once ascribed to them. Not only do failures occur in the adjustment of action to circumstance, but when these failures occur, or when the conditions are such as would lead to failure if the reactions took their ordinary form, animal behaviour has been found to be capable of modification. On the other hand, we have learnt that the behaviour of man is far less subject to reason and intelligence than was once supposed, and that his reactions to circumstance are often with difficulty to be distinguished from the behaviour of the unreasoning brutes. This absence or deficiency of reason is especially pronounced in those social reactions in which individual differences dictated by reason sink into insignificance before the mass-reactions of the crowd. We are learning, that the behaviour [p. 41] animals does not differ from that of Man in kind, but rather in the relative degree and importance of the different modes of reaction of which the behaviour consists.

A second way of distinguishing between instinct and intelligence is psychologically even less valid than the last. In the higher vertebrates, i.e., in those which have developed a cerebral cortex or neo-pallium as part of their central nervous system, instinct is regarded as the product of sub-cortical activity, while intelligence is held to depend on the activity of the cortex or neo-palium. It is an instructive commentary on the difficulties presented by current definitions of instinct that In the last resort even so psychological a writer as Lloyd Morgan is repeatedly driven to employ this anatomical distinction in his work on instinct and intelligence, thus virtually giving up the attempt to make a psychological distinction between the two.[2]

A third and most important distinction which has been made between instinct and intelligence is that the former is innate and the latter acquired. If an animal or man behaves in a way which is quite independent of any experience it can have acquired in its individual existence, the behaviour is regarded as purely instinctive. if, on the other hand, it were possible to say that the behaviour of an animal or man was wholly determined by the experience of the individual, we should regard the behaviour as an example of pure intelligence. Since, however, it is impossible to exclude innate factors, all that we can do is to recognise as intelligent those components of behaviour which can be ascribed to individual experience.

This difference between instinct and intelligence is one of great value and probably furnishes the best theoretical distinction between the two kinds of behaviour, but when we endeavour to use the theoretical difference as a guide in practice and research, we are met by several difficulties. The distinction is one which is difficult to utilise in practice, for, as soon as an animal has acquired experience of any kind, it becomes a matter of the greatest difficulty to distinguish between the innate and the acquired conditions, while, as already pointed out, in all [p. 42] examples of intelligent behaviour, it is impossible to exclude innate factors. Often, as in the case of insects and other animals which carry out actions of a most complicated kind, wholly independent of individual experience, the distinction is valid and useful. Thus, the butterfly which lays its eggs on a special kind of plant in the absence of any experience derived from the observation of this action by others of its species may be regarded as a typical example of instinct. An especially striking and often quoted example of this kind is that of the yucca-moth (Pronuba yucadella) which, preparatory to laying its eggs in the ovary of the yucca plant, cuts open the pistil and stuffs into it the pollen from another plant, so that at one stroke it both fertilises, and ensures the persistence of, the plant which is essential for the future welfare of its progeny. A still better example is given by the behaviour of the grub of the Capricorn beetle (Cerambyx miles). After a larval life spent wholly in the channels within a tree-trunk which it itself manufactures, this creature, little more than a piece of crawling intestine, as Fabre says, makes elaborate preparations to ensure that after the pupal state it shall escape from the woody prison in which it has itself been for all its life immured.[3] I call this insect a better example than the butterfly or the moth because it is quite impossible that the behaviour of the grub can have been in any way influenced by the imitation of its kind.

The exclusion of individual experience which is possible or even easy in the insect is beset with the greatest difficulties in the case of the higher animals. These difficulties become especially great in those animals, of which Man is the best example, which are born in a state of great-immaturity. The years spent by the child in acquiring experience, which it is impossible to record with any degree of accuracy, make it peculiarly difficult to analyse human behaviour into its innate and acquired components.

One other point about this mode of distinguishing instinct and intelligence may be mentioned. The distinction belongs to the field of biology rather than of psychology. If we were able [p. 43] to analyse every case of behaviour, whether human or animal, into its innate and acquired elements, we should still be little, if at all, nearer the solution of the psychological as opposed to the biological problem. We should not yet have begun to understand the place of consciousness in relation to behaviour, which, whatever may be our interest in the unconscious, must still remain the special task of psychology.

So long as we are considering the subject biologically we may be content with distinctions which depend on whether behaviour is exhibited by Man or animal, whether it is dependent on, or independent of, acquired experience, and on the locality of the physiological processes with which the behaviour is correlated. These modes of distinction, however, will not, or should not, satisfy the psychologist who requires something in the nature of the behaviour itself by means of which he may distinguish the instinctive from the intelligent. Nevertheless in the present state of the subject I believe we shall do best to take as the distinguishing mark of instinct its innate character, even though this character be biological rather than psychological. We shall do best if we devote our inquiries to the attempt to distinguish different kinds of instinct according to their psychological character. It should be our task to analyse the general group of instincts into its component parts just as it has been the main task of psychologists hitherto to analyse the different forms of intelligent behaviour.

In seeking for a criterion by which to distinguish different varieties of instinct, I propose to turn away for a time from the behaviour of insects or other invertebrate animals which are usually taken as our patterns of the instinctive. These animals differ so enormously from ourselves that it is too great an adventure into the unknown to base any distinction on differences between their behaviour and ours. Let us look rather to the behaviour of Man as compared with the animals to which he is more nearly related, and to the behaviour of adult man as compared with the infant, for our clue to the nature of the differences which will enable us to distinguish different classes of instinctive behaviour. [p. 44]

I will begin with a difference taken from the comparison of the human adult with the infant and the animal. An animal or child exposed to danger, which is so recognised as danger that it produces a reaction, tends to give itself to the reaction fully. If it runs away, it tends to run with every particle of the energy which it is capable of putting forth; if it cries, screams, or utters other sound, it tends to do so with all the vigour at its command. In these cases there is no discrimination of the degree of danger. The reaction by flight or cry is the same whether the danger be great or small. In the case of the animal the movement of a shadow thrown by a falling leaf may produce as strong a reaction as the full sight of its deadliest enemy. The child may scream as vigorously after some trivial touch as it does with the pain of a cut or burn. With no discrimination of the degee of danger, there may be complete absence of graduation of the reaction to the nature of the stimulus which occurs even in the animal in its more intelligent behaviour, and is characteristic of the behaviour of the adult man when danger threatens. If the danger is sufficiently great, or if certain lines of behaviour by which the danger would normally be met are frustrated, even the adult man will fail to discriminate the nature of the danger and to graduate his movements accordingly. He will devote every particle of his energy to flight or other form of primitive or instinctive behaviour. Thus, if he becomes angry and assumes an aggressive attitude, his anger and aggression will go far beyond those called for by the needs of the situation. If he flees, his flight may continue long after it has removed him to a safe distance from the source of danger.

In what I have just said I have spoken of the child as tending to scream and of the animal as tending to run away with all the force at their command, because I wish to make clear that the child or animal does not always behave in this thoroughgoing manner. All I wish to imply is that when these reactions take place in their most characteristic manner, they show a complete absence of proportionality between the behaviour and the conditions which call it forth. I assume that when the child and animal are so behaving, they are acting [p. 45] in a manner ill which they would act if their instinctive behaviour had not been modified by experience.

In the last chapter I have adopted the current view that such emotions as fear or anger, with the reactions characteristic of them, are expressions of instinct. When they occur in Man, these reactions are prominent, even the most prominent, elements in that part of his behaviour which can be ascribed to instinct. We have now seen that these reactions, when occurring in their most characteristic form, have the special feature that there is an absence of graduation according to the nature of the conditions by which the behaviour is produced. If they take place at all, they tend to occur in their full strength. This form of reaction is known in physiology as the "all-or-none" reaction,[4] and I propose to adopt this term for the special kind of behaviour I am now supposing to be characteristic of certain forms of instinct.

It may help us to understand this reaction if I give a brief account of its nature in physiology. For this purpose I will begin with the instance in which the principle was discovered by Keith Lucas and Adrian. I will not describe the somewhat complex experimental procedures which were needed to demonstrate the principle, and will give only the essential facts. When a weak electrical stimulus is applied to isolated nerve-fibre, and the impulse which in consequence travels along the nerve is measured, it is found that if the stimulus is weak there is no impulse at all, or more correctly, the electrical behaviour of the nerve gives no evidence of any impulse. If strength of the electrical stimulus is gradually increased, a point is reached when the nerve gives the response normally associated with an impulse passing along its length. If now strength of the stimulus is increased, there is no corresponding increase in the response, and this remains so, however great the increase of the stimulus. If the isolated nerve-fibre is set action at all, it reads with its full strength and produces all effect of which it is capable. [p. 46]

In previous chapters I have cited the work of Head as giving good examples of the process of suppression, and protopathic sensibility as a characteristic example of the content of the unconscious. It will greatly strengthen my argument and help to show that I am dealing with a real character of certain forms of instinct if protopathic sensibility should be subject to the "all-or-none" principle. As a matter of fact this is practically, though not completely, the case. When a region of the skin which is endowed only with protopathic sensibility is stimulated with cold, the intensity of the cold sensation is roughly the same whether the temperature of the stimulating surface is zero or 20°C., i.e., whether it is the temperature of ice or about the temperature of a summer day. The sensation due to the colder stimulus radiates over a larger area, which makes it difficult to be absolutely confident that there is no difference in the intensity of the sensation of cold, but we can be confident that when protopathic sensibility reacts to cold, it does so with appropriately or altogether the same strength so far as this can be tested by sensory experience,

The principle also holds good of certain forms of reflex action. Thus, the nature of the reflex known as the "extensor thrust" led Sherrington to think that the strength of the stimulus had no influence upon the amount of the response, and that the reflex occurred either not at all or fully.[5] The mass-reflex recently observed by Head and Riddoch, of which I gave an account in Chapter IV, also obeys the "all-or-none" principle fairly completely. Still more significant is the fact that the heart-muscle responds to stimulation either not at all or fully, this mode of reaction being of especial importance owing to the close relation between the heart and those affective disturbances which are closely connected with instinct.

Thus, the isolated nerve-fibre, the heart, certain forms of reflex action, and the protopathic sensibility of the skin all agree in having characters which only appear in the more complex behaviour of man or animal under conditions which bring instinctive processes into activity. [p. 47]

The "all-or-none" principle may be regarded as only a special case of a wider law holding good of the relation between stimulus and sensation, or between stimulus and reaction. Except at the limits of the range of intensities the normal sensibility of the skin or other sense-organs shows definite proportionality between stimulus and reaction, of which the most exact expression is given by Fechner's formula that the sensation is proportional to the logarithm of the stimulus. Any such exact relation is wholly absent in the case of protopathic sensibility, in the reactions of the "extensor-thrust" or the mass-reflex, and similarly, there is no such exact relation between the conditions setting an instinctive or emotional reaction into being and the strength of the reaction, at any rate in the child, or in the adult human being whose emotions have not been brought well under control by long training and practice.

The Fechner formula has been supposed to hold good of one affective state. It has been pointed out that the amount of pleasure derived from an accession of fortune stands in a definite relation to the fortune we already possess. A gift of half-a-crown will have a very different effect on a beggar and on a millionaire, and it has been supposed that this relation is subject to logarithmic expression; that equal increment of good fortune produce steadily decreasing increments of pleasure. Even if this law could be shown to apply with any degree of exactness, it conceals a highly-developed aspect of the affective life, one in which the crude emotional basis has been elaborated by the addition of highly complex intellectual factors. The states of pleasure and displeasure, at any rate in their more customary forms, are definitely graded. From the point of view here put forward, they must be regarded as states in which the crude emotional basis has undergone great development under the influence of individual experience. The nature of pleasure and displeasure, as well as the relation between what have been called physical and moral fortune, show a certain amount of definiteness of relation between stimulus and affect.

This definite and even quantitative relation is not true of the cruder [p. 48] passions which I connect with the instinctive behaviour of the man, and still less is it true of the passions of the child. Here there is not even an approach to any exact proportionality between the fear or other emotion and the condition or conditions by which the emotion has been produced.

I have chosen the "all-or-none " principle and the absence of the relation expressed by Fechner's formula as my examples of the kinds of character by which we may distinguish different forms of instinctive behaviour, because they furnish differences which are capable of exactness of expression and even of measurement. Another character, common to emotive reactions, to protopathic sensibility and to the forms of reflex action I have considered, is their immediate, and as it were unreflective, character. It is characteristic of emotion that it flares up at once and leads immediately to the behaviour characteristic of it. When, on the other hand, the crude affective tendencies which I associate with instinct have been brought under control, and even brief reflexion becomes possible, the emotion will only come into being if the conditions tending to produce it have such force as to sweep before them with their flood the obstacles interposed by intelligence. Similarly, it is characteristic of the reactions of protopathic sensibility that they tend immediately to result in movements approaching in nature those of reflex action, and are quite beyond the control which we normally exert over our more reasoned movements. One of the first signs of the return of the later epicritic sensibility is that this urgency goes, so that stimulation is followed by movements which are adapted to the nature of the stimulus.

I propose, therefore, to adopt as the distinguishing marks of one class of instincts: firstly, the absence of exactness of discrimination, of appreciation and of graduation of response; secondly, the character of reacting to conditions with all the energy available; and thirdly, the immediate and uncontrolled character of the response. It is interesting to note that Head and Gordon Holmes have found these characters to hold good in large measure of the activity of the optic thalamus, the essential nucleus of which they have shown to be the central [p. 49] representative of the protopathic aspect of peripheral sensibility and the central basis of emotive reactions. As I have already pointed out, it is clear that in this case we have to do with a structure which has come down from an early stage of the development of the nervous system. The optic thalamus is now hidden sway in the interior of the brain, overlaid and buried by the vast development of the cerebral cortex. Just as I have supposed that emotive and instinctive reactions are buried within the unconscious, hidden from consciousness by the vast development of those reactions which are associated with intelligence, so do we find that the organ of the emotions and instinctive reactions has been buried under the overwhelming mass of the nervous structure we know to be pre-eminently associated with consciousness.

It is interesting to note that the line of argument which I have followed has brought us to the view of Lloyd Morgan that instinct is the product of subcortical activity, but with the very important difference that I regard such structures as the thalamus as the organs only of certain forms of instinct, and have attempted to distinguish these forms of instinct by means of definite characters of the mental processes involved, and of the behaviour by which the instinct becomes manifest.

It must be remembered that this attempt to mark off one kind of instinctive behaviour by its psychological character has been based almost entirely on the study of human behaviour. It is now necessary to consider briefly how far these distinctions apply to the behaviour of those animals we have come to regard as our patterns of the instinctive. It is quite clear that the characters which I have taken as the special marks of certain instinctive aspects of human behaviour do not apply to those actions which are universally regarded as characteristic forms of the instinctive behaviour of the insect. It is certain that the "all-or-none" principle does not hold good of the activity of the bee when constructing the cells of the honeycomb, nor even the cruder art of such an animal as the grub of the Capricorn beetle which I have cited as a typical example of innate behaviour. The actions of these animals, certainly those of the [p. 50] bee, require in large measure the fine discrimination and delicacy of adjustment which remind us of epicritic rather than of protopathic sensibility. The way in which an insect will often carry out a set of activities dependent on its inherited tendencies when the external conditions are different from the ordinary, thus depriving these activities of all value, may perhaps be regarded as a sign that the insect is subject in some measure to the working of the "all-or-none" principle, but this is something different from the nature of the reactions themselves.

If we were to take the characters I have considered as marks of certain forms of instinct, it is evident that the behaviour of the insect could not be thus explained, but that some other principle must be in action, giving to its behaviour the power of discrimination and graduation of response. The lines taken by the development which has conferred this power are probably widely different from those which have been followed in the case of the vertebrata. The vast difference between the nervous system of an insect and that of a vertebrate animal would lead us to expect a correspondingly wide difference in the nature of the controlling and graduating mechanisms of the two kinds of animal. If the views here put forward seem worthy of adoption as a working hypothesis by students of insect-behaviour, it will become their business to seek out the nature of the controlling and graduating mechanism by which the originally crude modes of response of the insect have been modified and regulated.

I have in this chapter attempted to show that it is possible to distinguish two kinds of instinctive behaviour according as they do or do not exhibit certain characters. The characters which I have used as a means of distinguishing the instincts which are especially obvious in the innate behaviour of Man resemble in many respects the characters of protopathic sensibility, of a person who is dependent on the activity of the thalamus or of the isolated spinal cord, and in the domain of pure physiology the characters of the isolated nerve and of the heart. The discriminative and graduated activity of the more elaborate instinct of the insect, and also of certain forms of innate behaviour in Man, resemble in its general nature the [p. 51] epicritic sensibility of the skin and the activities of the body generally when fully under the influence of the cerebral cortex. It will be convenient to have terms for these two different kinds of instinct and instinctive behaviour, and I propose that they shall be named after the two kinds of characters which, through the work of Head, can be recognised in cutaneous sensibility. I shall, therefore, in this book, speak of instinctive behaviour as protopathic or epicritic according as it is or is not subject to the "all-or-none" principle, and according as it is not or is capable of graduation in relation to the conditions which call it forth.

Footnotes

[1] See the series of papers on "Instinct and Intelligence," Brit. Joun. Psych., vol. iii. (1910), pp. 209-270.

[2] Lloyd Morgan, Instinct and Experience, London (1912).

[3] J. H. Fabre, The Wonders of Instinct, London (1918), p. 49.

[4] See E. D. Adrian, Journ. of Physiol., vol. xlv. (1912), p. 389; ibid., vol. xlvii. (1914), p. 460; Brain, vol, xli. (2918), p. 26.

[5] The Integrative Action of the Nervous System, London (1906),p. 74.

Instincts my be classified as of three main kinds -- those of self-preservation; those which subserve the continuance of the race; and those which maintain the cohesion of the group, whether this group be a clump or herd of animals, or the more complex mass of individuals which makes up human society with its highly varied forms of grouping.

The instincts of self-preservation are concerned especially with the welfare of the individual. They may be divided into two main groups. One is of the more appetitive kind which subserves the function of nutrition, hunger and thirst being the chief representatives of the conscious states which accompany their activity on the side of attraction, while disgust is the mental correlative of the opposite state of repulsion from the harmful. This group of instincts includes not only the elementary instinct of sucking and the innate awareness of useful and harmful foods, but it is also concerned in the instinctive aspect of such a pursuit as hunting. It also takes a large part in the development of curiosity.

The other group of the instincts of self-preservation, made up of the reactions which serve to protect from danger, will be considered at length in this chapter.

The second main variety of instinct comprises those which subserve the continuance of the race. Here again they may be divided into two main groups-a more appetitive, making up the sexual instinct in the strict sense, while the chief constituent of the other group is the parental instinct with which, and with the sexual instinct, is associated the tender emotion. [p. 53]

The third main variety of instinct is concerned with the welfare of the group. Its main constituent is the gregarious instinct with its different aspects of suggestion, sympathy, imitation and intuition which I shall consider in a later chapter.

As in most branches of psychology, there are no sharp lines between these three varieties of instinct, and in many instinctive reactions more than one variety is involved. Thus, if we recognise acquisition as an instinct, this must be regarded as primarily an off-shoot of the instinct of self-preservation, which manifests itself strongly in connection with the sexual and parental instincts and plays a part in the higher developments the gregarious instinct. Again, if we acknowledge an instinct of construction, this can be regarded as primarily a manifestation of self-preservation, but its most complete and striking developments are connected with the parental occupation of nest-building, and with the social ends of the honey-bee. The gregarious instinct is closely interwoven with members of other two main groups of instinct. The instinct of play, which seems to be connected in some measure with self-preservation, as the practice of activities which will be useful to the individual in later life, manifests itself also in a striking manner in the playful performance of activities which have a strictly social purpose.

I propose to consider in this chapter that group of the instincts of self-preservation, the end of which is the protection or the animal or man from danger. I shall first describe the reactions to danger which can be objectively observed, and then attempt the more difficult task of connecting these with forms of emotion, or other forms of conscious response. Five chief forms of reaction to danger can be distinguished, other forms seeming to be modifications or combinations of these.

Flight. -- Flight from danger is probably the earliest and most deeply seated of the various lines of behaviour by which animals react to conditions which threaten their existence or their integrity. Flight may be regarded as a development of [p. 54] the reaction of repulsion from the noxious which is one of the fundamental modes of response to stimulation in those animals which are capable of mass-motion -- attraction towards the beneficial or useful; repulsion from the harmful. Those instinctive reactions in which animals seek special sources of safety may be regarded as developments, or modifications, of the instinct of flight, while the instinctive cry which so often accompanies flight is probably a still later development arising out of the gregarious habit.

Aggression. -- The second kind of danger-instinct is the reaction by aggression. This may be regarded as the opposite of flight. Since it will only come into play where the source of danger is another animal, this instinct must be later than that of flight, at any rate in its primitive form. Moreover, this kind of reaction would hardly be possible until an animal had reached a degree of development which endowed it with jaws and limbs fitted to act as instruments of offence and defence.

Manipulative Activity. -- I have had great difficulty in finding a term for the mode of reaction to danger I have now to consider. Originally I chose "pure serviceable activity," but since both flight and aggression are also serviceable, I have discarded this term in favour of "manipulative activity." This form of reaction is of great importance in the present discussion because it is the normal reaction of the healthy man. In the presence of danger Man, in the vast majority of cases, neither flees nor adopts an attitude of aggression, but responds by the special kind of activity, often of a highly complex kind, whereby the danger may be avoided or overcome. From most of the dangers to which mankind is exposed in the complex conditions of our own society, the means of escape lie in complex activities of a manipulative kind which seem to justify the term I have chosen. The hunter has to discharge his weapon, perhaps combined with movements which put him into a favourable situation for such an action. The driver of a car and the pilot of an aeroplane in danger of collision have to perform complex movements by which the danger is avoided. The beings which seem to come next to Man in this respect [p. 55] are the quadrumana or other animals with an arboreal habit, for this habit greatly increases the complexity of flight and needs a high degree of delicacy of adjustment of sense and movement. This must have formed a fitting ground for the development of the manipulative skill which forms Man's most natural response to danger.

Immobility. -- The three forms of reaction already considered resemble one another in that they involve definite activity on the part of the being, whether man or animal, threatened by danger. The mode of reaction now to be considered differs fundamentally from them in that it involves the complete cessation of movement, complete inhibition or suppression of the movements which would be brought into being by the instincts of flight and aggression, or by manipulation. The instinct which thus leads to the complete absence of movement seems to go very far back in the animal kingdom. It is often associated with purely physiological modes of reaction, such as changes in the distribution pigment, which increase the chances of safety of the animal by making it indistinguishable from its background. The instinctive reaction by means of immobility has the end of concealing the animal from the danger which threatens it, and this end of concealment is often assisted by other means, which may also be more or less instinctive in character.

Collapse. --This last form of reaction to danger is one which has greatly puzzled biologists. The reaction is usually accompanied by tremors or irregular movements which wholly deprive the reaction of any serviceable character it might possess through the paralysis of movement: Haller[1] has suggested that this form of reaction is useless to, or even prejudices the welfare of, the individual, it is useful to the race by eliminating, or helping to eliminate, the more timid members of the species. From this point of view the reaction would be a failure of the instinct of self-preservation in the interest of the continuance of the species. I think we shall take a more natural view of the reaction by collapse if we regard it as a failure of the [p. 56] instinct of self-preservation taking place in animals when instinctive reactions to danger have been so overlaid by reactions of other kinds that, in the presence of excessive or unusual stimuli, the instinctive reactions fail. It is noteworthy that collapse with tremor seems to be especially characteristic of Man in whom all the different modes of reaction to danger found in the animal kingdom are present in some degree, but no one of them so specially developed as to form an immediate and invariable mode of behaviour in the presence of danger.

There is evidence also that collapse and tremor occur especially when there is frustration of an instinctive reaction. Thus, Brehm[2] describes a motionless state, with staring eyes and tongues hanging out of their mouths, in seals which had been surprised in their favourite place of repose and cut off from their usual access to the sea. Again, as an example in Man, Mosso[3] observed collapse with violent tremor in a youthful brigand condemned to summary execution. Emitting a shrill cry, the boy turned to flee, and rushing against a wall, writhed and scratched against it as if trying to force a way through. Baffled in his attempt to escape, he at last sank to the ground like a log and trembled as Mosso had never seen another tremble, as "though the muscles had been turned to a jelly shaken in all directions."

I have mentioned several modifications or complications of these five main forms of instinctive reaction to danger. Some of them serve the end of concealment which may be attained by immobility or by flight to a place of safety, and concealment may serve as the end of a still more complex chain of reactions.

Having now considered certain modes of reaction to danger, I can consider how far it is possible to connect these with definite states of consciousness, positive or negative.

Flight and Fear. -- It is generally assumed without question that the instinctive reaction of flight is accompanied by fear, and human experience points to the truth of this conclusion, though the evidence is not as abundant as might be desired. [p. 57] There seems to be little doubt that fear becomes especially pronounced when there is interference with, or even the prospect of interference with, the process of fleeing, and the possibility cannot be excluded that the normal and unimpeded flight of animals from danger is not accompanied by the emotion of fear.

Aggression and Anger. -- The reaction to danger by aggression is definitely connected with anger. In Man acts of aggression, or acts which have the appearance of aggression, may be expressions of fear. A man in a state of sheer terror may do violence to others who stand in the way of his own safety. There is no doubt that such behaviour occurs, but in the main we may conclude that the primary instinct of aggression is bound up with the emotion of anger.

Manipulative Activity and Absence of Affect. -- There is abundant evidence, probably such evidence could be provided by the personal experience of everyone, that manipulative activity in response to danger is, or may be, wholly free from fear, or from any other emotion except perhaps a certain degree of excitement. Those who escape from danger by the performance of some complex activity bear almost unanimous witness that, while so engaged they were wholly free from the fear which the danger might have been expected to arouse. Highly complex acts designed to allow escape from, or to overcome, the danger are carried out as coolly as, or even more coolly than, is customary in the ordinary behaviour of daily life. There seems to be in action a process of suppression of the fear or other affective state. That there is such suppression is supported by the fact that fear may be present, perhaps in an intense form, if the experience is reproduced later in a dream.

That the absence of fear is due to suppression of the affect, which seems to accompany the primitive reaction to danger, is supported by the insensitiveness to pain which often occurs at the same time. Not only may an injury occurring in the presence of danger fail wholly to be perceived, but the pain already present may completely disappear, even if it depends upon definite organic changes. On one occasion I was in imminent danger of shipwreck while suffering from severe [p. 58] inflammation of the skin over the shin-bones, consequent upon sun-burn, which made every movement painful. So long as the danger was present I moved about freely, quite oblivious of the state of my legs, and wholly free from pain. There was also a striking absence of the fear I should have expected the incident to have produced.

It is evident that the occurrence of either pain or fear would interfere with the success of manipulations or other activities by which a creature escapes from danger. If a man or animal is to escape from a dangerous situation by means of delicate manipulations or other complex form of activity, success would be seriously prejudiced by the presence of fear or pain. When, as in arboreal animals, successful flight depends on a highly delicate adjustment of hand and eye, the occurrence of pain or fear would inevitably interfere with its success.

The complete suppression of pain and fear, even in the presence of imminent danger, may also take place when any form of serviceable activity is impossible. The best known case of this kind is that of the missionary and explorer, Livingstone, who experienced neither pain nor fear while his arm was being devoured by a lion, and others who have been mauled by animals while hunting have had a similar experience.

Immobility and Suppression. -- The suppression which occurs in the manipulative activity of Man, and may safely be assumed to occur in many of the higher mammals, seems also to afford the most natural explanation of the immobility which forms the chief instinctive reaction to danger in so many animals. If immobility is to be useful in the presence of danger, and especially in dangers threatened by other animals, it is essential that it shall be complete. It is a well-recognised character of animals that their vision is especially sensitive to movement. The perception of movement probably forms the most primitive form of vision,[4] and concealment by means of immobility would be of little use unless it were complete. If an animal capable of feeling pain or fear, in however crude a form, were to have these [p. 59] experiences while reacting to danger by means of immobility, the success of the reaction would certainly be impaired and would probably fail completely. I suggest, therefore, that the essential process underlying the instinct of immobility is the suppression of fear and pain. It is possible that the instinctive reaction to danger by means of immobility may have furnished one of the earliest motives for suppression. It may be that the suppression of the immediately painful or uncomfortable, the process by which the highly complex experience of Man becomes unconscious, is only a modification of a process going very far back in the animal kingdom, which was essentially the safety of animals in their reaction to danger by means of immobility.

Collapse and Terror. -- There is little doubt that the collapse, associated with tremor, which forms one mode of reacting to danger, especially in the higher animals, is accompanied by that excess of fear we call terror. This association, based on the experience of Man, may also be ascribed to animals. Though immobility and collapse resemble each other superficially, I suppose them to be poles apart so far as the accompanying affect is concerned. In dealing with collapse as a mode of reaction, I pointed to interference with flight or with some other form of serviceable activity as one of its most important conditions. In this obstruction to normal instinctive modes of reaction by which danger would be avoided, we have a satisfactory explanation of the excess of affect by which it is characterised. The conflict of different instinctive modes of their consequent failure would furnish an alternative explanation of the excessive affect. In most animals there is a special disposition towards some one of the various forms of reaction to danger, so that in them there is little room for conflict between alternative tendencies. Conflict leading to collapse occurs when the tendency proper to each is obstructed. In

Man, on the other hand, all the different tendencies found throughout the animal kingdom seem to be present. Man may flee, become aggressive, or adopt some other form of serviceable activity in the presence of danger, and there is reason to believe that he may show, at any rate in pathological [p. 60] states, the reaction of immobility. The conflict between tendencies in these different directions is probably a definite reason for his liability to collapse or other non-serviceable states, such as trembling, in the presence of danger. This is the penalty Man has to pay for the pliancy of his danger-instincts, for their failure to become systematised or fixed in any one direction.

In the sketch I have just given of the modes of reaction and associated mental states which make up what I have called danger-instincts, the feature I wish especially to emphasise is the suppression of affect which certainly accompanies the manipulative activity of Man, and has been assumed to accompany the immobility of the lower animals. These two modes of reaction differ from one another in one important respect. The suppression of pain and fear in the manipulative activity of Man is not necessarily accompanied by any failure of memory of the events which produced the reaction, or of the nature of the reactions themselves and their accompanying mental states. In some cases, however, as has not uncommonly happened in war, there is partial or complete amnesia for the period of activity. Soldiers have carried out, so skillfully as to earn the special commendation of their superiors, highly complicated processes of giving orders, directing operations, showing personal skill in attack and defence while afterwards their memories have been a blank for the whole series of events and their own behaviour in relation to it. Moreover, there is abundant evidence that the experience which had thus lost direct access to consciousness is still present and may show itself in some indirect manner.

Footnotes

[1] "Elementa Physiologicæ corporis humani," Lausanne (1763), t.v., p. 568.
[2] A. E. Brehm Thierleben, Leipzig (1877), vol. iii. p. 601.
[3] A. Mosso, Fear, London (1896), p. 145.
[4] W.H.R. Rivers, Schäfer's Textbook of Physiology, Edinburgh, vol. ii. (1900), p. 1146.

Some of the instinctive reactions to danger described in the last chapter are evidently subject to the all-or-none principle. If an animal is to flee from danger it is essential that this reaction shall be carried out as completely as possible. There is no opening for graduation of the degree and rapidity of flight, and probably in the most primitive forms there is little power of regulation of direction, while the flight may continue long after the animal is at a safe distance from the source of danger. Even in Man there is no graduation of the rapidity and length of a flight accompanied by definite fear. The extent of the flight is usually quite out of keeping with the nature of the danger, real or imaginary, to which the emotion and its reactions are due.

It is much the same in the case of the aggressive reaction its affective accompaniment of anger. If an animal, instead of fleeing from an enemy, stands and fights, it does so with all the energy at its command, and this is also true of Man in his natural state. It needs a prolonged course of training to enable a man to fight, whether with his fists or with weapons, yet preserve his composure so that he can discriminate the movements of his enemy and adjust his own actions accordingly. Even the practised fighter may allow the purely affective attitude to overcome him and, as we say, may lose his head, putting out all his powers blindly, and failing because he is no longer regulating his actions according to the nature of the situation. In such a case a crude instinctive impulse of aggression has mastered all the later developments due to his special training. This training consists in putting the crude actions of [p. 62] the primitive instinct of aggression under subjection to carefully discriminative and chosen actions based on intelligence.

I have now to consider how far the all-or-none principle applies to the process of suppression which forms so important an element in the reaction to danger by means of immobility and in that of manipulative activity. We have to inquire whether a principle which holds good of certain emotional reactions also applies to the process by which these reactions are controlled and suppressed.

In the case of the reaction of immobility, we can be confident that the all-or-none principle holds good. The reaction by immobility is radically opposed to the other two chief reactions by flight and aggression. If the animal is to flee or fight, suppression would be wholly out of place. Any trace of it could only interfere with the success of the more active reaction. If, on the other hand, the animal adopts the reaction of immobility, the process of suppression upon which this reaction depends must be complete. Even the slightest movement will endanger the success of the whole reaction. Any graduation of the process of suppression, any attempt to discriminate differences in external conditions and to adjust the degree of suppression accordingly, would be fatal to success. We have here a case in which the all-or-none principle applies most definitely and is essential to the working of the instinctive reaction.

The manipulative reactions of Man or of arboreal mammals also require that the suppression of tendencies to other kinds of reactions shall be thorough, though not necessarily as complete in the case of the reaction by immobility. The movements of flight from bough to bough, or from tree to tree, would be impaired if the animal were at the same time the subject of blind impulses of the same order as those which actuated ancestors who lived on the ground or underwater. In the case of Man, we know that where the efficiency of manipulative activity is greatest, there is no trace of impulses of other kinds, certainly no trace of fear or of emotional states associated with other kinds of reaction.

Thus far I have considered the process of suppression as it [p. 63] affects instinctive reactions to danger. Let us now turn to our earlier topics and consider the suppression of forgetting. The first point to notice is that forgetting, and especially that kind of active forgetting with which we are especially concerned, is not a graduated process; or, any graduation that it may possess is not adjusted to the needs of the situation. We may remember experience with different degrees of clearness, dependent on such factors as the time which has elapsed since the remembered experience, the intensity of the experience, and the interest given to it by association or meaning. But when an experience has been forgotten by means of the active process of forgetting, there is, so far as we know, no corresponding graduation of the process. An experience is either remembered or forgotten. There may, however, be different degrees of difficulty in bringing the experience again to consciousness, and these differences would seem to be due to different degrees of obstruction to recall. The experience of the psycho-analytic school goes to show that there are such differences of resistance, and this may be regarded as constituting different degrees of strength of suppression. Consequently these differences suggest that suppression of this kind is not subject to the all-or-none principle. If, as seems clear, the process of suppression was originally subject to this principle, the nature of active forgetting suggests that it has been modified in later evolution and that in Man, at any rate, the process of suppression has departed from the all-or-none principle and is, at any rate in some degree, capable of graduation. It is noteworthy that the most complete cases of forgetting seem to occur in early childhood, when we are justified in supposing that the later developed principle of graduation is still of little power. The forgetting of adult life may be regarded as an epicritic modification of the original instinctive or protopathic process of suppression, just as most our adult sensations are the result of the modification of the original protopathic forms of sensation by fusion with epicritic elements.

The application of the all-or-none principle may be examined from another point of view. We have seen that there is evidence [p. 64] that the process of suppression does not act merely on the special experience which is producing pain or discomfort, but when it suppresses this, it suppresses with it much other experience of a neutral or even beneficent kind. Thus, if I am right in supposing that the suppression of all memories and images of the upper floor in my own child-memory is due to the existence of some unpleasant event or events, the process has not been limited to that experience, but every memory of life on that upper floor has disappeared completely. Similarly, those whose memories of some painful experience of war have been suppressed have at the same time lost the memory of all that happened over a period much longer than that of the unpleasant experience itself. In getting rid of the memory of an unpleasant experience, the process of suppression tends to involve all experience associated in time and space with that which is the immediate occasion of the suppression.

The foregoing considerations seem to show that, while suppression in the primitive form revealed in the simple instinctive reactions to danger is definitely subject to the "all-or-none" principle, this principle does not hold good, or is much modified, in later development, so that the process becomes at any rate to some extent, capable of graduation. The idea that the all-or-none principle holds good of instinct, at any rate in its more primitive and cruder forms, was supported by the nature of primitive sensibility as revealed by the experiments of Head. It is, therefore, of great importance to note that the suppression of protopathic manifestations revealed by those experiments was far from being complete. Only certain elements of the protopathic complex have been suppressed, while others have been utilised to enter into the composition of the fully developed cutaneous sensibility. The process of suppression on the sensori-motor level has here shown that it possesses the capacity for discrimination, selection and graduation, and if this be so on the physiological level, it is not surprising that the relatively high development on the psychological level of active forgetting should reveal a similar process of development and modification. The evidence, therefore, goes to show that, while suppression was [p. 65] originally subject to the all-or-none principle, this principle has in the course of phylogenetic development been modified, and has become capable of graduation. But it is still liable to show itself in its original form when it occurs in infancy. I hope to show later that the all-or-none principle tends to reappear in disease, when the process of regression reduces mental activity to a state comparable with that which it possessed at an early stage of its development.

I propose in this chapter to consider a little more fully some features of suppression to which I have already referred in connection with the "all-or-none" principle. Some of the instinctive modes of reaction to danger which I have described would fall short of their full effect, or would even fail altogether, if they were not accompanied by the complete suppression of tendencies to other kinds of reaction and of any conscious states associated therewith.

Thus, the reaction to danger, which may be regarded as natural to the healthy man, a reaction characterised by complete absorption in the immediate task by which the danger may be averted, would be impossible if complete suppression, not only of any tendency to the reaction of flight, but also of any trace of the emotion of fear which is its normal conscious accompaniment, did not occur. A man whose attention is wholly absorbed in the business of flying an aeroplane, or directing the movements of a company of soldiers, would certainly fall short of full efficiency if his movements were complicated by impulses to flight or his composure disturbed by even a trace of fear.

I have suggested that this normal reaction to danger has been inherited by man from his arboreal ancestors. When these ancestors took to an arboreal existence the reaction to danger by flight, which had previously involved the simple and wholly instinctive movements of running, now required the delicate adjustments of eye and limbs involved in movements from branch to branch and from tree to tree. Any animal in which such movements were complicated by impulses to the simpler motion of running, or whose consciousness was disturbed [p. 67] by the emotion of fear, would certainly fail to perform successfully the complicated movements of its arboreal existence. Accidents of various kinds would furnish means by which a rigorous process of selection would eliminate those animals which were unable to suppress their instinctive tendencies and any conscious affective states derived from their earlier mode of existence on the ground. It is evident that such adaptation to an arboreal existence by the suppression of inappropriate instinctive tendencies would have but poor chances of success if the mechanism of suppression only came into existence in order to meet the special conditions with which the arboreal tyro was confronted. The process of suppression could only be expected to succeed if it had been developed to meet other needs and was already there, only waiting to be employed in helping the animal to overcome the obstacles presented by a new mode of existence. We can be confident that the mechanism of suppression had already come into being in the ancestors of the tree-dweller long before there arose the needs due to a life above the ground.

In our search for conditions which could have brought the need for suppression, let us continue to deal with the instinctive reactions to danger. One of these clearly brings out the need for suppression. The reaction to danger by means of immobility is one which would obviously be impossible if the inhibition which led the animal to become motionless were complicated by the presence of impulses to movement, and especially to those pronounced and violent movements which make up the other great fundamental reaction -- that of flight. In order that an animal shall lie wholly motionless in the presence of danger, it is essential that this motionlessness shall be complete. Such danger would generally come from another animal and owing to the primitive character of the cognition of movement in visual perception, to which I have already referred,[1] it is essential that the animal in danger shall avoid any movement whatever. There must be complete suppression of such impulses as would produce even a trace of the movements which make [p. 68] up the reaction by flight. Moreover, it is equally necessary that the consciousness of the animal reacting to danger by means of immobility shall not be disturbed by such feelings or images as would tend to set up movements, whether adapted to flight or of an irregular kind. It is essential that such consciousness as the animal may possess shall be wholly in harmony with the need for immobility which the instinct of the animal has led it to adopt. The need for suppression is all the greater in that animals which are accustomed to react to danger by immobility are usually, if not always, capable also of the reaction to danger by flight. We have not merely to do with an ancestral tendency to an incompatible kind of reaction, but with the need for the inhibition of an alternative mode of reaction. Moreover, there are many animals which flee till they have removed themselves from the source of danger, and only then resort to the reaction of immobility. In such a case it is necessary to inhibit a mode of reaction which, only a moment earlier, has been in full activity. The mechanism of suppression is thus one which must have come into being at a very early stage of animal existence. When, far later, an animal changed its habit of life, as in taking to an arboreal existence, it would already possess, waiting to be utilised when needed, a mechanism by which it could suppress instinctive impulses and conscious states which would interfere with the needs of its new life.

I have so far considered especially the needs for suppression which would be required when there is the possibility of two kinds of instinctive reaction incompatible with one another, or when an animal adapted to one kind of existence is forced by new needs to take up new modes of reaction which would be disturbed even by traces of its old behaviour. Still another opening for suppression is presented by those animals whose life-history is characterised by changes of habit so great that the modes of reaction proper to one phase could be seriously prejudiced if the tendencies of the earlier phase or phases were not suppressed. Thus, the metamorphoses of an insect produce existences so different from one another that if the impulsive [p. 69] tendencies and modes of consciousness proper to one phase were to continue in a later phase, they would greatly interfere with the behaviour proper to that phase. Thus, during the larval existence of the butterfly, the caterpillar reacts to the stimuli of certain leaves and plants in definite ways and exhibits certain movements adapted to the mode of progression proper to that stage of the life-history of the insect. If the impulses to such movements or the feelings and sensations which aroused the activity of the caterpillar were to persist in the imago, they could only interfere with the harmony of movements exquisitely adapted to the wholly different motions of flight. The harmony of its existence would be continually prejudiced if the memories of its larval existence were liable to intrude into the consciousness of the fully-developed butterfly with its vastly different needs and interests.

Again, to take an example from an animal nearer to ourselves, the movements of the frog could only be impaired if it were liable to be disturbed by impulses of such a kind as were needed by the tadpole, or if sensations referable to its caudal extremity were liable to complicate the sensations regulating the movements of limbs which did not exist in its larval stage.

I have so far spoken only of suppression of tendencies and conscious states as characters of early modes of animal reaction. In the case of Man, however, we have not only suppression of tendencies and of states of consciousness, but there is definite evidence that the suppressed experience and the tendencies I associated therewith, may have a kind of independent existence, and may act indirectly upon or modify consciousness even when incapable of recall by any of the ordinary processes of memory. Let us now inquire how far there is evidence of this continued existence in those animals in which we have found evidence for the process of suppression. One form of instinctive reaction, the suppression of which has been shown to be necessary under certain conditions, is that of flight, whether by movements of swimming in the water or of running upon the ground. Although these movements may need suppression, either in the interests of the alternative instinct of immobility [p. 70] or of a new mode of existence, the older instinct may still be needed at times. It is essential that its mechanism shall remain intact ready to be utilsed whenever it is needed. For most animals it is essential that the mechanism for each kind of reaction shall be present ready to be called into activity if the need should arise. This is so even if one mode of reaction is habitual, while the need for the other may only arise once in a lifetime or may always lie dormant.

The need for the continued existence in one phase of an instinctive mode of reaction proper to another phase of the life-history of an animal subject to metamorphosis is less obvious. There is no immediately obvious reason, for instance, why a butterfly should preserve among the potentialities of its existence the sensations or feelings which were aroused in the caterpillar by the leaves on which it feeds. One possible motive for such preservation, however, may be discerned. It is essential to the existence of the species that the female butterfly shall lay her eggs on or near the plant upon which the future larvæ will feed. In order that this shall happen it seems to be essential that the food-plant shall be capable of arousing such sensations in the butterfly as will make her choice possible. Professor Seligman has suggested to me that it may be to this end that the suppressed sensations of the larva persist during metamorphosis to be called once more into activity when, preparatory to its death, the imago carries out the act by which it perpetuates the race.

At the end of the last chapter I have referred to the activity of suppressed experience which is exemplified, for instance, by the case of claustrophobia which I have chosen to illustrate the nature of "the unconscious." This activity is usually known by the name of dissociation and it now becomes necessary to consider exactly what is meant by this term and how it may be used so as to be of most service in the study of psychopathology.

It is not unusual to find the terms "suppression" and "dissociation" used as if they denoted one and the same process. I have myself been guilty of this confusion, or have at any rate used language which might be supposed to indicate that I regard the two terms as synonymous.[1] I have now, I hope, made it clear what I mean by suppression, and it remains to make equally clear the sense in which I shall speak of dissociation.

Before I do so, one possible source of confusion must be mentioned. In their work on the nervous system, Head,[2] Riddoch and others use "dissociation" in a manner very different from that in which the term is used by writers on morbid psychology. When Head and his colleagues speak of "dissociation" they refer to a process, pathological or experimental, whereby one set of nervous functions are separated from others with which they are normally associated so that they become capable of independent study. A good example is given in the spinal cord where the selective action of certain [p. 72] morbid processes removes the activity of some forms of sensibility and allows others to remain. Thus, interference with the conductivity of the posterior columns will abolish the power of appreciating two points placed on the skin simultaneously while leaving touch unaffected, -and Head speaks of this occurrence as one in which the power of appreciating compass points has been dissociated from touch. Again, Riddoch finds[3] that in pathological states of the occipital cortex the power of appreciating movement may remain intact while other visual activities are destroyed, and he again speaks of this process of separation as "dissociation." To Head and Riddoch dissociation is pre-eminently a method provided by disease which makes it possible to analyse complex nervous processes into their component elements. It is a process which on the psychological side stands in a definite relation to the process of fusion, but has none of the special relation to suppression which is so definite in the connotation of dissociation as I shall use the term, and as it is used by most writers on morbid psychology. The dissociation of Head is predominantly a physiological rather than a psychological term, and it might therefore be thought that there is no danger of confusion, but the physiological processes for which the term is used stand in so close a relation to the psychological that there certainly is such a danger. I was at one time inclined to use dissociation as Head and Riddoch propose and find some other word for the psychological process, but the term is now so firmly established in psycho-pathology that it will be very difficult to give it up. Moreover, the word "dissociation" is particularly appropriate to the nature of the psychological process. I believe it would be more practicable for Head and his colleagues to find some other term for the process so essential to the method by which they are making such momentous contributions to the physiology of the nervous system and at the same time to the foundations of any scientific study of mental process.

I can now pass to the definition of "dissociation" as I shall use the term. I have already stated that I regard it as a [p. 73] process which experience undergoes when it has been suppressed. The special feature of dissociation, as I understand it, is that the suppressed experience does not remain passive, but acquires an independent activity of its own. It is this independence of activity which I wish to regard as an essential character of dissociation. The most characteristic example of dissociation is the fugue in which a person shows behaviour, often of the most complicated kind, and lasting it may be for considerable periods of time, of which he is wholly unaware in the normal state. The fugue usually comes into being owing to the fact that some unpleasant experience has become unconscious by the unwitting process of suppression or is tending to pass into the unconscious through the agency of the witting process of repression. One day the subject of this suppressed or repressed experience goes out for a walk and suddenly finds himself in some part of the town remote from that in which he had been, it seems to him, only a few minutes before. On looking at his watch he finds that it is an hour since he left home, though he would have thought he had only been out a few minutes. On putting his hand in his pocket he finds two cigars which were certainly not there when he left home, and on counting his change he finds that he has one shilling and eightpence less than when he put his money into his pocket in the morning. On going to his tobacconist he finds that he had already visited him that morning, although he had no recollection of the visit, and had bought three sixpenny cigars, although he was accustomed to smoke either a pipe or cigarettes. He may also discover, perhaps a week later, that he had met a friend with whom he had talked, and may be able to ascertain that the friend noticed nothing out of the way in his conversation or demeanour, he himself having no recollection whatever of the meeting. On piecing the evidence together it would seem that he had had a fugue in which he had visited a tobacconist and bought three cigars of which one had been smoked or given away during the fugue. He had then found his way to the distant part of the town where he, as we say, came to himself. The distance he had traversed made it probable that he had [p. 74] travelled by tram, thus accounting for the twopence he had spent in addition to his expenditure at the tobacconist's. The description I have given is not that of an actual case but is compounded by putting together incidents from several of the many fugues which I have had the opportunity of studying during the war. In such a fugue the dissociation is complete. On return to the normal state there is no memory of the behaviour during the fugue or of any conscious processes which accompanied this behaviour, though these memories can be recovered in the hypnotic or hypnoidal states or under other conditions which favour the recall of suppressed experience.

If we accept the fugue as a typical and characteristic instance of dissociation, we are at once faced by another problem of definition. The subject of a fugue is certainly not unconscious. So far as we know, he is capable of experiencing all the modifications of consciousness which are open to the mind in its normal state. We have not at all to do with an example of the unconscious, but with consciousness cut off or dissociated from the consciousness of the normal waking life. A person in a fugue usually behaves in a manner somewhat different from that of his normal state, and shows what is usually described as a difference of personality, but the difference may be very slight. I have myself met one of my own patients in a fugue without recognising that such was the case. I noticed that his manner was not quite as usual, but the difference was so slight that though I knew about his fugues, and had hoped to have the opportunity of observing him in one, I failed to recognise the occasion when it came. Slight, however, as the change of personality may be, it is certainly there. All gradations may he met between a change so slight as that which I failed to recognise in my patient, and the pronounced cases of double or multiple personality which are described in psychological literature, reaching their climax in the classical case of Miss Beauchamp.

The existence of independent consciousness which thus shows itself in the fugue, and in cases of double personality, separates [p. 75] these cases very definitely from those, such as that of my claustrophobic patient, in which experience becomes unconscious and, though active, gives no evidence of any independent conscious existence. It is wholly out of place to speak of the unconscious or of unconsciousness in the case of a fugue, and Dr. Morton Prince[4] has suggested that we shall use the term "co-conscious" and "co-consciousness rather than "unconscious" and "unconsciousness." These terms are especially appropriate to the examples of double or multiple personality such as that of Dr. Prince's patient, Miss Beauchamp. In this case there seems to have been definite co-existence of independent consciousnesses. One conscious personality performed acts definitely designed to act upon another personality which was also at the time conscious, the former personality being able to perceive and reflect upon the consequence of her acts. In an ordinary fugue we have no evidence of such co-existence of independent consciousnesses. The use of the terms "co-conscious" and "co-consciousness" in the case of the fugue would indicate a decision in a matter of the utmost difficulty in which it is essential to maintain an open mind. I do not propose, therefore, to adopt Dr. Morton Prince's terms for the more ordinary cases of dissociation, though I recognise them as appropriate to such a case as that of Miss Beauchamp. It will, however, be convenient to have a term for such examples of independent consciousness as characterise the fugue, and for this purpose I shall speak of "alternate consciousness." It is possible that during a fugue the normal personality may be independently conscious, and that the fugue-consciousness may persist beneath the surface in the normal state, though the two are so completely dissociated that neither ever become accessible to the other. We have, however, no evidence that this is so, and till we have such evidence it will be more satisfactory to speak of alternate consciousness, the reality of which is now well established.

If we accept the fugue as a characteristic example of dissociation, the question arises whether we should not include in [p. 76] its definition the character of alternate consciousness, and I believe that we shall best be meeting the needs of the situation by doing so. I propose therefore to use the term "dissociation," not merely for a process and state in which suppressed experience acquires an independent activity, but shall assume that this independent activity carries with it independent consciousness. In some cases in which we have obviously to do with independent activity as shown by behaviour, it may not be possible to demonstrate the existence of independent and dissociated consciousness, but I believe it will be convenient to limit the term "dissociation" to cases where there is evidence of this independent consciousness.

I propose now to consider some of the cases of suppression with which I have dealt in this book and inquire how far they do or do not bear signs of the independent activity and independent consciousness which I am taking as the signs of dissociation. In, several of the instances which I have taken as my examples of suppression, especially the definitely organised suppression which I have supposed to exist in the lower animals, there is no reason to suppose that there is either independent activity or independent consciousness. In the case of Man also there is every reason to suppose that in many instances suppression may be complete, and the suppressed content wholly free from any kind of independent activity and from any accompaniment of consciousness. Thus, in the normal healthy man the special kind of fear which reveals itself in night-terrors, or nightmares, seems to be wholly suppressed and devoid of any kind of independent activity. A person may pass through life, and even through dangers of an extreme kind, without showing any trace of this kind of fear, though its occurrence in nightmares or in other pathological states shows that it is there lying ready to appear in consciousness if the suitable conditions should arise.

Again, there is no reason to associate any independent activity, or any form of consciousness, with much of the suppressed experience of early childhood. The knowledge derived from psycho-analysis goes to show that this suppressed early [p. 77] experience may have a great effect on character and may play an important part in determining likes and dislikes and tendencies to special lines of activity in later life, but we may regard influences of this kind as due to fusion rather than suppression or dissociation. The most natural explanation of these influences is that they are due to fusion between the suppressed tendencies, or certain parts of them, and the products of later experience, exactly comparable with the fusion between protopathic and the later epicritic elements by which the sensibility of the normal skin is produced.

I assume, therefore, that suppression often exists without anything which we can regard as dissociation, that in many cases the suppressed content exhibits no form of independent activity with no evidence that it is accompanied by any form of consciousness. In other cases in which there is definite activity of the suppressed content, there is no clear evidence of consciousness accompanying this activity, but yet cut off from the general body of conscious experience. This seems to be so in the case of claustrophobia which I have taken as my most characteristic example of suppression. I shall now consider whether we ought to regard this disorder as an example of dissociation. The dreads to which the patient was subject are most naturally explained if the memories of his four-year-old experience existed in a state of suspended animation, always ready to be aroused whenever the boy or man was brought into contact with circumstances which resembled those of his experience with the dog in the narrow passage, circumstances which would tend to stir up the buried memory. The simplest way of regarding this case is to suppose that the suppression was not complete, but that the suppressed experience lay for thirty years so near the threshold of consciousness that it was capable of being roused into activity by any conditions resembling those of the events in which the suppression had its origin. On these occasions all that reached consciousness was the affective side of the experience and then only in a more or less vague form. To use a metaphor, it is as if the activity of the suppressed body of experience is accompanied by an affective disturbance which boils over on [p. 78] certain occasions, so that some of the steam reaches the conscious level, while the main disturbance still continues to be wholly cut off from consciousness.

I have now to consider whether we should or should not include such a state in our definition of dissociation. It is clear that we have to do in this case with suppression and with independent activity of the suppressed experience. If we regard independent activity as the distinguishing mark of dissociation we should clearly have to do with an example of the process. If, on the other hand, as I propose, we hold independent consciousness to be necessary to the definition, we cannot find any evidence of such independence. In this case we have clear evidence of consciousness associated with the activity of the suppressed experience, but this consciousness is clearly linked with the general body of consciousness of the normal life. So definitely was it linked therewith in the case of claustrophobia that it determined the behaviour of the patient in many respects, and especially in respect to the conditions which he knew from experience would arouse his dread. Not only was there no evidence of any dissociated consciousness, but there was clear evidence that such consciousness as accompanied the activity of the suppressed experience was associated with the consciousness of the normal mental life. I propose, therefore, to exclude this case of claustrophobia, and, of course, with it other similar states, from the category of dissociation. I believe that this course could be justified on other grounds: The object of using such technical terms as "dissociation" is to conduce to clearness of thought and to assist the classification of psychological and psycho-pathological states according as they resemble or differ from one another in their essential nature. A phobia and a fugue are so unlike one another that it should be comforting to be relieved of the necessity, which would follow on the ordinary use of the term "dissociation" of regarding both as exemplars of this process. I shall return to the nature of the phobias later. I am only concerned here to show why they should be excluded from the category of dissociation.

The conclusion to which I am tending is that the definition [p. 79] of dissociation, which will make the term of most service to psychology and pathology, is: one which lays special stress on the feature of alternate consciousness. The term "dissociation" will then be used for a process of activity of suppressed experience in which this activity is accompanied by consciousness so separated from the general body of consciousness that the experience of each phase is inaccessible to the other under ordinary conditions, in which the two phases can only be brought into relation with one another by means similar to those by which experience can be recovered from the unconscious.

Having now, I hope, made clear what I mean by dissociation, it becomes my task to attempt to fit the process into the biological scheme which I am formulating in this book. I have to show that there has been some biological need to account for the presence of dissociation among the potentialities of human behaviour. I have given examples of suppression from several different aspects of animal psychology and have attempted to show that it is a process essential to the success of many of the reactions by which animals, even animals very low down in the scale of development, adapt behaviour to the needs of their existence. I regard dissociation as one of the modifications which suppressed experience may undergo, and it is now necessary to inquire whether it is possible to discern any similar biological significance in this process.

I have already considered[5] the need for suppression which is created in the amphibian by the complex nature of its life-history. I have supposed that it is essential to the comfort, if not to the existence, of the frog that it shall not be disturbed by the memories of its experiences as a tadpole, and that it is convenient, if not necessary, that these memories shall be suppressed. Let us now carry our imagination to the two kinds of existence which enter into the life of the adult amphibian. The frog has a certain set of experiences which arise out of its life in the water and another set of experiences which arise out of its life on dry land. I now suggest that the amphibian has [p. 80] associated with these two modes of existence two different sets of memories, dissociated from one another. If the amphibian when in the water should only be liable to recall experience associated with this mode of existence and when on dry land should similarly not be liable to be disturbed by memories of his aquatic existence, but is only open to memories of a terrestrial kind, we should have a perfectly characteristic example of dissociation and of alternate consciousness amounting to double personality. If, as there is every reason to believe, Man in the course of his evolution has passed through such an amphibian phase, one in which it was necessary that he should be adapted to two very different kinds of existence, we seem to have the clue to the presence in his make-up of the property of dissociation of behaviour and splitting of consciousness.

I have taken the frog as an instance of an amphibian because it is one with which we are especially familiar, but the process of dissociation and the property of alternate consciousness would be still more necessary to such an amphibian as the newt, which is for long spaces of time the subject of purely aquatic experience and then for long periods leads a life upon the ground. In such an animal, the process of dissociation might be expected to be even more complete than in an animal, such as the frog, which passes habitually and quickly from one mode of existence to the other.

At a later stage of human development we come to a transition which must clearly have provided another occasion for dissociation. Whenever the ancestors of Man took to an arboreal existence, there would have been another opportunity for the occurrence of dissociation between the experience proper to life upon the ground and that of the existence in trees. It seems however, far more likely that in this case there was no dissociation. The transitions between the two kinds of existence would be so habitual that in place of dissociation we might expect a very full integration of the experience connected with the two modes of existence, an integration perhaps more complete than any which had been present in consciousness up to [p. 81] this stage in animal development. Professor Elliot Smith has pointed out[6] how greatly the necessities of an arboreal existence, with the need for delicate co-ordination of eye and hand, must have acted as the stimuli to cerebral development. I now venture to suggest that another motive and stimulus to such development are to be found in the need for the integration of experience connected with two different modes of existence in place of the independence of experience and absence of integration which I assume to have accompanied the prolonged phase in which the ancestors of Man were passing from an aquatic to a terrestrial existence.

It may be worth while to point out a corollary of the proposition that the process of taking to an arboreal existence was accompanied by a substitution of fusion and harmonious integration for the dissociation which had been characteristic of earlier phases of development. On the one hand, the need for integration would lead to the formation of many and complex nervous connections, thus making up the association-tracts which form so large a part of the neo-pallium. On the other hand, the need for the delicate co-ordination of movements of eye and hand would, as Elliot Smith has pointed out, naturally lead to other developments of the kind we call intelligent. Thus, furtherance of the growth of intelligence would follow even more naturally from the substitution of a process of integration for an earlier phase in which experiences which did not readily harmonise were kept in the separate compartments provided by the process of dissociation. If at this point of Man's development, a process of fusion and integration were substituted for dissociation as the normal means of dealing with experiences difficult to reconcile with one another, we seem to have a most important clue to the vast development which at this stage led, on the one hand, to the growth of intelligence and on the other to the growth of the cerebrum. If we assume that before this point of development it was habitual to keep in separate compartments bodies of experience such as those arising [p. 82] out of an amphibian existence, we shall not only be provided with an explanation of the potentialities of dissociation in Man, but we shall also be enabled the better to understand the great development of intelligence and of the neo-pallium which is the distinctive feature of Mankind.

It is one of the principles of psycho-pathology, with which I shall deal more fully later under the heading of regression, that in morbid states early instinctive modes of reaction tend to reappear. If the occurrence of dissociation under morbid conditions is such an example of regression, we are not only enabled to understand its occurrence, but light is also thrown upon one of the most important periods in the history of human development.

I will close this chapter on dissociation by considering its relation to certain features of normal mental process. We are all familiar with experiences of ordinary life which have much similarity with dissociation, and especially those in which we switch off from one occupation to another of a very different kind, and are in no way disturbed by impulses or memories proper to the occupation which has been given up in favour of another. The case differs from one of morbid dissociation in that the experience of each phase is readily accessible to the consciousness of the other. The passing from one phase to the other has not the unwitting character of the morbid process, but takes place wittingly, and under full control, so that it can be produced and repeated at will.

This power of switching from one set of interests to another may perhaps be regarded as a kind of epicritic dissociation in which Man has utilised the instinctive property of, or tendency to, dissociation, in which he has brought it under control and to a large extent graduated it to meet the special needs of the developed mental life. At the least we seem to have here a feature of normal mental process, with certain points of resemblance to morbid, or, as it may be called, protopathic, dissociation, which may help us to understand its nature. There is little doubt that different persons possess the power of keeping their mental processes in distinct compartments in very different [p. 83] degree, and it would be interesting to know with what other mental characters this power is correlated.

Another feature of the normal mental life may be mentioned which probably stands in an even closer relation to dissociation. All of us in some degree, and many persons in a high degree, keep their beliefs and thoughts in separate compartments which have been called "logic-tight compartments." In these cases each of two sets of beliefs or thoughts is accessible to the other, but no effort is ever naturally made to bring them into relation with one another. The special feature of these cases is a failure of fusion or integration which brings them definitely into relation with dissociation. The state may be regarded as another epicritic form of dissociation in which any suppression is of a very incomplete kind. This form of imperfect integration is of great importance in psycho-pathology because it shows itself in a most pronounced form in cases of delusion. In such cases a system of thoughts, affects, and beliefs may exist definitely connected with the delusion, the different parts of which are in harmony with one another. This system co-exists with another set of thoughts, affects, and beliefs which are of the same order as those of the rest of the society to which the person belongs. When this latter system is dominant the person seems to be a normal member of society, but if anything happens to arouse the delusion-system, his conduct may be wholly inappropriate to social needs, and he is regarded as insane, or rather whether such a person is or is not regarded as insane depends on the degree in which the delusional system is out of harmony with the conventions of the society to which he belongs.

I have pointed out that different persons differ in respect to the degree in which their opinions are subject to logic, and it has been supposed that similar differences characterise different races of Mankind, or at least varieties of Mankind differing in cultures. It has been supposed by the French writer, Lévy-Bruhl, that savages are incapable of integrating their beliefs, and are so prone to accept ideas which are incompatible with one another that he has supposed savage Man to be in what he calls the prelogical state of development. It is probable that [p. 84] the ideas of people of lowly culture are rather more shut off from one another by logic-tight compartments than those of the members, at any rate the more educated members, of a civilised community, but most of the examples upon which Lévy-Bruhl founds his prelogical stage are capable of explanation on other lines. Many of the ideas and practices which Lévy-Bruhl believes to be logically incompatible with one another are found to be perfectly logical, sometimes even more logical than our own ideas and practices, when we understand their real meaning.[7] In other cases, especially in the religious sphere, ideas are held by many savage peoples which are definitely incompatible with one another, but in such cases the incompatibility seems never to have been questioned. According to the interpretation of the school of ethnology to which I belong, these incompatible beliefs belong to different cultural influences, indigenous or introduced, which have never been harmonised and integrated. They have been accepted uncritically and in this respect do not differ from the religious beliefs of many a more civilised people, or at any rate from those of the less educated members of their societies.

Footnotes

[1] Brit. Jour. Psych., vol. x. (1919), p. 5·

[2] Brain, vol. xli. (1918), p. 57.

[3] Brain, vol. xli (1917), p. 16.

[4] See The Unconscious, New York (1914), p. 249.

[5] Page 69.

[6] Presidential Address, Section H, British Association, 1912; Rep. Brit. Ass., 1912, p. 583.

[7] See W.H.R. Rivers, "The Primitive Conception of Death," Hibbert Journal, vol. x. (1912), p. 393.

It will be convenient at this stage to consider a term for a concept which is now widely current in psycho-pathology and has so caught the general fancy that it is becoming part of popular language. I propose to consider what we mean when we speak of a complex. In its original significance, as used by Jung, the term referred to experience belonging to the unconscious which, though inaccessible to consciousness, is yet capable of influencing thought and conduct, especially in directions which may be regarded as pathological.

Bernard Hart, who more than any other English writer has made the psychology of the unconscious part of general knowledge, has greatly extended the meaning of the term and uses it for any "emotionally toned system of ideas" which determines conscious behaviour, taking the hobby as his special example, while he also instances political bias as a complex. During the war the term has come to be used very loosely. Worries and anxieties arising out of recent and fully conscious experience have been spoken of as complexes. In fact, the word is often used in so wide and loose a sense that my own tendency at present is to avoid it altogether, and this course will have to be followed in scientific writings unless we can agree upon some definition which will make the term "complex" really serviceable as an instrument of thought. I propose now to do what I can towards the formulation of such a definition.

In the last chapter I attempted to make clear the sense in which we should use another term, dissociation, which is also in danger of becoming useless through the inexactness with which it is employed. I reached the conclusion that the term "dissociation" will be most useful if it is defined as [p. 86] the independent activity of suppressed experience accompanied by alternate consciousness. The first possibility which occurs to us is that we should connect the term "complex" with the process of dissociation as so defined. A complex would then be a body of suppressed experience with an activity independent of the behaviour of normal life and accompanied by consciousness dissociated or separated from the consciousness which accompanies that behaviour.

An alternative is that the term "complex" shall be used in a wider sense for any body of suppressed tendencies and experience which shows any form of independent activity. This usage would certainly come nearer to that at present in vogue. Used in this wider sense it would be applied to such experience as that of my claustrophobic patient whose experience in the passage, together with the accompanying affect, would be a complex. In my own childish experience the nature of the "complex" is as yet unknown, but if it should be found that the suppression of my imagery is due to some one especially painful event, that event with its associated experience would then be spoken of as a complex. If it can be shown that this suppressed experience has had any influence on my character and mental constitution, this influence would be said to be due to the complex. In the case of war-experience the term "complex" would apply to any events which, having become inaccessible to consciousness, can yet be held directly responsible for fugues, nightmares, terrors, or other manifestations of a psycho-neurosis or for minor peculiarities of a similar order which are not ordinarily regarded as pathological.

The term "complex" is especially useful where we are seeking for the explanation of a specific mental manifestation such as a phobia, a fugue, a specific anxiety, or a specific feature of a dream. It is distinctly useful to be able to speak of the complex in such a case in place of having to refer every time to the body of suppressed tendencies together with the associated experience and affect which are determining the course of behaviour. [p. 87]

It will have been noted that both the senses in which I have considered the term "complex" are narrower than that proposed by Bernard Hart. There is no reason to suppose that political bias has any special relation to suppression or to dissociation in the sense in which I use the terms. In so far as our political opinions are determined by underlying preferences and prejudices, the "political bias" of Bernard Hart, they are the result of a large number of influences of childhood, youth, and adult age, many of which are fully conscious, while others may be determined, at any rate in part, by experience which has been suppressed. The bias as a whole, however, is a very complicated affair which in the main is a product, not of suppression, but of fusion, a fusion between trends of certain lines of thought and conduct which may or may not be determined by unconscious experience, together with other influences, such as those of parents, teachers and friends, which have never been either suppressed or repressed, but very much the opposite.

In the broad sense which Hart proposes for "complex," the term becomes almost identical with the "sentiment" of the orthodox psychologist. Used in this definite sense, the term and concept of "sentiment" are among the most recent and valuable acquisitions of psychology, but in my opinion it will only tend to confusion of thought to include in one category sentiments and the bodies of suppressed experience to which I should like to see the term "complex " limited, if it is going to be used at all.

It may perhaps help to make clear how I distinguish sentiments from complexes if I illustrate by similar products on the sensori-motor level. Such an experiment as that of Head shows that certain forms of protopathic experience, such as the radiation and reference of sensation in space, are suppressed while other elements are fused with later developed forms of sensation to make up the normal modes of sensibility of the skin. Let us consider for a moment what we mean when we speak of the sensibility for cold. We mean that the skin is endowed with "something" which, when a body with certain [p. 88] physical properties touches the skin, determines both our experience of cold, and the special kind of behaviour which is adapted to this experience. What we mean by sensibility is thus comparable to the "something" in our mental constitution which determines that when we read in the paper of a certain event, we experience the specific kind of affect and special tendency to behaviour, which determine the relation of that event to our political conduct, which help, for instance, to determine how we shall vote at the next election. This "something" which thus determines our feelings and conduct is what the orthodox psychologist knows as a sentiment.

We have seen that the sensibility of the normal skin is produced by the process of fusion of different kinds of tendency and experience. This fusion is a process of a wholly different order from the suppression by which certain features of early experience have been put out of activity. The whole process of development of cutaneous sensibility which is made clear and intelligible by distinguishing suppression from fusion, and by defining the proper place and share of each, would be hopelessly obscured if we confused the two very different processes of suppression and fusion under one heading. And yet this is what in my opinion has been done by Bernard Hart when he includes under the term "complex" the highly complicated product of fusion, which by other psychologists is called a sentiment, and the suppressed experience which probably, indeed certainly, enters into the process of fusion, but only as one of its elements. Using the terms as I propose, both complex and sentiment determine thought and conduct, but differ from each other profoundly in other respects. They differ first in complexity, the sentiment being far more complex in its nature than the process which has been denoted according to this feature.[1] Secondly, to use the special terminology of this book, the sentiment is a far more epicritic product than [p. 89] the complex. The sentiments are features of the mind which take part in the most finely graduated processes and are connected with discrimination of the most delicate description. The complex, on the other hand, being the result of suppression always partakes in some degree of the crude "all-or-none" character which we have been led to associate with suppression. Months or years may pass without its showing any effects at all and then it may reveal its presence by some profound and far-reaching disturbance of the mental life.

Lastly, it is not without importance that the sentiment is an absolutely necessary and constant feature of the normal mental life. Most of our sentiments come into action daily and influence the behaviour of every moment of the life of every day. The complex, on the other hand, in the sense in which I should like to use the term, has essentially a pathological implication. It is not only a result of suppression, but the product of independent activity of the suppressed content, whether accompanied by alternate consciousness or wholly within the region of the unconscious. There is, of course, no hard-and-fast line between the healthy and the morbid, and it is possible, if not probable, that the complex will in some cases shade off into the sentiment, but I believe it is useful that pathology shall have its own terms and concepts. I believe that it will be best to reserve the term "complex" for products which partake, in some degree at any rate, of a morbid quality and that nothing but confusion can result from the inclusion in one category of definitely pathological processes and such absolutely normal and necessary processes as the sentiments.

Footnotes

[1] It is very unfortunate that the complex should have been so named. Its two characteristic features are its relation to the unconscious and its affective importance, and a suitable term should have reference to one, if not to both, of these features.

Until now I have only been considering the relation between instinct and the unconscious from the standpoint of the individual. Taking the various forms of instinctive reaction to danger as my examples, I have illustrated the need for suppression and the value of the unconscious as means of preserving the life and the integrity of the individual, I have now to consider the additional factors which come into action when danger threatens a group of animals associated together, factors which in the case of Man will contribute to maintain the cohesion of society.

The instinct which has come into existence in order to produce and maintain the cohesion of the group is commonly known as the gregarious or the herd instinct. This is a complicated instinct which, according to the current opinion,[1] is represented in Man by three chief processes according as it is viewed from the three aspects from which we are accustomed to regard mental process. The essential function of the gregarious instinct is that it shall lead all the members of a group to act together towards the common purpose of furthering the welfare of the group. On the motor side this common action is regarded as a process of imitation. The actions of every member of the group are said to be determined by the "imitation" of those of some one member of the group, this process of imitation being especially definite when the group has a definite leader.

Viewed from the side of feeling or affect, the gregarious instinct is seen as "sympathy," which in its most characteristic form is the process which produces in every member of the group [p. 91] any affective state which may arise in one of its number. Here, again, the sympathy is especially important from the standpoint of the welfare of the group when the member of the group whose affect is the object of the sympathy is its leader.

The third aspect from which it is possible, on the lines of human psychology, to view the gregarious instinct is the cognitive, including within the connotation of this word the cognitive aspect of sensation. The feature of the instinct which stands out from this point of view is usually known as "suggestion." Thus, McDougall defines suggestion as "a process of communication resulting in the acceptance with conviction of the communicated proposition in the absence of logically adequate grounds for its acceptance."[2] If I were to use suggestion as a term for the cognitive side of the gregarious instinct I should prefer to define it as the process which makes every member of the group aware of what is passing in the minds of the other members of the group.

The chief object of this chapter is to point out that, though processes derived from the gregarious instinct may enter into the composition of conscious states, just as constituents of protopathic sensibility enter into the fully-developed cutaneous sensibility, they thus lose any individuality they may possess. When they are not thus fused with other later processes, they act unwittingly, and are to be numbered among the processes of the unconscious. When looked at from this point of view it is convenient to use the term suggestion, not as a name for the cognitive aspect of the gregarious instinct, but as a comprehensive term for the whole process whereby one mind acts upon another unwittingly. From this point of view suggestion can be put side by side with suppression as one of the processes of instinct. It is a process or mechanism of instinct rather than part of its content. Just as I have supposed that the process of suppression takes place unwittingly and cannot be produced, though it may be assisted, by witting repression, so do I now suppose that the process of suggestion works unwittingly and is not primarily set in action by voluntary process, though an effort of the will can [p. 92] set in action mental processes which assist suggestion and further its activity.

The unwitting character of suggestion also holds good of its three aspects, the motor or effector, the affective, and the cognitive. Thus, if "imitation" is used as a term for the motor or effector aspect of the gregarious instinct, it must be clearly recognised that the imitation is unwitting. It is this kind of imitation who is especially important in the life of the infant and in all those reactions upon which depend the special characters of the collective behaviour of Mankind. It is in this form that imitation is most effective. Witting imitation can never attain the completeness and harmony which follow the action of the instinctive process.

The use of one term for two processes, one witting and the other unwitting, is unsatisfactory, and another difficulty in the use of the term "imitation" for the instinctive process is that this term as ordinarily used applies especially to the person who, or the animal which, acts in the same manner as another, while in the unwitting process the attitude of the person whose actions are copied is just as important and requires denoting as much as that of the person who copies.

The differences between the witting and unwitting forms of imitation are so important that there is great danger of ambiguity and confusion if one term is used for the two processes. It would be far more satisfactory if a new term were employed for the unwitting process, and I propose in this book to speak of "mimesis" when I refer to it.

In the case of the affective aspect of the gregarious instinct the current term "sympathy" is more appropriate, for it implies the reciprocal and unwitting character of the process. It is generally recognised that, to be effective, sympathy must be spontaneous and wholly free from any voluntary forcing. It is the more real and the more effective the more unwittingly it comes into being.

In the case of the cognitive aspect of imitation the need for a new term is essential if the term hitherto used for this aspect is to be employed is a more general sense. If, as I propose, [p. 93] the term "suggestion" is to be used for the sum-total of the processes by which one mind acts upon, or is acted upon by, another unwittingly, it will be necessary to have another term for the process by which one person becomes aware unwittingly of any cognitive activity taking place in the mind of another. I propose to use the term "intuition" in this sense. Intuition will thus rank with mimesis and sympathy as one of the three aspects from which it is possible to view the comprehensive process of suggestion. It may be objected that this nomenclature leaves undenoted the cognitive activity which is intuited. This objection will come from the physician who, when he uses the term "suggestion" in a definite sense, usually has this active aspect in mind. He will object that the kind of suggestion he knows best is that which takes place in the consulting-room where he "suggests" and the patient reacts. From the standpoint of this book the process of the consulting-room is a specialised and artificial variety of the general process of suggestion, the artificiality lying in its witting use of a process which normally takes place unwittingly. If, as is probable, the physician prefers to continue to use "suggestion" in this limited sense, it will be necessary for him to find some other term for the more general process by which one mind acts upon, or is acted upon by, another unwittingly.

It may be remarked here that the uncertainty, if not confusion, which is so general concerning the meaning of suggestion is due to the failure to recognise that it belongs to a category of mental process widely different from the cognition, association, imagination, volition, and other concepts derived from the study of conscious mental states. As soon as we recognise that suggestion is essentially a process of the unconscious, and that its different aspects also have this nature, we have to renounce the clearness of definition which is possible in the case of the processes and products of consciousness. We have to be content with a concept which has a certain vagueness when considered from the purely psychological standpoint, while still remaining capable of exact use from the standpoint of biology. In the following argument, therefore, I propose to [p. 94] use suggestion with its three constituent processes as a term for a mechanism of the unconscious, for that aspect of the gregarious instinct whereby the mind of one member of a group of animals or human beings acts upon another or others unwittingly, to produce in both or all a common content, or a content so similar that both or all act with complete harmony towards some common end.

Assuming that animals whose common action is thus determined possess something we call mind, the effect of suggestion is to produce in all the members of the group a mental content so similar that all act with complete harmony towards some common end. There is reason to believe that the harmony so produced is more complete than is ever produced by the common possession of an idea or other form of intellectual motive. It is no great assumption that the more gregarious is a species of animal, the more perfect is its gregarious instinct. Since Man is very far from being completely adapted to the gregarious life, it will follow that the harmony produced by the action of suggestion in fully gregarious animals is more complete than is ever produced in Man, either by suggestion or by the presence in the social group of a common idea or other form of intellectual motive.

There is reason to believe that this superiority of the unwitting process of suggestion over intellectual process remains good among the different varieties of Man. Existing families of Mankind differ greatly in their degree of gregariousness and with this there seem to go different degrees in the potency of suggestion as a means of producing uniformity of social action. Thus, the Melanesian is distinctly more gregarious than the average European. His whole social system is on a communistic basis, and communistic principles work throughout the whole of his society with a harmony which is only present in certain aspects of the activity of our own society, and even there the harmony is less complete than in Melanesia. As an example of such harmony I give the following experience. When in the Solomon islands in 1908 with Mr. A. M. Hocart we spent some time in a schooner visiting different parts of the island of Vella [p. 95] Lavella. Whenever we were going ashore five of the crew would row us in the whale-boat, four rowing and the fifth taking the steer-oar. As soon as we announced our intention to go ashore, five of the crew would at once separate from the rest and man the boat; one would go to the steer-oar and the others to the four thwarts. Never once was there any sign of disagreement or doubt which of the ship's company should man the boat, nor was there ever any hesitation who should take the steer-oar, though, at any rate according to our ideas, the coxswain had a far easier and more interesting task than the rest.

It is possible that there was some understanding by which the members of the crew arranged who should undertake the different kinds of work, but we could discover no evidence whatever of any such arrangement. The harmony seems to have been due to such delicacy of social adjustment that the intention of five of the members of the crew to man the boat and of one to take the steer-oar was at once intuited by the rest. Such an explanation of the harmony is in agreement with many other aspects of the social behaviour of Melanesian or other lowly peoples. When studying the warfare of the people of the Western Solomons I was unable to discover any evidence of definite leadership. When a boat reached the scene of a head-hunting foray, there was no regulation who should lead the way. It seemed as if the first man who got out of the boat or chose to lead the way was followed without question. Again, in the councils of such people there is no voting or other means of taking the opinion of the body. The people seem to recognise instinctively, using this much misused word in the strict sense, that some definite line of action shall be taken. Those who have lived among savage or barbarous peoples in several parts of the world have related how they have attended native councils where matters in which they were interested were being discussed. When after a time the English observer has found that the people were discussing some wholly different topic, and has inquired when they were going to decide the question in which he was interested, he has been told that it had already been decided and that they had passed to other business. The [p. 96] decision had been made with none of the processes by which our councils or committees decide disputed points. The members of the council have become aware at a certain point that they are in agreement, and it was not necessary to bring the agreement explicitly to notice.

I am aware that the explanation of these examples of the great harmony of social life in savage peoples as due to suggestion rests upon evidence of doubtful value, and might be explained on other lines if our knowledge of the people, their language and behaviour, were more complete. It may be noticed, however, that this explanation has much to support it in our own society. The examples I have given are similar to the so-called process of thought-reading among ourselves.[3] It is noteworthy that these processes are especially exemplified in the minor everyday behaviour of our community, behaviour comparable in some measure with the harmony of the boat's crew which so excited my wonder in Melanesia. A speculative Melanesian who watched the traffic in the streets of a great English town would be greatly struck by the harmony of the passage of people on the pavements in which the rarity of jostling is to be explained by an immediate intuition of the movements of others which takes place unwittingly with all the signs characteristic of instinctive behaviour. In the case of the roadway, the Melanesian would on inquiry learn the existence of definite regulations, but they would seem to afford insufficient explanation of the harmony of the traffic and the rarity of collisions. These examples are peculiarly appropriate to the present argument in that they have a definite relation to the welfare of the group and, at any rate in the case of the roadway, promote its safety as well as its comfort.

Another example among ourselves of suggestion, in the sense in which I am using the term, is social tact. This is of exactly the same order, though on a higher level of behaviour, as the social adjustments which are necessary in traffic or even [p. 97] in the ordinary intercourse of the home. Tact depends essentially on processes which take place unwittingly. It is a process in which one person becomes aware of what is passing in the mind of another or others, and it is noteworthy that this tact comes especially into play when the mental content thus intuited has the affective quality which, according to the argument of this book, is so strongly associated with instinctive reactions.

Having made as clear as its nature allows the sense in which I shall use "suggestion," I ran proceed to consider its functions, in relation to the danger-instincts. When a group of animals react to danger by means of flight it is certainly for the welfare of each individual that it shall act with the rest, but it is not so clear that complete uniformity is necessary in this mode of reaction. It may even be that in some cases individual safety, as well as the safety of the greatest number, would be promoted by flight in different directions rather than by the absolute uniformity which would result from a perfect process of suggestion. In the reaction by aggression again, absolute uniformity is not imperative. The safety of the greatest number may even be promoted if some members of the group adopt an aggressive attitude while the rest save themselves by flight.

It is when we come to the reaction by immobility that we meet with the most imperative need for uniformity of behaviour. It will, of course, be to the advantage of the greater number if a few members of the group take to flight while the rest become motionless, but among those who adopt the latter reaction, uniformity is essential. If the reaction by immobility were absent, or even imperfect, in only one member of the group, it would endanger the safety of the whole. The factors, such as the high degree of visual sensibility for movement, which make the avoidance of all motion so essential for the safety of the individual, would be equally necessary for the safety of the group. The function of suggestion is to ensure the absolute uniformity which is essential to the welfare of the group. There is thus an especial reason for the close association [p. 98] of suggestion with the instinctive reaction to danger by means of immobility, and for its special potency in this association.

The close association between suggestion and the instinct of immobility also furnishes a clue to the continued activity, or potentiality for action, of the suppressed tendencies to other forms of reaction. If the reaction by immobility fails, it is essential that it shall be at once replaced by some other mode of reaction, such as flight or aggression. The potentiality for one or other of these reactions must be there ready to come at once into play if the need arises. It is essential that suppression and the potentiality for full readiness of the suppressed activity shall go hand in hand. If, therefore, the association between suggestion and the suppression of the instinct of immobility is especially close, there will also be an association between suggestion and the potential activity of suppressed tendencies. We should expect to find suppressed tendencies to be especially prone to independent activity when they are derived from, or connected with, the reaction to danger by means of immobility. Moreover, the activity of animals who suddenly replace immobility by another kind of reaction has some similarity with the process of dissociation. The change from the reaction by immobility to that of flight is so great that animals practising the two kinds of reaction might be regarded as two personalities. One activity, when compared with the other, has some similarity with a fugue or other example of dissociation.

In an earlier chapter I have considered how far the "all-or-none" principle applies to the process of suppression to which I ascribe so great an importance in relation to instinct. I have now to inquire whether this principle applies to suggestion which I regard as the characteristic process of the gregarious instinct.

It will be evident at once that the examples I have given of suggestion imply a high degree of delicacy of appreciation of the states to which an animal or human being reacts, together with a corresponding graduation of the activity in which the reaction consists. If we regard suggestion as an instinctive [p. 99] process, it becomes necessary to give up completely the idea that the "all-or-none" principle is a character of instinct in general. The nature of suggestion shows with certainty that the principle cannot apply to all the processes or mechanisms of instinct. When considering suppression from this point of view it was found that though this process seems originally to have been characterised by the "all-or-none" principle, its reactions have ceased to show this character as the process became adapted to more complex conditions. Until now I have assumed that this process of adaptation depends upon the influence of the factors we group together as intelligence. The fully graded character of suggestion raises the question whether this process may not provide another means for giving a discriminative and graded character to suppression, the discrimination and graduation differing from those associated with intelligence in that they belong to the sphere of instinct and take place unwittingly.

It is important to note in this connection that suggestion belongs to an instinct which is concerned with collective as opposed to individual needs. This suggests that the protopathic forms of instinct characterised by the "all-or-none" principle are especially concerned with the welfare of the individual and that this principle had to be modified as soon as the collective or social life gave birth to new needs. As soon as it became necessary to adjust behaviour to that of other members of a group, the original "all-or-none" reactions had to be modified in the direction of discrimination and graduation. The presence in Man of both suggestion and intelligence shows that the early protopathic forms of instinctive behaviour were modified in two directions, one leading towards intelligence and the other towards suggestion and intuition. In Man the former has become, or perhaps more correctly may be gradually becoming, the more important, but suggestion still remains as a factor of the greatest potency in determining human behaviour, especially under certain conditions. In an earlier chapter I have suggested that the grading mechanism by which the protopathic reactions of the insect, or other exemplar of pure instinctive [p. 100] behaviour, have been graded are of a different order from that which has been effective in Man, and that it is the business of the student of insect behaviour to discover the nature of this grading principle. I have now to suggest that this grading principle may belong to the order of suggestion. It is noteworthy that the highest examples of innate discrimination and graduation occur in animals, such as ants and bees, in which the social life is especially developed. I now put forward the idea that we must look to suggestion and intuition for the clues through which we may hope to understand the nature of the powers by which the discriminative and graded character of the innate behaviour of the insect has been produced.

Footnotes

[1] See W. McDongall, Social Psychology.

[2] W. McDougall, op. cit., p. 97.

[3] I use "thought-reading" as a name for the unwitting transmission of ideas from person to person in the presence of one another as distinguished from the problematical telepathy or distant thought-transference.

I have already mentioned hypnotism in this book on more than one occasion as a means of recalling to memory suppressed experience. I have now to consider more fully its relation to instinct and the unconscious.

I will begin with a brief general account of the nature of hypnotism. The first point to be noted is its intimate relations with suggestion. When hypnotism was first studied the general tendency, as is usual in such cases, was to regard it as a manifestation of some new force, and in accordance with the prevalent conceptions of the day, a force of a physical kind allied to those which were already known. Misunderstood observations in which hypnotic manifestations were produced by means of magnets led to the choice of magnetism as the prototype of the new force, and animal magnetism was widely used, and is still sometimes heard, as a term for this state. It was not long, however, before it was established, chiefly through the work of the Nancy school, that the chief or only agency by which hypnotic manifestations are produced is suggestion. Moreover, one of the most important features of the hypnotic state is the greatly enhanced suggestibility of the hypnotised person. It is one of the characteristic features of hypnotism that the receptivity of a hypnotised person towards suggestion is greatly increased, and there is reason to believe that this increase is especially great in relation to suggestions given by the hypnotiser unwittingly.

A second feature of the hypnotic state, which is closely linked with the heightened suggestibility, is a great increase in sensitiveness [p. 102] to sensory stimuli, or at least to certain kinds of sensory stimulus. A hypnotised person may become aware of and utilise indications given by organs of sense which produce no effect whatever upon his consciousness in the normal state.

A third feature of hypnotism is that it affords a characteristic example of suppression. When a person is hypnotised it is possible to blot out from his memory experience which in the normal state is directly accessible to consciousness, while, as already mentioned on more than one occasion, other experience which is normally inaccessible to consciousness may by means of hypnotism be brought to the surface. Moreover, any experience gained during the hypnotic state may become inaccessible to memory when the hypnotic state comes to an end, and seems to do so spontaneously unless special suggestions are given that it shall be remembered. A striking feature of this aspect of the hypnotic state is the ease with which it is possible to produce suppression of sensibility. Any sensory surface may be rendered wholly insensitive to stimuli to which it ordinarily responds. It is especially striking that this anæsthesia may occur in conjunction with the heightened sensibility which I have already mentioned. A hypnotised person may be wholly insensitive to certain kinds of sensory stimulus and show a vastly exaggerated receptiveness to others.

In the fourth place hypnotism affords a characteristic example of dissociation. During the hypnotic state in response to suggestion a person performs acts, it may be of a highly complex kind of which he is completely unconscious when the hypnotic state is over. The hypnotic state only differs from a characteristic attack of dissociation or a fugue in having been produced by the suggestion of another person.

Hypnotism is thus not only a means by which it is possible to tap the unconscious, but through its agency it is possible to produce at will the two most characteristic mechanisms of the unconscious, suppression and dissociation, and study them experimentally. Moreover, hypnotism is closely linked with suggestion which in the last chapter I have regarded as another mechanism or process of the unconscious. [p. 103]

I have now to consider whether these four characters of hypnotism allow us to bring it into relation with instinct and with the general scheme of this book. I will begin by considering whether the views concerning suggestion put forward in the last chapter help us to understand the very difficult problem of the nature of hypnotism.

In the first place the idea that suggestion is a process of the unconscious evidently accords with its relation to hypnotism. It is not so obvious how the phenomena of hypnotism fit in with the view that suggestion is essentially the expression of the gregarious instinct. At first sight there seems to be no obvious relation between hypnotism and the instrument working unwittingly by means of which unity of purpose and unity of action are given to a group or herd of animals. In the form in which we know it best, hypnotism is an individual and not a collective process. In the instances which usually come before our notice one person is hypnotised by another person, and in general the aim is individual and is directed to affect the health or character of the person who is hypnotised without any necessary relation to the society to which he or she belongs. Collective hypnotism occurs, but it takes a place in our experience insignificant beside the individual relation.

I believe, however, that the individual character of hypnotism, in the form in which it is most familiar to us, only masks and has by no means obliterated its essentially collective character. Especially instructive from this point of view is the heightened sensibility to sensory stimuli which we have found to accompany the heightened suggestibility. For perfect harmony of action among the members of a group of animals, it is necessary that they shall divine or intuit how the rest of the group is going to act before it does so. It will not do to wait until the actions of the rest are in full swing. It is essential that every member of the group shall be ready to react with the rest, this readiness being dependent upon awareness of the minute and almost imperceptible movements which accompany the impulse preceding a definite act.

Some degree of a similar process is needed for the success of [p. 104] the social reactions of man of which I gave several examples in the last chapter. If my interpretation of their actions is right, my Melanesian boatmen must have become aware of the intended movements of their fellows before there was any movement sufficiently great to become the object of conscious attention, and some degree of such intuition is necessary for the success of the daily reactions upon which depends the harmonious character of the traffic of our crowded streets.

Whether we consider animals or Man, it is natural that suggestion should be associated with a high degree of sensory acuity and that the enhanced suggestibility of the hypnotic state should be accompanied by heightening of the sensibility to which suggestion owes so much of its peculiar power. The heightened sensitiveness of the hypnotic state is thus altogether in accordance with its relation to the gregarious instinct.

This relation is less obvious when we turn to the third character of the hypnotic state -- its connection with suppression. I have supposed that the process of suppression in its most complete form is associated with the instinctive reaction to danger by means of immobility. Moreover, I have tried to show that unity of action, or rather of inaction, is essential to the success of this instinct and have therefore put forward the view that, in this connection at least, suggestion and the instinct of immobility are intimately associated with one another. Let us inquire, therefore, whether any connection can be found between hypnotism and the instinct of immobility.

It has long been recognised that a state resembling hypnotism may be induced experimentally in animals. A fowl placed in front of a chalk line will become quite motionless and remain so for a considerable time. A frog stroked on the back will also become, and for a time remain, motionless. It has been supposed that these states depend on the paralysis of fear,[1] but the view more widely taken is that the suppression of movement is of the same order as that which can be induced in Man by suggestion and that the whole process is allied in nature to hypnotism. [p. 105] If the existence of an instinct of immobility is accepted, it will involve no great stretch of the imagination to see in these animal reactions expressions of this instinct. The hypnotic or quasi-hypnotic manifestations of animals thus furnish an intermediate link between hypnotism and the instinct of immobility. They may be regarded as manifestations of the instinct of immobility occurring in the individual animal under the influence of a human being.

The question which is suggested by these animal reactions is whether the hypnotism of the human being may not have a similar connection with the instinct of immobility. It is possible by means of hypnotism to produce a very large range of sensory and motor reactions, but it is noteworthy that it seems especially easy to produce anæsthesias and paralyses, or what is more to the point, there is a great tendency for these states, and especially anæsthesias, to occur as the result of unintended and unwitting suggestion on the part of the hypnotiser. I hope to deal with this topic later from another point of view. I must acknowledge that in so far as hypnotism itself is concerned, it may seem to be stretching the facts to suggest that there is a special tendency for the manifestations of hypnotism in the human subject to take the form which would be dictated by the instinct of immobility, though this form is definite in the allied behaviour of animals which has been so widely regarded as hypnotic.

I have now to consider the fourth character of hypnotism, its exhibition of the process of dissociation. It is one of the dangers of hypnotism, especially when unskilfully employed, that the state may come to occur spontaneous, a person passing into the hypnotic state as the result of some condition which resembles, or seems to resemble, that by which the state was originally produced. In this spontaneous hypnotic state a person may carry out complex actions and behave in a manner wholly indistinguishable from that of the subject of a fugue. We may regard hypnotism as a process by means of which it is possible to produce and study experimentally the process of dissociation. Moreover, there is little doubt that most of the classical cases of [p. 106] multiple personality, such as that of Miss Beauchamp so fully recorded by Dr. Morton Prince, are largely artificial products of hypnotism or have had their characters largely determined by this process.

At this stage it will be useful to sum up the conclusion to which the argument has led. I have given reason to suppose that the hypnotic state is a complex blend of four processes; (a) suggestion with heightened suggestibility; (b) heightened sensibility; (c) suppression; and (d) dissociation. Or perhaps, rather, hypnotism may be viewed from these four different aspects. Moreover, I have advanced arguments to explain why there should be this association of processes or aspects. I have regarded the heightening of suggestibility and of sensibility as being essentially manifestations of the gregarious instinct, arising out of the need of animals as soon as their association in groups required harmony of purpose and action. I have supposed that they are additions to, or modifications of, the earlier process of suppression which had already come into being as a means of meeting certain individual needs, and I have explained the connection of suggestion with suppression as due to the importance of common action in relation to the instinct of immobility. From this point of view the primary aspect of hypnotism is its suppression with the accompanying dissociation, and in the so-called hypnotism of animals there is little more than this, the only feature pointing to the influence of suggestion being the fact that the state is produced by the activity of Man.

According to the view here put forward the complex hypnotic state has arisen through the influence of certain factors which became connected with the primary states of suppression and dissociation through gregarious needs, through the needs of animals when associated together in groups. These factors are heightened sensibility as a means of reading immediately to sensory indications given by other members of the group and heightened suggestibility as a means of responding immediately to the more complex states existing in the minds of the other members of the group. If we put the so-called hypnotism of animals on one side, hypnotism is a process in which Man has [p. 107] discovered how to utilise the processes of suppression and dissociation by turning to advantage the power of suggestion. Hypnotism is an artificial process in which Man has wittingly utilised a process, or group of processes, which normally take place unwittingly.

In the last chapter I have put forward the view that suggestion has been one of the means by which the crude "all-or-none" reactions of primitive instinct have become subject to the principle of graduation. If this were the sole graduating principle, we may suppose that the two more or less conflicting principles would have long ago reached a modus vivendi, a state of stable equilibrium in which such a phenomenon as dissociation could not occur. If, as I have supposed, suggestion forms the essential controlling factor in such creatures as insects, one may suppose that in them such stable equilibrium has been attained. The high degree of adaptation of means to ends in these animals and the perfection of their social organisation would be results and aspects of this equilibrium.

In Man, however, suggestion does not exist alone as an instrument of discrimination and graduation, but is accompanied, and even surpassed in efficacy, by the principle of graduation belonging to the order of intelligence. In the ordinary life of Man there has been produced a state of fairly stable equilibrium in which the graduating activity of intelligence is able successfully to control instinctive tendencies. From this point of view we may regard hypnotism as a process in which Man has discovered that he can direct the instinctive process of suggestion and annul the activity of intelligence, thus giving the mastery to suggestion with its three aspects of mimesis, sympathy and intuition. According to this view, the essence of hypnotism is the annulment of one of the two lines of activity by which the cruder instinctive processes are brought under subjection, leaving in full power those other activities which we subsume under the heading of suggestion.

Those who are acquainted with the subject will have noticed that I have said nothing about one feature of hypnotism which must be explained if the view I have put forward is to hold [p. 108] good. I refer to the process known as post-hypnotic suggestion. If a person in the hypnotic state is told to perform a certain act at a given interval of time after being awakened from the state, he will do so in spite of the fact that he has no knowledge in the normal state that he has received the suggestion. He performs the act at or about the time indicated without knowing why he is so acting, though he will often rationalise and give reasons for an act which, without the knowledge of the suggestion in the hypnotic state, would appear to be irrational. We have here a striking example, in the first place, of what I call unconscious experience, and, in the second place, of the independent activity of such experience. The hypnotised person when in the hypnotic state has a definite experience which becomes inaccessible to his consciousness when he awakes, and this experience has so definite an independent existence that it determines conduct of a highly specific kind. The behaviour has a highly organised and complex character. Not only may the actions carried out be very complex, but the estimation of time involved in the operation may be more accurate than the similar operation carried out wittingly and with full consciousness.

The complexity of the operation raises the questions whether there is not only independent activity but also independent consciousness, and whether there may not be true co-consciousness in Morton Prince's sense. We have no direct evidence of such independent consciousness, but if we accept Morton Prince's account of such a case as that of Miss Beauchamp, in which the different personalities had such independent consciousnesses that one was able to act upon and torment the other, we should expect to find other similar examples. It is a question whether the hypothesis which will best meet the facts of post-hypnotic suggestion is not one which assumes the co-existence of an independent system of experience carrying out the post-hypnotic suggestion. This may be regarded as the germ of the far more highly organised system which makes up an independent personality.

Moreover, this hypothesis would naturally lead us to an [p. 109] interpretation of the fugue on similar lines. It would lead us towards, if not to, the view that in a fugue the normal consciousness is there underlying the split-off consciousness accompanying the activity of the fugue, in which case the terms "co-conscious" and "co-consciousness" would be appropriate. Though I regard this hypothesis as possible and even legitimate, I do not propose to adopt it, but to continue to speak of the fugue as an example of alternate consciousness and to reserve "co-consciousness" for cases of double or multiple personality. When speaking of post-hypnotic suggestion, I shall regard it as an example of the independent activity of suppressed experience, and leave it an open question whether this experience is or is not co-conscious.

Footnotes

[1] See especially W. Preyer, Die Kataplexie und der thierische Hypnotismus, Jena (1878)

In the last chapter I have made no reference to an aspect of hypnotism which is of much importance and must now be considered. I have described how it is possible in the hypnotic state to apply the power of suggestion so as to produce acts of various degrees of complexity as well as the cruder paralyses and anæsthesias, but I have not mentioned a state which is so frequently produced by means of hypnotism, or so often follows its application, that it may be regarded as an almost necessary part of its nature. Not only is the suggestion to sleep one of the most frequent measures which are used when it is desired to produce the hypnotic state, but when this state has been produced, it is often difficult to distinguish it from normal sleep, the chief difference being that the time-limit of the sleep may be determined by the suggestion of the hypnotist and has not the free character possessed by the customary process of sleep. We may assume with some confidence that sleep is a state which is allied to hypnotism, and therefore stands in some relation to the process of suggestion. This raises the problem of the nature of sleep, which I must now consider.

Sleep is an aspect of life which has been strangely neglected by the psychologist. Students of psychology are profoundly interested in the dreams which occur during sleep and in their more abnormal varieties, such as nightmares and somnambulism, but they seem to have been content to regard sleep itself as a process which belongs to the realm of physiology. Even those who have come fully to recognise that external stimuli to the organs of sense or internal visceral disturbances are insufficient as explanations of the dream, are yet content to refer sleep to [p. 111] such purely physiological causes as alterations of blood-supply to the brain, accumulation of the toxic products of activity, or other similar material agencies. They fail to recognise that sleep is much more than a mere negation of psychological activity, and that, quite apart from the occurrence of dreams, sleep has characters of a positive kind which must be fitted into any scheme of mental happenings which seeks to be consistent and complete.

I have already mentioned the resemblance of the hypnotic state to sleep. I have now to consider other points in which sleep resembles the state which follows the hypnotic suggestion of another person. Several features of sleep have led students to believe that it is the result of suggestion exerted by the conditions of time and space with which sleep is habitually associated. There is no question that such conditions as fatigue within certain limits, warmth, the toxic influence of the products of respiration, etc., act as agents in the production of sleep, but they cannot explain the occurrence of sleep under any conditions of time and space of which certain persons are capable, or the immediate occurrence of sleep, even in the absence of sleepiness, which in many people immediately follows going to bed. In such cases it is customary to speak of auto-suggestion. This term may seem in some degree appropriate when applied to the sleep of persons who are able to sleep at will. In the case of those who sleep immediately after going to bed, on the other hand, we should have to regard the suggestion as coming from the pillow, the darkness, the silence, or other habitual feature of the surroundings in which a person is accustomed to sleep.

The conditions of awaking from sleep point more definitely to the influence of suggestion. The selective action of certain conditions of awaking cannot be explained on physiological lines, but demands some kind of discriminative and selective activity on the part of the sleeping person. As examples of such selective activity I may cite the doctor who is awakened even by the movements of wires which precede the ringing of his night-bell, while he is undisturbed by the crying of his [p. 112] child to whose slightest sound the mother immediately responds. Awaking is determined, not by physiological demands but by conditions the efficacy of which is determined almost entirely by predispositions of a psychological kind.

We may regard the conditions which awake a person as suggestions determined by special systems within the personality of the sleeper. It may be noted that such awaking stimuli seem to be especially effective when they stand in a close relation to affective states of the sleeper. The awakening of the mother at the slightest sound or movement of her child may be regarded as a reaction of the parental instinct. The reaction of the doctor to his night-bell bears a less direct relation to instinctive process, but in spite of its more complex character can usually be traced to affective factors connected with instinctive means.

An even closer relation of sleep to suggestion appears in cases in which a sleeping person responds to the questions or commands of another person, especially one with whom he is habitually in intimate relation. A sleeping person may converse with another and may yet be completely unaware of what he has said and done when he awakes. The absence of memory is altogether comparable with that which accompanies the suppression of the post-hypnotic state when no suggestion has been given that the hypnotic experience shall be remembered.

An interesting point of resemblance between hypnotism and sleep may be noted here. Probably everyone has at some time or another experienced how, when sleepless, the difficulty in sleeping is greatly enhanced if doubt arises in the mind whether sleep will come. Going to sleep is an act which normally takes place unwittingly. If we once begin to think whether we are going to sleep, a state of mind is induced which works strongly against the occurrence of the sleep so greatly desired. Sleep is essentially a process which, like forgetting, takes place unwittingly. It is, therefore, interesting to note that those with much experience in the practice of hypnotism have found that if a person who wishes to be hypnotised has doubts whether his wish will be realised, success is definitely prejudiced.[1] Instead [p. 113] of falling into the receptive and passive state which forms the best background for the efforts of the hypnotiser, the doubter becomes agitated and the hypnotic process fails or is delayed. Forel remarks that the more frequently and the more energetically a person endeavours to become passive, the more certainly will he fail, and he compares this state, not only with sleep, but also with affective states. Thus, we cannot force ourselves to become pleased. Pleasure and other affective states must arrive spontaneously. They come without invitation or conscious direction, and resemble in this respect sleep, hypnotism, and active forgetting.

I have so far considered the relationship of sleep and suggestion. I have now to deal with the relation of sleep to other processes of the unconscious. Sleep affords a striking example of suppression. Not only does the conscious activity of the waking life disappear, but any experience acquired in sleep is forgotten, or tends to be forgotten, when we awake. The sleeping experience which is suppressed may be of the kind I have already mentioned in which a person may be wholly unaware of what he had said or done in sleep. Dreams provide an equally characteristic example of forgetting. One of their most definite features is the ease with which they are forgotten. It often happens that we only become aware that we have dreamed owing to some event of the day which recalls an image or incident of a dream which has occurred during the preceding night, or even on some more remote occasion. This has often raised the question whether sleep is not habitually accompanied by dreams, only a small proportion of which are remembered. Whether this be so or not, we can be confident that dream-experience bulks largely in the content of the unconscious. We all know that dreams differ greatly in the ease and completeness with which they are forgotten. The memory of the special variety, which is known as the nightmare, may be as vivid and persistent as that of the most poignant and striking events of the waking life, and all degrees occur between this realistic persistence and the complete forgetting of a dream which is present only for a few moments after awaking. It is significant [p.

114] that the dream which persists in memory is one which has been accompanied by a definite affect, especially of a painful kind.

The process of disassociation is also definitely present in sleep. This is especially obvious in those dreams which are accompanied by acts ranging in complexity from the elaborate behaviour of the sleepwalker to the apparently disjointed utterances of one who talks in his sleep. The most elaborate of these performances may be regarded as a pattern of dissociation, but the difference between it and the slightest movement or utterance in a dream is one only in degree and not in kind.

Somnambulism is of especial interest as an example of dissociation on account of its very close resemblance to a fugue. One who is walking in his sleep is carrying out a series of activities, often of the most varied and complicated kind, which are wholly independent of the activities of his normal life. In some cases the sleepwalker is aware of these activities in the form of a dream when he awakes, but more often any consciousness which may have accompanied the somnambulistic acts becomes inaccessible as soon as the sleeper awakes. Its recovery in the hypnotic or hypnoidal states, however, shows that we have to do with independent consciousness as well as with independent activity, so that the state answers completely to my definition of dissociation. There is, in fact, no difference between a fugue and a somnambulistic attack except that one occurs in sleep and the other in the waking state.

A point which is of the greatest interest in the light of the present argument is that the somnambulistic state is much more frequent than the fugue. In other words, the state of sleep predisposes to the occurrence of dissociation. Moreover, sleep-walking is especially frequent in childhood. The sleep of childhood is especially prone to be disturbed by activities accompanied by consciousness cut off from the activities and consciousness of the ordinary life.

I have supposed dissociation to be an instinctive process. I regard it as a process necessary for the welfare of some of the ancestors of Man which still comes into action in Man himself [p. 115] under certain special circumstances. The special tendency of somnambulism, as a special kind of dissociation, to occur in childhood accords thoroughly with its instinctive character, for it is one of the main theses of this book that instinctive reactions are especially liable to occur, or are liable to occur in an especially pure form, in childhood. In the same way the special liability of dissociation, in the form of somnambulism, to occur in sleep points to the instinctive nature of sleep already brought into view by its close relation to suppression.

At this stage of the argument I should like to call attention to two distinct varieties of somnambulism. In one, with which we have become very familiar during the war, a sleeper reproduces the activity of some experience, while in other cases the actions of the sleep-walker have no such definite relation to one another, but have rather the apparent inconsequence and incoherence of the dream. If, however, the somnambulistic behaviour is an acted dream, we should expect to find it showing varieties of the same kind as those shown by the dream itself.

If, now, we consider the relation of sleep to the three processes of suppression, dissociation and suggestion, it is clear that the primary position belongs to suppression. Sleep is pre-eminently a process in which certain mental processes are put in abeyance for the purpose of recuperation and restoration of the sleeper to full mental as well as bodily efficiency. The dissociation of sleep is the result of the action of lower activities which are released by the suppression of the higher controlling processes, while the enhancement of suggestibility which accompanies sleep is not a necessary, and may even be only an occasional, feature.

Sleep, therefore, may be regarded as primarily an example of the instinctive process of suppression coming into action for the purpose of affording rest to those parts of the mind and body which, being less organised and less stable than the lower instinctive processes, are more liable to fatigue and more in need of the opportunity of rest. Sleep may be regarded as of essentially the same order as the instinct of immobility, but as having through the wide scope of its beneficent action become [p. 116] an almost universal attribute of animal life. Sleep is, in fact, an instinct, allied to the instinct of immobility, which, instead of coming into action only in the presence of danger, is normally of daily occurrence. When it takes place under the influence of certain external surroundings, it is no more appropriate to regard their action as an example of suggestion than it is appropriate to speak of a danger as "suggesting" the special kind of behaviour which is dictated by the instinct of immobility. I do not propose, therefore, to adopt "auto-suggestion" as a term for the process by which external objects induce or help to induce sleep. Nor is it necessary to use the term for the cases in which a person sleeps at will, or apparently at will. This power depends on the ease with which the person can fall into the passive attitude which forms the best opportunity for sleep or hypnotism, but there is no reason to connect the power itself with the process of suggestion which yet undoubtedly takes a part both in sleep and hypnotism. Because, however, I exclude from the category of suggestion certain features of sleep which have frequently been ascribed to it, we must not blind ourselves to the large part which is taken by suggestion in sleep. The selective nature of awakening especially brings into notice features which are closely related to this process.

It is not difficult to see why there should be this relation. The conditions which induce sleep in the individual will also induce it in the group, but there is no special reason why going to sleep should be influenced by factors promoting the welfare of the group as distinguished from that of the individual. With waking, however, the case is different. Here it is essential to the safety of the individual that he shall respond in sleep, not merely to sounds or movements which threaten danger, but also to the sounds or movements of the other members of the group. Moreover, it is necessary that this response shall be discriminative and selective. If each member of the group awakened in response to any kind of stimulus, it would conflict seriously with the recuperation which is the special function of sleep. It is essential that each species of animal shall react in sleep, as in the waking life, to those stimuli which indicate danger, [p. 117] and shall not react to stimuli of an indifferent kind. The power of discrimination and selection which is shown in the process of awakening in Man may be regarded as the direct descendant of the similar power which is essential to the safety of gregarious animals.

Before I leave the subject of sleep, I must consider whether, and if so to what extent, it is subject to the "all-or-none" principle. A moment's consideration will show that the principle does not apply. Sleep is a definitely, and even finely, graded process. It is often difficult to say whether a person, including oneself, is or is not, or has or has not been, asleep. Moreover, the process of waking, as I have just said, implies the presence of the processes of discrimination and selection. I have regarded sleep as allied to the instinct of immobility, but we can now see the essential difference between the two. If I am right, sleep is an example of the instinctive process of suppression in which this process has become capable to a very high degree of being graded and of reacting to delicately-discriminated and selected stimuli. Since this power of gradation and selection appear especially in relation to awaking, and since the process of awaking stands in a close relation to the welfare of the group, it is no great assumption to suppose that the grading stands in a definite relation to gregarious needs and to the process of suggestion by means of which these needs are satisfied. I suggest, therefore, that sleep is an example of instinctive behaviour in which the process of suppression, originally subject to the "all-or-none" principle, has become capable of gradation in a high degree, not through the action of intelligence, but through the working of the power of suggestion which is itself an instinctive process of a graded and discriminative kind. If we are to classify instinctive processes into protopathic and epicritic varieties, sleep belongs pre-eminently, and in a high degree, to the latter group.

There is some reason to believe that one phenomenon of sleep must be excepted from this generalisation, and must be regarded as an example of the "all-or-none " reaction. I refer to the nightmare. In this form of dream, the dreamer is [p. 118] liable to experience affects of extreme intensity. The fear which forms its usual content is more intense and is accompanied by more pronounced physical manifestations than are ever known in the waking state. We seem to have here a form of reaction in which the suppressed experience which underlies the dream reappears with all the force of which it is capable. While some subjects of psycho-neurosis are liable to intense reactions of this kind, others whose general history is very similar show complete suppression of similar experience which may, however, underlie somnambulistic attacks. The completeness of the suppression in some cases, side by side with the extremity of affective disturbance in others, suggests that in the instinctive state to which persons are reduced in psycho-neurosis, the suppressed experience either manifests itself with all its available force or undergoes complete suppression, thus exhibiting a feature which reminds us of the "all-or-none" reaction.

Footnotes

[1] See A. Forel, Hypnotism, London and New York (1906), p. 67.

The aim of the study set forth in this book is to provide a foundation for a biological theory of the psycho-neuroses. Thus far I have been attempting to establish this foundation and I can now turn to the task of formulating the theory the stability of which I have been trying to ensure.

According to this theory mental health depends on the presence of a state of equilibrium between instinctive tendencies and the forces by which they are controlled. The psycho-neuroses in general are failures in the maintenance of this equilibrium. When such a failure occurs, certain processes, some instinctive and some of the order of intelligence, come into activity as attempts to redress the balance. The special form of the psycho-neurosis depends partly on the nature of the failure and the processes by which it has come about, partly on the nature of the restorative processes which come into activity, and partly on the degree of their success. The psycho-neuroses may be regarded as attempts, successful or unsuccessful, to restore the balance between instinctive and controlling forces, attempts to solve the conflict between these warring elements.

Let us first consider the nature of the failure upon which the psycho-neuroses primarily depend. Theoretically the failure in balance and the resulting conflict might be produced in two ways -- by increase in the power of the suppressed tendencies or by weakening of the process by which they are controlled. There is little question that both factors take a part in the production of neurosis.[1] Thus, the frequency of functional [p. 120] nervous disorders about the time of puberty may be ascribed to the increased power of tendencies connected with the instinct of sex. Again, the frequency of neurosis in the recent war has certainly been due in part to the call made upon instinctive tendencies which in the usual peaceful character of our modern civilisation receive no stimulus so that the more adventurous have to resort to excessive speed, dangerous sports, big game hunting, and other similar pursuits to excite their danger-instincts, and give that spice of conflict which redeems the monotonous calm of our modern life in times of peace.

While increase in the activity of instinctive tendencies thus plays an important part in the production of neurosis, this part is, as a rule, overshadowed by the second factor -- weakening of the controlling forces. Both in peace and war the immediate factor in the production of neurosis is weakening of control by shock, strain, illness or fatigue. The chief cause of the frequency of neurosis in the war has been the excessive nature of the strains to which modern warfare exposes the soldier.

As already mentioned, the special form taken by the psycho-neurosis is to some extent dependent on the nature of the conflict and the causes to which failure in this conflict is due. Thus, the differences between the neuroses of war and those of civil life are due in large measure to differences in the nature of the instinctive tendencies which have escaped from control. The relative simplicity of the war-neuroses is due to their origin in disturbance of the relatively simple instinct of self-preservation, while the great majority of the neuroses of civil practice depend on failure of balance between the less simple sexual instinct and the very complex social forces by which this instinct is normally controlled.

Factors arising out of the nature of the failure are, however, of far less influence in determining the form of the neurosis than are the processes by which the organism attempts to amend the failure. The form taken by the neurosis depends mainly upon the nature of the process by which it is attempted to solve the conflict between the instinctive tendencies which have escaped from control, and the forces by which this control has been [p. 121] exerted. I propose in later chapters to consider some of these modes of solution in detail. In this chapter I shall deal, and that only very briefly, with two lines of activity by which attempts, one successful and the other unsuccessful, are made to redeem the failure of balance. In both these cases the organism takes the simple course of attempting to reimpose the state of suppression in a form more or less complete, by means of which the instinctive tendency has previously been held in check. In the successful attempt the neurosis, perhaps only present in an incipient form, disappears, while in the other case a definite form of neurosis develops, the special characters of which are determined in large measure by the process which is put into action in the attempt to solve the conflict.

Successful Suppression. -- I will begin with the mode of reaction which succeeds in utilising the mechanism of suppression, the instrument so fully considered in this book, by which the organism puts out of action tendencies incompatible with more developed ends. There is good reason to believe that in many cases suppression is reinstated in a healthy manner, or at least in a manner which is compatible with health and efficiency. Thus, a frequent form of the conflict by which the neuroses of war are produced is that between the re-awakened instinct of danger with its accompaniment of fear and the ordinary standard of our social life that fear is disgraceful. There is no doubt that this conflict has often been solved during the war by the spontaneous reassertion of the mechanism of suppression so that the fear and its associated tendencies to certain lines of behaviour have been again put into abeyance. In such a case, tendencies which are incompatible with warfare and the military life are restored to their seclusion in the unconscious by the process of suppression, taking place in the unwitting manner which I have supposed to be its characteristic mode of action. I give an example from a life of profound interest in which this seems to have happened. In one of his letters from the front Frederic Keeling mentions[2] that he had never been depressed since coming out to France except on the third and fourth days [p. 122] in hospital, after he had received wounds from a shell-explosion such as must have given him a severe shock. On these days he got a fit of funk and dread of the firing-line. Later letters[3] show that the wound and shock left their mark on him, but it is clear that the manifest fear soon left him. In Keeling's case we do not know whether the disappearance took place by an unwitting process of suppression or was assisted by some witting end conscious process. In many similar cases into which I have been able to inquire, the disappearance of the fear has been greatly assisted by measures similar to those by which we treat an anxiety-state. The subject of the fears has faced the situation and brought the experience associated therewith into relation with other experience of his normal mental life. It is possible that in some cases the suppression may be effected, or at least assisted, by voluntary repression, in which the subject of the fears wittingly thrusts out of his consciousness the painful experience together with the affects and conative tendencies connected therewith. Whether this mode of solution is ever successful I do not know. I have not myself met with a case, but most of my experience has lain with failures to solve the conflict, and it will need a wider survey than has been possible to myself before we can discover whether mere witting repression ever succeeds in producing or helping the suppression of fear which seems to be the normal state of the healthy adult.

Whatever may be its mechanism, however, it seems certain that the process of suppression as a means of solving a conflict may take place in a healthy manner and produce a thoroughly efficient result.

Anxiety- or Repression-Neurosis. -- The other case which I shall consider in this chapter is that in which an unsuccessful attempt is made to reinstate the suppression by which the instinctive tendency with its accompanying affect is in health controlled. As I have already mentioned on more than one occasion, there is much reason to believe that suppression, being an instinctive process, normally takes place unwittingly. Though it is possible that in some cases the attempt wittingly to subdue [p. 123] instinctive tendencies and to banish painful experience associated therewith may be successful, it stands beyond question that this process is as a rule wholly unsuccessful. It not merely fails to still the conflict, but greatly increases its severity. The conflict from which the neurosis starts tends to produce a state of general mental discomfort which may range from mere malaise to definite depression. This discomfort and depression tend to crystallise round some unpleasant experience, either some painful or horrible incident, some fault which has been committed by the sufferer or some misfortune which has come into his life. In those who suffer thus from the effect of war-experience, one party in the original conflict is usually the re-awakened danger-instinct in some form or other with its accompanying affect of fear, but this is often wholly displaced by the affect of horror associated with some peculiarly painful incident of war, or by the affect of shame following some situation which the sufferer fears that he has failed to meet in a proper manner. Whether the dominant affect be fear, horror or shame, the sufferer strives with all his strength to banish it from his consciousness. The process of witting repression is often assisted greatly by the occupations and activities of the day, and may be apparently successful so long as occupation is able to fill the day and the fatigue it brings leads to sleep at night. But if sleep fails, the repressed content may acquire such power as wholly to gain the upper hand, and when sleep abrogates control, the repressed content finds expression in the form of painful dreams or nightmares. On these occasions the painful affect, together with the experience round which it has crystallised, dominates the mind. The disturbed sleep only exhausts the sufferer's strength and makes still more unequal the struggle between the fear, horror or shame, and the forces by which the attempt is made to subdue the ever-rising storm. The sufferer may throw himself into still greater activity or may attempt to drown the conflict by excesses of various kinds, but only succeeds in still further sapping his strength till some comparatively trivial shock, illness or wound, removes him from the possibilities of such attempts to solve the conflict. He [p. 124] becomes the victim of the fully-developed state, formerly called neurasthenia, but now, following Freud, more generally known as anxiety-neurosis from the special exaggerated anxiety, the Angst of the German language, which forms one of its most striking and characteristic symptoms.[4]

The process of witting repression plays so large a part in the development of this state that it might well be styled repression-neurosis, and if our pathological classification is to be founded on ætiology, as all such classifications should, I am coming to believe more and more that repression-neurosis is the proper term, for this mode of denotation has reference to the ætiological process upon which many of its chief manifestations depend. The state is essentially one in which the normal processes of integration and suppression have failed, in which the attempt to use wittingly a process, which, if it is to be successful, should be unwitting, has only magnified the conflict in which the morbid state has had its origin.

In speaking of repression and suppression as processes by which it is attempted to solve conflicts between instinctive and controlling forces I have so far referred only to their characters as respectively witting or unwitting. I can now consider the matter from another aspect. I have dealt fully in this book with the instinctive character of suppression and have regarded it as itself a process belonging to instinct. I have now to consider more fully the nature of repression. It may be noted, in the first place, that repression is a process of which its subject is fully aware. In its most characteristic form it is definitely under his control, and is even, to a certain extent, capable of having its degree discriminated and its strength graduated. In the terminology often used in this book, it is an epicritic rather than a protopathic process, or, to use the language of orthodox psychology, it is a process which belongs to the order of intelligence as opposed to suppression which I hold to be definitely instinctive. In accordance with this [p. 125] intelligent character the patient is not merely aware of the conflict, but both the factors in the original conflict and the various symptoms which the conflict produces tend to become the subject of rationalisation, and to act as the nuclei of morbid intellectual processes, of the nature of delusions but differing therefrom in their being open to criticism and capable of being removed by knowledge and appeals to intelligence. This character of anxiety- or repression-neurosis has two very important results. One of these is the painful or unpleasant nature of the process. In several other forms of solution, and especially in that to be considered in the next chapter, in which the solution is on instinctive lines, there may be little or no mental discomfort, but anxiety- or repression-neurosis is a state in which mental depression is always present and is often both deep and intense. Consciousness tends to be filled with thoughts of a painful kind which either centre round the factors in the original conflict, or have their basis in the unpleasant nature of the symptoms in which the conflict finds expression, while other events which provide ground for grief, worry or apprehension produce these manifestations in exaggerated form.

The other result is more satisfactory. It is that the state is peculiarly amenable to treatment based on factors of an intelligent order. The patient is able to examine for himself many of the processes, such as repression and rationalisation, upon which his disorder depends, and through his power of criticism and witting control is able to influence these processes and thus do much to abolish their malign influence and set himself upon the path of recovery. The essential feature of anxiety- or repression-neurosis is that it is not only due a conflict between instinct and intelligence, but that subject of the morbid state is able wittingly to act upon factors which enter into this conflict.

Before I close this chapter I should like to point out one feature of anxiety- or repression-neurosis which helps us to understand the relation between repression and suppression. Painful experience which has been repressed and is yet capable [p. 126] of recall without any special difficulty is able to produce nightmares and other morbid symptoms which may in other cases depend on the activity of experience which has been suppressed. Repression and suppression seem here to run into one another. One possibility may be suggested for this close relation and for the failure of repression as a means of solving a conflict between instinctive tendencies and the forces by which they are controlled. I regard suppression as an instinctive process. As an instinctive process it is natural that it should be especially potent and effective in childhood, and should become less potent and effective with advancing years. Moreover, if suppression be an instinctive process, it is natural that it should occur unwittingly, and should be less successful if an attempt is made to put it into action wittingly. The symptoms which follow repression, and seem to be directly due to it, may be ascribed to the failure in the adult of a process which takes place naturally and without any special conflict in childhood. Anxiety- or repression-neurosis may be regarded as an unavailing attempt to solve a conflict by using, in an ineffective manner, a process which is only efficacious when it is exerted instinctively.

Footnotes

[1] The term "neurosis" is only used here for the sake of brevity. The distinctions which have been made by many writers between psycho-neurosis and neurosis have no sound logical basis.

[2] Keeling, Letters and Recollections, London (1918), p. 233.

[3] Ibid., pp. 240, 250, 264.

[4] For a more detailed account of the genesis and nature of this form of neurosis, see

Functional Nerve Disorder, edited by H. Crichton Miller, London (1920), pp. 89-98.

In the last chapter I have considered two modes of solving the conflict between instinctive tendencies and controlling forces which furnishes the basis of the psycho-neuroses. In each case the mode of solution, which is successful in one case and unsuccessful in the other, is an attempt to reinstate the suppression which had previously existed in health. In other forms of neurosis the solution is attempted on different lines, and in this chapter I shall deal with the case in which the organism seeks to escape from the conflict by substituting another form of instinctive reaction for that which has been brought into activity, or which tends to be brought into activity, by the conditions which have acted as the immediate precursors of his disorder. This mode of solution is one in which the sufferer regains happiness and comfort, if not health, by the occurrence of symptoms which enable him to escape from the conflict in place of facing it. The form of neurosis to which I refer is that usually known as hysteria. As this term is ordinarily used it applies to a very large and varied group of manifestations of which paralyses, contractures and anæsthesias are among the most frequent and characteristic. These physical manifestations have been regarded by Freud as due to the conversion of the energy engendered by conflict, and in consequence he has proposed "conversion-neurosis" as a term for the state. This term is now widely used and seems to be in many respects appropriate, but I hope to bring the subject into line with the biological scheme put forward in this book in such a way as to suggest a more appropriate term. [p. 128]

I will begin by referring to the chief manifestations of the process by which the conflict is solved or the solution attempted. I will at first limit my attention to the form which the disorder assumes when it occurs as the result of the accidents of war. Among the most frequent results of shock and strain in war are paralyses, often accompanied by contractures and anæsthesias. The paralysis may attack almost any part of the body, but paralysis of speech is especially frequent, while the anæsthesias may affect not only the skin, but also the special senses of sight and hearing, and less frequently of taste and smell. All these occurrences have the common feature that they unfit their subject for further participation in warfare, and thus form a solution of the conflict between the instinctive tendencies connected with danger and the various controlling factors which may be subsumed under the general heading of duty.

Paralysis and anæsthesis may be regarded as crude reactions by means of which a person is protected from danger. It has been objected to this view that when these states occur on the battlefield, they do not protect, but may even increase the danger by producing conditions incompatible with the activities which form Man's normal reaction to danger. To this objection there are two answers. One is that in the vast majority of cases these protective reactions do not occur on the field of battle, but it may be a few days, it may be months, after the shock, wound, or other event of which they are the sequel. When they occur in this manner they fulfil in great perfection the protective purpose which is the special function of the danger-instincts.

Sometimes, however, these disabilities immediately follow some shock or strain and occur on the field of battle. It then becomes necessary to find some other answer to the objection that these reactions which I suppose to be instinctive fail of their protective purpose, or at the least are but ill-adapted to this purpose. This is one of the problems which will have to be settled by any scheme of explanation which can be regarded as satisfactory. I shall begin the study of the subject [p. 129] by considering the relation of the state characterised by the occurrence of these paralyses and anæsthesias to the processes of suppression, dissociation and suggestion.

One prominent manifestation affords a most definite example of suppression. Anæsthesia is one of the most frequent accompaniments of hysteria. Insensitiveness of the skin ranging from mere blunting to complete loss of all sensibility is a very general symptom and loss of hearing or vision often occurs. The paralyses may also be regarded as examples of suppression, the character of suppression being especially obvious when the paralysis affects the organs of speech, but it is really quite as definite in a monoplegia or an astasia. Equally striking is the suppression of affect. In the most characteristic form of hysteria, as it occurs in warfare, there is no anxiety or depression. The patient is relatively or positively happy. He is unaware of any relation between his apparently physical disability and any of the dangers of warfare preceding the event which acted as the antecedent of his illness. He is content to regard his illness as the natural result of the shock or injury after which the paralysis or other hysterical manifestation developed. If we regard hysteria as a solution of the conflict between instinctive tendencies and controlling forces, we must regard the state as one in which there is suppression of the affect accompanying the instinctive tendencies, while in many cases there is suppression of all memory of the events in which the morbid state had its origin. That there is such suppression of affect is strongly supported by a frequent consequence of curing the paralysis or other physical manifestation. In many cases, especially where the disappearance of the morbid symptom raises the probability that the patient will again have to take part in warfare, a definite state of anxiety and depression takes the place of the physical disability.

Several of the most characteristic manifestations of hysteria can thus be regarded as results of the process of suppression. The paralyses and anæsthesias are characteristic examples of this process, while the contractures are due to the overaction of certain mechanisms which takes place when the activity [p. 130] of other mechanisms has been suppressed. In dealing with hypnotism I suggested that the suppression of motility and sensibility which are so characteristic of this state might be regarded as manifestations, highly modified it is true, of the instinct of immobility, and it is evident that such a conclusion holds still more naturally of the suppression of hysteria. In the case of hypnotism we do not know of any direct connection between its exhibition of suppression and the presence of danger, but in the case of the similar suppressions of the hysteria of warfare this connection is definite. The paralyses and anæsthesias of this state may be regarded as partial manifestations of a process which, if it were complete, would produce immobility and insensibility of the whole body. According to this view the paralysis and anæsthesia of hysteria are modifications of one of the most definite of the various instinctive processes by which animals react to danger.

The view that hysterical symptoms are modified forms of the instinct of immobility has been reached by attending only to one aspect of hysteria, viz., the production of certain of its symptoms by the process of suppression. It is now necessary to attend to other aspects of the disease, and especially to its intimate connection with suggestion. According to current views suggestion is the most prominent agency in the production of hysteria, and I myself have laid such stress on this feature that I have proposed "suggestion-neurosis" as a term for the state.[1]

Moreover, hysteria is undoubtedly accompanied by greatly enhanced suggestibility, and it is therefore natural to regard this suggestibility as an important, if not essential, factor in the production of the state. I have attempted to show that an important factor in the production of the hysteria of war is the enhanced suggestibility which results from military training.[2] One of the chief purposes of military training is to enable the individual soldier to act immediately and automatically to command so as to ensure unity of purpose and action in the section, platoon, company or other group of [p. 131] which the individual is a member. The success of such a training depends upon the utilisation of instinctive tendencies promoting unity within the group, and since the chief of these agencies is suggestion, the result is enhancement of suggestibility. It is, therefore, absolutely necessary that any theory of hysteria shall take into account its close connection with suggestion and suggestibility.

In this connection it will be useful to consider a characteristic feature of hysteria, viz., its mimetic character. According to the definition of suggestion employed in this book, mimesis is a special aspect of the more general process of suggestion, the term being used for the motor or effector side of the process whereby one animal or person influences another unwittingly. The tendency of the hysteric to exhibit symptoms similar to those of other persons in his environment is thus thoroughly in accord with the close relation between hysteria and suggestion. It would seem as if the chief difference between hysteria and hypnotism is that, while in hypnotism the manifestations are due to the suggestion of another person, they are in the case of hysteria the result of the unwitting process of mimesis which forms one aspect of suggestion.

When considering hysteria in relation to suppression I was led to regard the disease as a modification of the instinctive reaction to danger by means of immobility. It is now necessary to consider through what means the original instinctive process has been modified. According to the views put forward in this book, the primitive instincts subject to the "all-or-none" principle have been modified in two directions and by two different agencies, one intelligence and the other suggestion. We have seen that anxiety- or repression-neurosis, at any rate in some of its forms, is due to conflict between the primitive instinctive tendencies and factors based largely or altogether on intelligence. Intelligence may be regarded as a modifying principle, highly successful in the usual calm of our modern civilisation, which has broken down as the result of the excessive strains and shocks of modern warfare. I have now to suggest that hysteria is the result of the abrogation of the modifying [p. 132] principle based in intelligence, leaving in full power the other and more or less opposed principle of suggestion.

Let us now consider in more detail whether there are any reasons why suggestion should be so prominent in the production of hysterical manifestations, and whether its activity is able to explain some of the more characteristic features of the hysteria of warfare. Warfare is essentially a collective form of activity. As I have already pointed out, military training is especially directed towards the perfection of collective activity and towards the consequent increase of suggestibility which is essential to the success of the gregarious instinct. There are thus definite factors in warfare which tend to produce the predominance of suggestion and assist the abrogation of the more intelligent forms of reaction which are so prominent in the production of repression-neurosis. As I have-pointed out elsewhere,[3] hysteria tends to occur especially in the private soldier, and repression-neurosis in the officer.

I have explained this, partly by the greater intelligence and education of the officer, partly by the fact that it is the private soldier whose suggestibility is especially enhanced by military training and his military duties, while the training and duties of the officer are directed more to the development of initiative and independence.

If now we turn to the symptoms which are especially prominent in the hysteria of warfare, we find that some of these can be referred definitely to the protective end which I suppose to be the essential function of hysteria. One of the most frequent features of the hysteria of warfare is mutism. A soldier who has been buried or otherwise disabled by a shell-explosion will emerge from his experience with complete absence of all power of speech, which may continue for months or even years. Let us consider how the prominence and frequency of this symptom can be connected with the view that the protective function of hysteria is connected with the gregarious instinct.

It will be remembered that when describing the reaction to danger by means of flight, I mentioned the cry as one of its manifestations, and I assigned to this cry the function of warning the other members of the group. It would seem as if the individual reaction by flight has become closely associated with a mode of reaction, by means of which the individual warns the rest of the group of the danger from which he is himself reacting instinctively by means of flight. The cry may be regarded as a feature of the flight-instinct arising out of the gregarious habit. If however, a group of animals should adopt the reaction to danger by means of immobility, the cry would be wholly out of place. If only one of the herd or other group were to utter the warning cry which belongs to the instinct of flight, it would wholly destroy the virtue and success of the alternative instinct of immobility upon which the group is now dependent for its safety. If a group of animals is to adopt successfully the instinct of immobility, it is not only essential that all tendencies to the movements of flight shall be suppressed; it is just as essential that every one of its members shall suppress the warning cry which serves so useful a purpose on other occasions. If, therefore, hysteria be primarily a variant of the instinct of immobility, it is natural that one of its earliest, if not its earliest, need should be the suppression of the cry or other sound which tends to occur in response to danger. I suggest, therefore, that the mutism of war-hysteria is primarily connected with the collective aspect of the instinct of immobility. When it persists, as it often does, after removal from immediate danger, this is because it provides a means of protection from further participation in danger, and is therefore utilised, not consciously, but in that unwitting manner which is characteristic of instinctive forms of behaviour.

In those rare cases in which paralysis of a limb, or even of all limbs, occurs on the field of battle, and thus prevents the movements by which the soldier would normally escape from danger, it is necessary to suppose that the reaction is due to the coming into play of an instinctive form of behaviour, which is ill-adapted to the special conditions by which it has been produced. It may be regarded as an incomplete, and therefore unsuccessful, adoption of an instinctive form of reaction to danger. It is obvious that, if in such a case the reaction of immobility were [p. 134] complete, it might be successful as a means of simulating death, and the whole reaction of immobility may be, and often has been, supposed to have this end. Where the immobility is only partial, therefore, we may regard it as an incomplete form of reaction which if it were complete would serve a useful purpose.

I have now considered the rôle in hysteria of the instinctive processes of suppression and suggestion. I have regarded the state as primarily one of suppression, as a means of promoting safety, which has been greatly modified through the process of suggestion coming into action through gregarious needs. I have now to consider its relation to another instinctive process -- that of dissociation. According to the customary method of using the concept of dissociation, hysteria is a manifestation of this process. It is customary, at any rate in this country, to speak of the hysterical symptoms as the result of dissociation. It is therefore necessary to consider this point, and to inquire how far the hysterical state accords with the definition of dissociation adopted in this book.

If dissociation implied only the independent activity of suppressed experience, there might be some justification for the idea it underlies the paralyses and anæsthesias of hysteria. If we regarded these states as positive phenomena, we might look on them as the results of the activity of suppressed experience. But even here the position would not be altogether satisfactory, for we should be driven to regard the process of suppression to which the paralyses and anæsthesias are due as itself a mode of activity of the suppressed experience. If, in place of regarding dissociation as a state of independent activity, we hold independent consciousness to be a necessary part of the concept of dissociation, it is evident that hysteria wholly fails to answer to the definition, for there is no evidence whatever of such independent consciousness. In the absence of any evidence of alternate consciousness, it is doubtful whether anything is gained by bringing hysteria within the category of dissociation.

I have, therefore, no hesitation in excluding dissociation from the connotation of hysteria, and in regarding this state as a [p. 135] product of the two processes of suppression and suggestion. I have already pointed out its close relation to hypnotism, from which it differs in being unaccompanied by independent consciousness, thus bringing it still nearer than the hypnotic state to the instinctive reaction to danger by means of immobility. I have pointed out that the paralyses and anæsthesias, which are the most characteristic manifestations of hysteria, may be regarded as localised manifestations of the suppression of the instinct of immobility, of which sleep and hypnotism are other forms. According to this view the symptoms of hysteria are due to the substitution, in an imperfect form, of an ancient instinctive reaction in place of other forms of reaction to danger. If this way of regarding the matter were accepted, the term "substitution-neurosis" would become an appropriate and convenient term for the "hysteria" of general usage or the "conversion-neurosis" of Freud.

I have so far treated hysteria, or substitution-neurosis as we know it through the effects of warfare. The theory of this state which I have put forward differs so profoundly from that generally held that I cannot abstain from considering how far it can be utilised to explain the hysteria of civil practice.

According to my view hysteria is primarily due to the activity of a danger-instinct, to the coming into action of an instinct whose primary function is protection from danger. I have now to consider whether the hysteria of civil practice can also be referred to danger, or whether it is the result of the transference of the reaction from a connection with the danger-instincts to some other instinct. My own experience of civil practice is too small to enable me to deal adequately with this problem, and I must leave it to those with more knowledge to discover how far this form of hysteria can be led back to an origin in the awakening of the danger-instinct.

Even if some cases of hysteria in civil life can be referred to onslaughts on the danger-instincts, there can be little doubt that factors connected with sex take a most important part in the ætiology of this state. I can only here deal with the matter very briefly, and will begin by considering a fact which [p. 136] must be explained by any theory of hysteria, but of which current explanations are not satisfactory. It is necessary to explain why hysteria in civil life affects women to so far greater an extent than men. The idea that only women are affected has long been given up, but the experience of war has shown how very prone men are to succumb to hysteria when the suitable conditions arise, viz., conditions which make too great a demand on their danger-instincts. We have to discover why hysteria should be so frequent in women, and so rare in men, under the ordinary conditions of civil life. I have already mentioned the rarity of severe demands on the danger-instincts in the ordinary routine of our modern civilisation. In so doing I see now that I was thinking only of the male element in the population. Women are always liable to dangers in connection with child-birth to which men are not exposed, while the danger-element, real or imaginary, is more pronounced in them than in the male in connection with coitus. That the greater prominence of danger with the consequent tendency to awaken fear should be potentially present in connection with the normal functions of women seems to afford a definite motive for the more frequent occurrence in them of a form of neurosis which, according to the view here put forward, is due to the occurrence, though in modified form, of a definite mode of reaction to danger.

One difficulty for my view of the nature of hysteria is so important that I cannot pass it over in silence. One of the symptoms which has always been regarded as a characteristic manifestation of the hysteria of civil practice is the occurrence of convulsive seizures which are sometimes with difficulty to be distinguished from epilepsy, and share with that disease the exhibition of movements, often of a very violent kind. Such seizures are, of course, wholly incompatible with the purpose in which I suppose hysteria to have had its origin, and they must raise serious doubts concerning the validity of my hypothesis that hysteria is connected with the instinctive reaction to danger by means of immobility. Other manifestations, such as the globus hystericus and the violent emotional expression so frequently associated with the current concept of hysteria, [p. 137] would also be wholly out of place in a state which has the origin I suppose.

In considering this difficulty I must first point out that in my experience, and I believe the experience is general, convulsive seizures of the kind which are known in the hysteria of civil practice are of exceptional occurrence in the hysteria of warfare. The seizures called "fits" which occur in this state are very different from those of civil practice. The patient lies motionless and silent, and in a state quite consistent with a relation to the instinct of immobility. The stupors and cataleptic states which so frequently occur immediately after the shocks of warfare are also, I need hardly say, completely in harmony with the view that the hysteria of warfare is an expression of this instinct.

The convulsive seizures which stood out so prominently in the concept of hysteria held before the war must, however, be accounted for if the hypothesis I am putting forward is to explain all the facts. I can only regard the difference between the two forms of hysteria as dependent upon the modification which the primary process has undergone in the course of its utilisation in the interests of another instinct, although I suppose that many of the manifestations of civilian hysteria can be referred to demands upon the danger-instincts, I have assumed that in general this state depends on disturbances of the sexual instinct. It will be necessary to inquire whether the convulsive seizures, globus hystericus, and emotional attacks do not occur especially in cases which can be definitely referred to a sexual cause. Owing to my own ignorance of civilian hysteria I can only raise this possibility and leave its investigation to others.

I venture, however, to suggest that it would conduce to clearness of thought, and to successful practice, if two distinct varieties of hysteria were recognised, the two differing in the nature of their ætiology. It may then become apparent that two very different concepts have been confused under the heading of hysteria. Here, as is the rule in psychological medicine, intermediate cases will occur, in which convulsive [p. 138] seizures are associated with paralysis, contractures and anæsthesias. It seems possible that the two concepts will turn out to be as capable of distinction from one another as most of the other concepts of psychological medicine where shading and gradations are peculiarly liable to occur owing to the great complexity and intimate inter-relations of the psychical processes concerned.

I should like at this stage to point out an important difference between the psycho-neuroses of civil life and those which follow the events of warfare, which has a definite bearing on the possibility I have just raised. The instinctive tendencies which manifest themselves in the psycho-neuroses fall into two definite classes. One class is composed of the tendencies which in a state of nature would promote the happiness of the individual or the crude necessities of the race, but are in conflict with the traditional standards of thought and conduct of the society to which the individual belongs. The other class of tendencies have a protective character. Their function is to produce immediate pain or unpleasant affect as a means of warning against and avoiding danger. In the psycho-neuroses of warfare the second group of tendencies are predominantly or even exclusively involved, while, if we accept the position that the psycho-neuroses of civil life depend mainly upon disturbances of the sexual instinct, they will involve tendencies of the first class, This difference is so great and far-reaching that it is amply sufficient to account for the different natures of the two kinds of psycho-neurosis. It would alone go far to justify the separation of the two forms of disorder in a scientific classification.

Footnotes

[1] See p. 223.
[2] See p. 217.
[3] See p. 207.

In the last two chapters I have considered three of the more important means by which the human organism attempts to solve the conflict between re-aroused instinctive tendencies and the forces by which they are normally controlled. I have considered the healthy solution by the reinstatement of suppression, the ineffectual attempt at solution by witting repression, and the solution in which modification of an ancient form of reaction to danger is substituted for that which is the more natural mode of response in Man.

Dissociation. -- I can consider other modes of solution more briefly. The occurrence of definite dissociation with altered personality may be regarded as an attempt at solution, especially when it takes the form of the fugue with its independent activity and its independent consciousness. Sometimes the fugue is combined with an anxiety-state, in which case the attempt at solution by means of dissociation has been ineffectual, but in other cases the fugue may be the chief or only manifestation of the conflict, the patient being otherwise healthy and happy except in so far as he is disturbed by the possibilities which are always open to the subject of a fugue. In such a case the conflict finds expression in an occasional escape into another life, a life which is in effect that of another person shut off from all memory of the conditions upon which the conflict depends.

The Phobia. -- In another mode of solution by a process in which painful experience is suppressed, but yet maintains the potentiality for activity whenever conditions arise which resemble those of the experience which has been suppressed. [p. 140] The various phobias in which the suppressed experience finds expression are of a kind which makes this mode of solution unsatisfactory if the conditions which re-arouse the dreads are liable to be frequently encountered, but if they are of exceptional occurrence it is possible for the subject of a phobia to lead a normal and comfortable life, though there is always the possibility that his life may take a course which will expose him to conditions which arouse the phobia and make the solution altogether ineffectual. Thus, the sufferer from claustrophobia who has been so often mentioned in this book was but little disturbed by his dread in his life at home, but it played a large part in the production of an anxiety-neurosis when his work in France during the war exposed him to conditions which brought his phobia into activity. Similarly, the subject of a snake-phobia may be hardly disturbed by it in his own home, but the disorder may take a very serious turn if circumstances oblige him to live in a country where snakes abound.

According to Freud many phobias are due to the transference of a conflict from an object by which fear was originally aroused to that which forms the subject of the dread. If this view be right, we have an excellent example of a solution which completely disguises from the patient the real nature of his trouble. The original fear is objectified in the snake or the rat through a process of symbolisation similar to that by which similar fears find expression in the dream.

A somewhat similar, though far less satisfactory, attempt at solution is presented by a case recorded in Appendix III in which a subject of war-neurosis suffered from sudden attacks of intense depression, in the intervals of which he was relatively healthy and cheerful. There was no evidence that these attacks of depression were aroused by any conditions similar to those of the experience he was repressing, but the case bears some resemblance to a phobia in that the repressed experience only found occasional expression and left the patient more or less comfortable in the intervals.

Compulsion-Neurosis. -- Another mode of solution of the conflict between awakened instinctive tendencies and controlling forces [p. 141] is by the performance of meaningless acts such as counting, touching things, arranging objects of the environment in certain ways, etc. These acts have a compelling character, and failure to carry them out produces intense discomfort, while their unimpeded performance makes the life of their subject comparatively happy and calm so long as the acts to which he is compelled are not obvious to others and do not come into conflict with ordinary social standards. Many persons perform these compulsive acts in such a manner that they do not attract anyone's notice, and they are often regarded by the subjects themselves as natural and normal, so that they do not come under the notice of the physician, but when they are associated with other morbid manifestations, or are of a kind which conflict with social standards of conduct, the state is known as compulsion-neurosis, and the compulsions form a frequent feature of the state formerly, and still often, known as psychasthenia. In many cases it is possible to discover that these compulsive acts go back to some definite experience, usually of childhood, which has been suppressed, and it may be possible to ascertain that their special features have been determined by the nature of the forgotten experience. The compulsive acts seem, however, in many cases to be only subsidiary and comparatively unimportant features of the original experience. In these cases they may be regarded as more or less symbolic expressions of the activity of the suppressed experience. In some cases the symbolism is very near the original tendency or impulse. Thus, one of my patients had a compulsion to cut himself, which was satisfied as soon as he had drawn blood. This compulsion followed definite thoughts of, and impulses to, suicide, following the suicide of his company-commander, and cutting himself was a kind of symbolic act which gave relief. In this case there was no suppression, but the thoughts and impulses out of which the compulsion developed were clearly present in consciousness and memory.

Rationalisation. -- This is a process by which the solution of a conflict is frequently attempted. As already mentioned, this process enters largely into the composition of anxiety- or [p. 142] repression-neurosis, but it may form the most prominent feature of a psycho-neurosis, and, as we shall see presently, it is the leading feature of one of the most clearly-defined psychoses. The process of rationalisation often plays a large part in the production of states, as means of escape from conflict, which, being more compatible with health, can hardly be included under either head.

It is hardly surprising that the process of rationalisation should often centre round the relation of the patient to medicine, the social institution which has to do with disease. In searching for something by means of which to explain his troubles, the patient is apt to fix upon the advice and measures given or recommended by his physician or physicians. He argues more or less correctly that if his troubles had been taken in time and corrected when they were slight, the task of getting well would have been comparatively easy. He concludes that his illness is due in the main to mistakes made by his medical advisers, who allowed the faulty trends to remain in activity or even enhanced their evil effects by the measures they recommended. Since the advice and measures which are thus held to blame come in the majority of cases from practitioners of the orthodox art of medicine, this mode of solving the conflict often takes the form of a violent reaction against the medical profession. In this situation the patient is liable to become the prey of quackery, or he may become a disciple of one or other of the systems which, at any rate until lately, have recognised more adequately than orthodox medicine the principles of psycho-therapy. Such a movement as Christian Science owes its success, partly to its recognition of certain truths which physicians have been slow to learn, partly to its providing a nucleus for the rationalisations by which patients are so often apt to explain their morbid state. If at the same time the new doctrines give the opportunity for wide application and proselytism, the patient will be provided with an interest in life, the absence of which may have previously formed one of the conditions of his illness. The success of Christian Science, the New Thought, and other similar cults is due in the first [p. 143] place to the materialism of orthodox medicine and its failure to recognise the vast importance of the mental element in disease, but these movements would never have attained their success if they had not furnished the basis for systems of rationalisation by means of which sufferers from psycho-neurosis have been enabled to escape from the conflicts to which their troubles were in the first place due.

Hypochondriasis. -- In some cases the patient may solve his conflict in a manner more painful to himself by becoming unduly interested in the various pains and discomforts of his morbid state. His absorption in these allows him to escape from the deeper conflicts to which the symptoms upon which he dwells so insistingly are ultimately due. He becomes a hypochondriac, and such hypochondriasis is only one of tile many means by which the process of rationalisation enables escape from conflict.

Alcohol and Psycho-neurosis. -- Another frequent mode of attempting to solve a conflict is by taking alcohol or some other drug. Alcohol produces its effects by removing or lowering the efficiency of the highest levels of mental activity. Where, as in some cases, it appears to increase mental accomplishment, this is almost certainly due to removal of inhibiting forces, such as anxiety, which interfere with success. Its more noxious effects are directly due to weakening of control, and, probably without exception, the altered behaviour which follows the taking of excessive amounts of alcohol can be traced to the overaction of instinctive or other early tendencies normally kept under control by the higher levels of mental activity.

It is a striking feature of anxiety-neurosis that its subjects are especially liable to have their behaviour influenced by alcohol. This altered behaviour can be explained by the more complete abrogation of controlling factors already weakened by the pathological process producing the neurosis. The more morbid effects of alcohol fit easily into the scheme of the relation between instinctive and controlling forces which I have put forward in this book.

Another interest of alcohol in relation to our subject is that it [p. 144] and other substances which inhibit the higher controlling levels are frequently used in the attempt to still the conflict between instinctive tendencies and controlling forces. The immediate success which follows their use is due to the removal or lessening of the anxiety and depression which are among the first indications of the anxiety state, thus making possible the proper performance of duties which are being prejudiced by this anxiety and depression. The failure which sooner or later follows the attempt to solve a conflict by resort to alcohol is due to the fact that the injurious action of this substance only reinforces the weakening influence of strain and fatigue, while it may set up the habit which we call dipsomania. The nature of this process is now so fully recognised by those with special experience that modern treatment depends on making the patient understand the nature and history of his trouble. By solving the original conflict in some other manner scope is given for the breaking of the habit which has been the outcome of the crude solution attempted by the sufferer.

Paranoia. -- I have so far dealt only with the psycho-neuroses and I must now briefly consider the psychoses or insanities as attempts to solve conflicts between instinctive tendencies and the forces by which they are normally controlled. One of the most characteristic of the modes of solution of this order is paranoia. In this disease, which often seems to start from a state of inferiority, real or supposed, the sufferer enters upon an elaborate process of rationalisation, partly to explain his inferiority, partly to still the conflicts to which certain forms of inferiority render their subjects peculiarly liable. The usual course of such a paranoia is from suspicions and forebodings arising out of inferiority to explanations which tend towards delusions of grandeur. The course of the disorder appears to be that the rationalisations, developed by the subject to explain his inferiority, become so intimately connected with the affective basis of his trouble that they attain a reality and effectiveness which greatly relieve, or even wholly remove, the painfulness of the conflict. The state produced furnishes a solution of the conflict which seems wholly satisfactory to the patient [p. 145] himself. In the case of paranoia the results of the rationalisation are so out of harmony with the ideals and traditions of the society to which the sufferer belongs that they are called delusions, and if the delusions led to conduct incompatible with social standards, their subject is called insane. If, on the other hand, the process of rationalisation produces beliefs in the sufferer which differ from those of the majority of his fellows, intellectually rather than morally or socially, and lead to behaviour which is not obviously out of harmony with the general standards of conduct of the community, we call the product of rationalisation a fad or a crank. Beliefs of this kind furnish a vast number of gradations which pass insensibly from states which everyone would regard as healthy and normal to others not differing appreciably from paranoia in so far as their psychological, as distinguished from their social, character is concerned. The crank and the paranoiac may be regarded as two definite types of person who have resorted to rationalisation in the attempt to solve the conflict between instinctive tendencies and social forces.

Dementia Præcox. -- Another frequent method by which it is attempted to solve, or rather to escape from, a conflict, is by means of day-dreams in which the subject of the conflict fancies all kinds of situation in which he is playing a part different from that in which he is, in fact, placed by his conflict. When this mode of attempted solution is adopted by persons with low powers of resistance, it is apt to produce the definite hallucinatory and delusional states which make some of the chief forms of dementia præcox. The occurrence of this mode of solution, as a means of escaping from the conflicts aroused by warfare, has not only produced a vast number of cases which conform to the generally accepted class of dementia præcox, but cases have been frequent in which this mode of solution has produced minor degrees of a similar disorder, which would have been called dementia præcox without hesitation in civil practice, but which have run a course very different from that civil experience would have led one to expect. In these forms of insanity, as in paranoia, there is often some inferiority, real or [p. 146] imaginary, which puts the subject of the conflict at a disadvantage in relation to his fellows.

Disintegrative Psychosis. -- In some cases the conflict is so severe, or the resistive power of the organism so slight, that the mental balance breaks down completely. The older psychiatry regarded such a complete breakdown, which it labelled acute mania, as the expression of a mere disorderly jumble of disintegrated mental process, but if we look on the whole situation as a means of reacting to the conflict between suppressed instinctive tendencies and controlling forces, it becomes a question whether the acute psychosis, with all its apparent disorder, is not merely the expression of a victory of the instinctive forces running riot after their escape from a lifelong period of suppression and control. There is little question that if we knew the complete life-history of a person suffering from acute mania, his ravings, which, without this knowledge, seem to be mere wild incoherence, would be found to have a sense, though one perhaps disguised by disorder of expression and omission of many of the links by which the associations would normally be expressed. The view that a psychosis of this kind is due to the complete abrogation of the control, which is normally exerted over the lower instinctive tendencies, is rendered probable by the study of the exaltation and excitement which make up its milder forms. All gradations may be seen between the apparently meaningless ravings of acute mania and such mild examples of exaltation as convert an ordinarily subdued and reticent person into a talkative and excitable busybody, who in such a state reveals thoughts and tendencies of thought which in health he would not allow himself to entertain.

All the gradations of mania may be regarded as merely different degrees of expression of modes of thought and behaviour which, owing to their incompatibility with social traditions and ethical standards, are in health subdued and suppressed. It may be noted that a case of acute mania provides a natural means of psycho-analysis in which all kinds of suppressed experience and tendencies come to the surface spontaneously. It fails in general to be capable of utilisation in diagnosis or [p. 147] treatment, partly because it often goes too deep and reveals tendencies which would only become intelligible if we knew the intermediate steps in the process by which the tendencies came under control; partly because the patient is unable to provide the clues which would enable the physician to piece together the disjointed fragments which find their way to the surface.

In dealing with the various means by which the human organism seeks to solve the conflict between instinctive tendencies and the forces by which they are controlled, I have so far been considering the psycho-neuroses only as examples of failure of equilibrium and of various modes of attempting to redress the balance. In this chapter I propose to treat the psycho-neuroses from another point of view and see how far they may be regarded as examples of regression, as processes which enable us to study the general course of mental development on the assumption that in disease the organism tends to retrace the steps through which it has passed in its development. This aspect of disease is one to which special attention was paid by Hughlings Jackson, whose "devolution" corresponds closely with the "regression" of present-day students of nervous and mental disorder.

I will begin by considering the modes of solution considered in the last three chapters as examples of regression. I have regarded hysteria as a state dependent upon the coming into activity, in a modified form, of a mode of reaction which dates back to a very early stage of animal development. If I am right in looking upon this morbid state as due to the substitution of the instinct of immobility for other forms of reaction to dangerous or unpleasant situations, we have in it not merely an example of regression, but of regression to a very primitive form of reaction. There will be not merely regression to a character of the infancy of the individual, but to a character which must go very far back in the process of development by which Man has become what he is. [p. 149]

The mimetic nature of hysteria provides another characteristic indication of regression. The mimesis of hysteria may be regarded as a throw-back, partly to the dramatic character of the activity of early life, partly to the mimetic aspect of the activity of the gregarious instinct.[1] According to the view put forward in this book hysteria depends on the recrudescence of a very early form of reaction to danger modified by factors arising out of gregarious needs, and both the original activity and the force by which it is modified provide characteristic examples of regression.

In anxiety- or repression-neurosis the regression is less complete, but since in this case the regressive features are of a kind with which we are acquainted in the individual life, the process is more obvious and presents a feature which is now widely recognised. One of the most striking features of this regression is presented by the strength and urgency of emotional reactions. Expressions of affective activity which are frequent in infancy, but have been brought under complete control in later life, are apt to reassert themselves in the state of anxiety-neurosis. Some of the most frequent and distressing symptoms of this state are due to the reawakening of these affective reactions. In slight cases the change may be limited to irritability and undue liability to lose the temper, while in more severe cases the patient may with difficulty restrain himself from violence on slight provocation. There is little doubt that this regression to states in which the primitive emotional impulses have escaped from control has been a definite factor in producing the increase in the frequency of crimes of violence which exists at the present time. In another direction the regression may show itself in great increase of the tendency to give way to grief. One of the most trying of the symptoms of the anxiety-neurosis following warfare is the liability to give way to grief on occasions which would not have moved at all in health, and here the regression to a character of infancy is obvious. In this case it is not so much that emotions occur in greater strength, but they are accompanied by a mode of expression, natural in childhood, to the control of which the [p. 150] influence of parents, teachers and tradition is directed from the earliest years.

A striking manifestation of regression is to be found in dreams. The nightmares of anxiety-neurosis are of exactly the same order as the night-terrors which are so frequent in childhood. In many cases which have come under my own observation they have even been exact reproductions of these childhood states. Thus, one of my patients after an aeroplane crash had dreams in which a Chinaman figured prominently. He remembered having been frightened by a recurrent dream in childhood in which the Chinaman appeared in exactly the same surroundings as those of the adult dream, and similar examples of regression to the dreams and night-terrors of childhood are frequent. The terrifying animals which appear so often in the nightmares of war-neurosis may be regarded as the result of regression to a character especially frequent in the dreams of children.

Another frequent feature of anxiety-neurosis may be an example of regression to a more deeply-seated instinct. One of the most frequent symptoms of war-neurosis is a desire for solitude and inability to mix in the usual way with one's fellows. In many cases this may be explained by feelings of shame which are apt to trouble sufferers from neurosis as the result of their failure to understand that their excessive reactions or other troubles are the natural results of their morbid state and give no real ground for self-reproach. Often, however, it would seem that the desire for solitude and inability to mix with others cannot be explained by such conscious process, but is an instinctive reaction of the same kind as that which leads animals, when ill, to withdraw from their fellows in order to die in solitude. This view may be regarded as fanciful, but the desire for solitude in sufferers from war-neurosis is often so strong and so devoid of rational grounds that I am inclined to regard it as an example of regression to an instinctive reaction dating far back in the history of the race.

Compulsion-neurosis affords an excellent example of regression. There is reason to believe that the acts which are [p. 151] especially prone to be carried out compulsively in this state are frequent in childhood. When they become insistent in adult life, this is only an outcrop of a mode of reaction which is characteristic of infantile mentality.

There is little doubt also that the failure to appreciate reality which is so frequent in psychoses, and also occurs in anxiety-neurosis, is another example of regression. Children often, if not always, pass through a stage of development in which they fail to distinguish the products of their imagination from the features of the real world in which they find themselves. There must be a definite stage of mental development in which the child is learning to distinguish imagination from reality, and there can be little doubt that this stage must be accompanied by some degree of the doubt and discomfort which so often occur as features of the psychoses and psycho-neuroses. I have seen cases in which the regression in childhood in this respect has been very definite. I have seen more than one soldier with a history of having been very imaginative in childhood, when they had amused their relatives by tales of the wonderful adventures in which they had taken part. There had always been some difficulty in distinguishing between imagination and reality, and when they began to suffer from war-strain, this failure became pronounced and they laid themselves open to serious trouble by relating adventures in which they had taken an honourable and distinguished part for which there was no foundation. As in the case of other mental anomalies, all gradations may be met between such a regression and cases of pathological lying and swindling in which the person affected has never learnt properly to distinguish imagination from reality and has utilised this imperfection for the satisfaction of his instinctive tendencies.

The most characteristic form of dementia præcox may be regarded as another example of regression in which the sufferer gives way to day-dreams as a means of escape from conflict. The day-dreams which in this state pass insensibly into definite hallucinatory and delusional states may be regarded as regressions to the fancies which are so habitual in childhood. [p. 152]

Lastly, mania may be regarded as an example of regression to a still more primitive state, but one in which the regression is accompanied by such disorder and disintegration as to make this feature less obvious than in the milder forms of psychosis and in the psycho-neuroses.

It is an interesting question how far the process of suppression which has been found to be of such fundamental importance in psycho-neurosis can be regarded as an example of regression. In this book I have regarded the process of suppression as one which goes far back in the history of the animal kingdom, and corresponding with this antiquity I have regarded it as a process which is especially apt to come into action in the infancy of the human being. There is reason to believe that suppression is especially liable to occur, and when it occurs to be complete, or relatively complete, in the first few years of life. All the characters of anxiety-neurosis, on the other hand, are most satisfactorily explained as due to the attempt to put wittingly into activity in adult life a process which normally takes place unwittingly and instinctively in the first few years of life. Cases in which suppression occurs in adult life may be regarded as examples of regression in which an instinctive process characteristic of infancy persists in its capacity for activity in later years. It may be objected that I have supposed the reinstatement of suppression to be the normal way in which a temporary failure of balance is redressed, and if this is held to be an example of regression, we shall have to accept the situation that a regressive process need not necessarily be pathological, or rather, that in order to get rid of a pathological state, the organism sometimes utilises with success in adult life a process which is especially liable to occur in infancy. When suppression occurs in adult life it more frequently happens that the suppressed experience preserves an independent activity either with or without independent consciousness, and such cases may more fitly be regarded as examples of regression. I have suggested that this independence of activity, and the occurrence of independent consciousness, have come down from an ancestral stage of development when a change was taking place in the [p. 153] environment, and if there be anything in this suggestion, the independent activity of suppressed experience and the process of dissociation would also he examples of regression.

Regression and the "all-or-none" principle. -- If the psycho-neuroses are to be looked upon as examples of regression, we should expect them to show definite signs of the "all-or-none" reaction. According to the view put forward in the chapter on "the Nature of Instinct" the "all-or-none" character is the sign of the earlier and cruder forms of instinct which serve the immediate needs of the individual, especially such as manifest themselves in the presence of danger. We should, therefore, expect to find reactions conforming to this type in those varieties of neurosis which depend upon reawakening of the danger-instincts. Thus, if "hysteria" is primarily due to the substitution of the reaction to danger by means of immobility for other forms of reaction, we should expect to find that its symptoms would have the "all-or-none" character, for the reaction by immobility is one for the success of which in its original form this principle is essential. It must be noted, however, that I do not suppose "hysteria" to be a simple manifestation of the reaction to danger by immobility, but that the original instinctive reaction has been greatly modified by needs arising out of the gregarious habit. In other words, I suppose the symptoms of hysteria to be manifestations of the instinct of immobility greatly modified by suggestion, and since suggestion is a graded and discriminative process, we should not expect to find that hysteria would show the "all-or-none" character in a pure form. Nevertheless, in some of the features of hysteria the "all-or-none" character is distinctly present. Thus, the symptom of mutism involves not merely suppression of utterances which tend in some relation to the shock or strain by which the disability has been produced, but it extends to the whole of speech. In order to wipe out manifestations of speech which stand in a relation to the needs by which the mutism has been produced, it is necessary to suppress all expressions of the organ of speech, even those of the most useful and pleasant kind. In general, however, it must be acknowledged that the [p. 154] "all-or-none" principle appears only exceptionally in hysteria, and that the morbid process is largely subject to the processes of discrimination and graduation. According to the scheme of this book the slightness of the activity of the principle indicates how greatly the original instinct, which I suppose to underlie the disease, has been influenced and modified by later changes arising out of gregarious needs. We may fitly regard hysteria as dependent on a process whereby the organism, in response to gregarious needs, has utilised an old instinctive form of reaction, but while so utilising it has, at the same time, modified it greatly in so far as the features of graduation and discrimination are concerned. According to the view put forward in Chapter XV anxiety- or repression-neurosis is due to the ineffective action of the instinctive process of suppression, the ineffectiveness being due to the witting character of the process in which it is employed. We should, in consequence, not expect to find this morbid state exhibiting the "all-or-none" principle in any pronounced degree. The excessive emotional reactions of this disease do, indeed, show the "all-or-none" character and are wholly out of relation to the conditions which call them forth, and this want of relation between cause and effect runs through many features of the behaviour of those suffering from repression-neurosis. But there is no one symptom which can be regarded as a pure example of the "all-or-none" principle, at any rate in the waking state. In sleep, however, the principle is more potent as might indeed be expected, since sleep, by removing the higher controlling factors, will allow any instinctive manifestations to appear in the form natural to them. Thus, the nightmare clearly exemplifies the "all-or-none " principle. This state is characterised by an excess of emotion and emotional reaction. The affect, whether of fear, horror or grief, may be altogether out of proportion to the incident of the dream, which is its immediate occasion, and the emotion occurs with a force and urgency which are never experienced, even in the most acute emotional situations of the waking life. In dealing with sleep in Chapter XIV it was found that the normal process is clearly subject to the principle of graduation, but in the sleep accompanying [p. 155] pathological states such as repression-neurosis, instinctive tendencies with their affective accompaniments are apt to show the working of the "all-or-none" principle in an especially pure form. The process of dissociation is especially interesting and instructive in connection with regression and the "all-or-none" principle. I have considered in Chapter X the relation between the pathological process of dissociation, such as is manifested in the fugue, and several phenomena of the normal mental life. One of the chief differences between the pathological and the normal process is the greater completeness of the barrier between systems of dissociated experience in the pathological examples, and this greater completeness seems to bear a definite relation the "all-or-none" principle. Thus, in a definite fugue the suppression is complete. There is no graduation of memory so that certain incidents of the fugue are remembered and others forgotten, but the memory of experience gained during the fugue is lost as a whole. In the examples taken from the normal life, which were compared with the fugue, there is no such completeness of separation, and there is a power of choice between what shall and what shall not be recalled which is wholly absent in the fugue. Thus, if I switch off my attention from one set of interests and turn it to another, I do not thereby exclude the former from memory, but elements of the first set are readily capable of recall if they should come into associative relation with any of the second set of interests. I have spoken of the two kinds of dissociation as protopathic and epicritic respectively, and the protopathic form shows, at any rate in certain respects, the "all-or-none" character which belongs in general to protopathic manifestations. The "all-or-none" character is also present in the dissociation which exists in insanity between a delusional system and the experience which is in harmony with the beliefs of the society to which the deluded person belongs. It is a definite character of a delusional system that it does not admit of compromise. The subject of a delusional system when under its influence is wholly dominated by it and excludes from attention everything in his environment which conflicts with the system.

Footnotes

[1] See also p. 235.

I have so far considered only the conflicts arising out of the activity of instinctive tendencies as agencies in the production of pathological states or of states, such as hypnotism, which lie outside the ordinary lines of human activity. I cannot leave the subject without some indication of the part which these conflicts may take in some of the more useful and beautiful aspects of life. Hitherto we have considered the solution of conflicts by such crude means as paralysis, delusion or crank, but if properly directed the conflict may have a very different outcome.

The main purpose of this book has been to consider the success and failure of suppression as a means of dealing with instinctive tendencies out of harmony with the needs of social life. I have said nothing of a process, which not only forms one of the chief therapeutic agencies by means of which we try to meet the failures of suppression, but is one which underlies success in all the higher accomplishments of life, especially in art, science, and religion. In this process which is called sublimation, the energy arising out of conflict is diverted from some channel which leads in an asocial or antisocial direction, and turned into one leading to an end connected with the higher ideals of society.

We are accustomed to think of sublimation as a process of a more or less artificial kind, by which the physician directs the energy of a conflict into a channel more healthy and beneficent than that it has taken under the influence of those natural forces we denote collectively by the term "disease." We are accustomed to speak of this therapeutic process as re-education, [p. 157] and this is a most appropriate term, for it is essentially of the same order as the process of education in childhood which consists, or should consist, in the direction of innate or instinctive tendencies towards an end in harmony with the highest good of the society of which the child is to be an active member. Childhood is one long conflict between individual instinctive tendencies and the social traditions and ideals of society. Whether the outcome of this conflict is to be a genius or a paranoiac; a criminal or a philanthropist; a good citizen or a wastrel; depends in some measure, we do not yet know with any degree of exactness in what measure, on education, on the direction which is given by the environment, material, psychological and social, to the energy engendered in the conflicts made necessary by the highly complex character of the past history of our race.

To some of those who have been studying, during the last few years, the nervous and mental havoc produced by the ravages of warfare, one great interest lies in the light which this study has thrown on the process of education. Through our work we have been led to see how great a part is taken in the formation of character by influences, especially those of early childhood, which do not lie on the surface but are embedded in the unconscious strata of the mind.

In concluding this book I should like to suggest the possibility that the unconscious may have a still wider scope. Many lines of evidence are converging to show that all great accomplishment in human endeavour depends on processes which go on outside those regions of the mind of the activity of which we are clearly conscious. There is reason to believe that the processes which underlie all great work in art, literature, or science, take place unconsciously, or at least unwittingly. It is an interesting question to ask whence comes the energy of which this work is the expression. There are two chief possibilities; one, that it is derived from the instinctive tendencies which, through the action of controlling forces, fail to find their normal outlet; the other, that the energy so arising is increased in amount through the conflict between controlled and controlling [p. 158] forces. Many pathological facts, and especially the general diminution of bodily energy accompanying so many forms of psycho-neurosis, point to the truth of the second alternative. Whatever be the source of the energy, however, we can be confident that by the process of sublimation the lines upon which it is expended take a special course, and in such case it is not easy to place any limit to its activity. We do not know how high the goal that it may reach.

We have, I think, reason to believe that the person who has attained perfection of balance in the control of his instinctive tendencies, in whom the processes of suppression and sublimation have become wholly effective, may thereby become completely adapted to his environment and attain a highly peaceful and stable existence. Such existence is not, however, the condition of exceptional accomplishment, for which there would seem to be necessary a certain degree of instability of the unconscious and subconscious strata of the mind which form the scene of the conflict between instinctive tendencies and the forces by which they are controlled. During the last few years we have been driven to attend to the instability produced by the conditions of war in its rôle as the producer of disease. Now that the struggle is over, I believe that we may look to this instability as the source of energy from which we may expect great accomplishments in art and science. It may be also that, through this instability, new strength will be given to those movements which under the most varied guise express the deep craving for religion which seems to be universal among Mankind.

FREUD'S PSYCHOLOGY OF THE UNCONSCIOUS [1]

The usual course of scientific progress has been well exemplified, though perhaps in an exaggerated form, by the history of the theory of the unconscious put forward by Sigmund Freud, of Vienna. Few scientific theories escape the fate of being pushed by their advocates beyond the positions which they are fitted to hold, with the result that, failing to fulfil the expectations thus aroused, their merits are under-estimated or they are even thrust into the limbo reserved for dead hypotheses, only to be rescued therefrom by some later generation. If we are to trust the contemporary medical literature of Great Britain, this fate is now in store for Freud's theory of the unconscious. His views, or perhaps rather their applications, have stirred up such a hotbed of prejudice and misunderstanding that their undoubted merits are in serious danger of being obscured, or even wholly lost to view, in the conflict produced by the extravagance of Freud's adherents and the rancour of their opponents. This paper is an attempt to deal with the subject dispassionately from the point of view of one who has only temporarily been drawn by current events into the neighbourhood of the maelstrom of medical controversy.

The first point which may be noted is that Freud's theory of the unconscious is of far wider application than the perusal of recent medical literature would suggest. It is true that Freud is a physician and that he was led to his theory of the unconscious by the study of disease, but his theory is one which [p. 160] concerns a universal problem of psychology. If it is true, it must be taken into account, not only by the physician, but by the teacher, the politician, the moralist, the sociologist,[2] and every other worker who is concerned with the study of human conduct. Not only does the medical controversialist fail to recognise that he is dealing only with one corner of the subject, but too often he looks on the whole matter entirely from the so-called practical standpoint and judges a theory of universal interest by the consequences which follow the application of the theory in the hands of the more extravagant of its adherents. It is possible, even probable, that the practical application of Freud's theory of the unconscious in the domain of medicine may come to be held as one of its least important aspects, and that it is in other branches of human activity that its importance will in future be greatest. I may perhaps mention here that my own belief in the value of Freud's theory of the unconscious as a guide to the better understanding of human conduct is not so much based on my clinical experience as on general observation of human behaviour, on evidence provided by the experience of my friends, and most of all on the observation of my own mental activity, waking and sleeping.

In the mixture of invective and witticism which may pass for a serious contribution to the subject in the medical literature of this country, an objection frequently put forward is that in postulating unconscious mental states Freud is putting together incompatible and contradictory ideas. One possible course is that those who make this objection should see whether it is not possible to enlarge their conception of the mind, but to those who find this impossible a way out of the difficulty may be suggested. It would be an advantage if, instead of speaking of unconscious mental states, we were to speak of unconscious experience. Everyone would acknowledge that adult human beings have been the subjects of a vast body of experience of which they have no manifest memory, which does not enter into their manifest consciousness. Everyone would, I think, also be [p. 161] prepared to acknowledge that this body of unconscious experience influences our thoughts and actions, our feelings and sentiments. When we speak of such unconscious experience, we are keeping within the realm of obvious fact, although we are ignoring the problem concerned with the form in which the experience exists. Whether this unconscious experience is, or is not, to be included within the connotation of mind is largely verbal and depends on the definition of mind which we adopt. Since the science of psychology has until lately been almost exclusively concerned with problems of definition and description, it is natural that such a concept as that of Freud should meet with opposition, because it does not fit immediately into current systems of definition. The matter will perhaps become clearer if we consider the closely related body of experience which we term heredity. This term is only the name we have adopted for ancestral experience. When we discuss whether a given phenomenon, such as a morbid mental state, is due to heredity, what we are really discussing is how far the morbid state is the consequence of the experience of the ancestors of the patient. There have been those, such as Hering and Samuel Butler, who have extended the connotation of a psychological term so as to include this ancestral experience, and have regarded heredity as a species of memory. According to the more generally accepted usage this vast body of unconscious experience is not thought of as a whole in psychological terms. There are, however, certain elements in this ancestral experience which psychologists have singled out from the rest and; have termed instincts, and they are agreed in holding that instincts form part of the subject-matter of psychology. If such unconscious elements derived from ancestral experience are by universal assent included within the scope of the mind, it is difficult to understand how it is possible to exclude unconscious experience acquired in the lifetime of the individual. It would be humorous, if it were not pathetic, that many of those who object most strongly to Freud's views concerning the rôle of unconscious individual experience in the production of abnormal bodily and mental states should be loudest in the appreciation of the part [p 162] taken by that ancestral experience for which they use the term, too often the shibboleth, heredity.

Far more important than the largely verbal question, whether the unconscious influences which mould our conduct are or are not to be regarded as constituents of: the mind, is the question concerning that which distinguishes Freud's theory of the unconscious from other theories which deal with this subject. A favourite statement concerning Freud's theory is that its fundamental idea is mental conflict. Standing out prominently in the system of Freud is the idea of conflict between the mental tendencies of the individual and the traditional code of conduct prescribed by the society to which the individual belongs. This conflict, however, was fully recognised by psychologists long before Freud. if this idea were the chief characteristic of his theory, no great claim for novelty or originality could be advanced. If a writer were to point to conflict as characteristic of human society, few would regard the proposition as either profound or especially illuminating, and the idea of mental conflict is in much the same case. The feature which makes Freud's theory noteworthy is his scheme of the nature of the opponents in the conflict, and of the mechanism by which the conflict is conducted.

Another concept characteristic of Freud's psychology is that of dissociation, but here again the idea is older than Freud, and forms part of systems of psychology very different from his. The special merit of Freud's theory in this respect is that it provides a psychological theory of dissociation, of the factors upon which it depends, acid of the processes by which its effects can be overcome.

There is much to be said for a view which would regard as a distinctive feature of Freud's system his theory of forgetting. According to the views long current in psychology, forgetting is a passive process which stands in no special need of explanation. According to these older views, experience is remembered in so far as it is frequently repeated and according as it is interesting and arouses emotion, pleasant or unpleasant. It has been frequently recognised, however, that it is forgetting rather than [p. 163] remembering which needs explanation. It is, perhaps, the greatest merit of Freud's theory that it provides us with such an explanation. According to Freud, forgetting -- and especially the forgetting of unpleasant experience -- is not a passive but an active process, one in which such experience is thrust out of consciousness and kept under control by a mechanism which by a metaphorical simile Freud has termed the censorship. This censorship is Supposed to act as a constant guard, only allowing the suppressed experience to reach consciousness in sleep, hypnotism, and automatic or other states in which the normal control of the censorship is removed or weakened. Even when the censorship thus permits the suppressed experience to become manifest, the experience is often only allowed to show itself in an indirect and often symbolic manner. It is this belief in a process of active suppression of unpleasant experience which is the special characteristic of Freud's theory of the unconscious, and it is his doctrine of the part taken by such suppressed experience in the production of bodily and mental disorder which is the leading feature of his theory in its relation to medicine. According to Freud many morbid mental states and many bodily states dependent on mental disturbance are due to a conflict between bodies of suppressed experience, now usually called "complexes" and the general personality of the sufferer.

Still more important than nomenclature m theoretical basis as a cause of prejudice and misunderstanding has been the stress which Freud and his followers have laid upon sexual experience as the material of morbid complexes. In his theory Freud uses the term "sexual" with a far wider connotation than is customary, using it to comprise anything which is either directly or indirectly connected with the process of reproduction. His followers, however, and to a large extent Freud himself, have become so engrossed with the cruder side of sexual life that their works might often be taken for contributions to pornography rather than to medicine. In some of Freud's followers this absorption in the sexual has gone to such lengths that perverse tendencies and prurient ideas are scented in every thought, waking or sleeping, of the patients who came under their care. [p. 164] To a certain extent this excess is a reaction from the timidity and prudery of the great mass of the medical profession in relation to sexual matters, and is a protest against the ignorance of this side of life which so often exists. The mistake which is now being made by many is to regard this excess as a necessary part of the Freudian scheme instead of an unfortunate excrescence, probably due in large measure to the social environment in which the theory had its origin. There are even those who are so obsessed by the sexual aspect of Freud's pyschology[sic] that they regard sexuality as its basic principle and have fallen into a state of mind which wholly blinds them to its merits.

It is a wonderful turn of late that just as Freud's theory of the unconscious and the method of psycho-analysis founded upon it should be so hotly discussed, there should have occurred events which have produced oil an enormous scale just those conditions of paralysis and contracture, phobia and obsession, which the theory was especially designed to explain. Fate would seem to have presented us at the present time with an unexampled opportunity to test the truth of Freud's theory of the unconscious, at any rate in so far as it is concerned with the part taken by sexual factors in the production of mental and functional nervous disorder. In my own experience, cases arising out of the war which illustrate the Freudian theory of sexuality directly and obviously have been few and far between. Since the army at the present time would seem to be fairly representative of the whole male population of the country, this failure to discover to any great extent the cases with which the literature of the Freudian school abounds might well be regarded as significant. If my experience is a trustworthy sample, it would seem as if the problem was already well on the way towards settlement.

There me, however, certain features of the situation which must be taken into account before we should accept this conclusion. First, it must be noted that, while the proportion of the population from which cases of war-strain are now being drawn is very large, it is not wholly representative, but has been selected, though in a very rough manner, by the medical [p. 165] examination preliminary to enlistment. There is some reason to think that many persons who would be likely to support the Freudian point of view, have for one reason or another escaped inclusion in the army, or if they have joined are given work which does not expose them to the more severe shocks and strains of warfare. Another and more important reservation depends on the fact that warfare tends to produce states of anxiety and apprehension so deep-seated and far-reaching that they obscure causes of a different kind. Cases arising out of the war do not for this reason furnish satisfactory material whereby to test the truth of the Freudian position. Persons who break down under the strains of ordinary life, in whom other states are not hidden by the overpowering emotional conditions arising out of modern warfare, provide material which shows far more readily the influence of unconscious factors of the kind which are held to be so important by Freud and his school. Even when these reservations are taken into account, however, there remains little to support the Freudian position in the form in which it is usually presented to us by its advocates. We now have abundant evidence that those forms of paralysis and contracture, phobia and obsession, which regarded by Freud and his disciples as pre-eminently the result of suppressed sexual tendencies, occur freely in persons whose sexual life seems to be wholly normal and commonplace, who seem to have been unusually free from those sexual repressions which are so frequent in modern civilisation, especially among the more leisured classes of the community. It is, of course, obvious that the evidence in this direction, being negative, cannot be conclusive. The point is that while we have over and over again abundant evidence that pathological nervous and mental states are due, it would seem directly, to the strains and shocks of warfare, there is, in my experience, singularly little evidence to show that, even indirectly and as a subsidiary factor, any part has been taken in the process of causation by conflicts arising out of the activity of suppressed sexual complexes. Certainly, if results are any guide, the morbid states disappear without any such complexes having [p. 166] been brought to the surface, while in other cases the morbid states persist in spite of the discovery of definite complexes, sexual or otherwise, going back to times long before the war.

The denial of the validity of Freud's theory of the unconscious in the farm currently held by its adherents, as the means of explaining nervous and mental disorders, is, however, something very different from the denial of the validity of this theory altogether. While in my experience instances of the kind which abound in the Freudian literature sue rarely met with among the cases arising out of the war, there is hardly a case which this theory does not help us the better to understand -- not a day of clinical experience in which Freud's theory may not be of direct practical use in diagnosis and treatment. The terrifying dreams, the sudden gusts of depression or restlessness, the cases of altered personality amounting often to definite fugues, which are among the most characteristic results of the present war, receive by far their most natural explanation as the result of war experience, which by some pathological process, often assisted later by conscious activity on the part of the patient, has been either suppressed or is in process of undergoing changes which will lead sooner or later to this result. While the results of warfare provide little evidence in favour of the production of functional nervous disorders by the activity of suppressed sexual complexes, T believe that they will be found to provide abundant evidence in favour of the validity of Freud's theory of forgetting, which in the earlier part of this paper I have regarded as the most striking and characteristic feature of his psychology.

I do not attempt to deal generally with the practical consequences which must follow, if we accept the view that many of the symptoms which follow the: strains and shocks of warfare depend an the suppression of painful experience. I am content now to point out one consequence if we accept the position that certain symptoms of war-strain depend on the activity of suppressed experiences arising-directly out of the war. I believe that I am: stating the orthodox view of the medical profession, I am certainly expressing that of the man in the street, if I say [p. 167] that the forgetting of unpleasant experience is held to be the obvious and natural line of procedure. The advice given takes such forms as: "Put it out of pour mind," "Try not to think of it." Moreover, if the advice is not successful and the solitude of the night allows the painful thoughts to force themselves on the attention of the patient, hypnotic drugs, hypnoidal suggestion, or perhaps even definite hypnotism, are employed to assist the process of driving the painful thoughts below the threshold of consciousness. When hypnotism or hypnoidal suggestion is employed, there is definite danger of producing just those states of dissociation which it should be our most vital duty to avoid, while it is a moot question whether the employment of hypnotic drugs does not tend to produce the same effect though in a different and more gradual way.

If the view I have put forward has any validity the proper line of conduct should be the direct opposite of that which, is usually taken. Instead of advising repression and assisting it by drugs, suggestion, or hypnotism, we should lead the patient resolutely to face the situation provided by his painful experience. We should point out to him that such experience that of which he has been the subject can never be thrust wholly out of his life, though it may be possible to put it out of sight and cover it up so that it may seem to have been abolished. His experience should be talked over in all its bearings. Its good side should be emphasised, for it is characteristic of the painful experience of warfare that it usually has a good or even a noble side, which in his condition of misery the patient does not see at all, or greatly under-estimates. By such conversation an emotional experience, which is perhaps tending to become dissociated, may be intellectualised and brought into harmony with the rest of the mental life., or in more technical language, integrated with the normal personality of the sufferer. As a matter of practical experience the relief afforded to a patient by the process of talking over his painful experience, and by the discussion how he can readjust his life to the new conditions, usually gives immediate relief and may be followed by great improvement or even rapid disappearance of his chief [p. 168] symptoms. It is in grave cases in which the painful experience of warfare has come to persons of somewhat neuropathic tendency, liable to the occurrence of dissociation, that this line of treatment is especially useful, but in slighter cases and more normal subjects there is much to be said for encouraging the patient to become familiar with his painful experience instead of treating it by the process of taboo, surrounding it, and assisting the tendency of the patient to surround it, with a halo of mystery. What is rather needed is the encouragement of that kind of familiarity which breeds indifference, if not contempt.

I have only dealt superficially with some of the misunderstanding in which Freud's theory of the unconscious has been enveloped, especially in this country, while briefly considering the place which this theory seems destined to take in relation to the vast mass of clinical experience which modern warfare is providing. I must conclude by considering in the most general manner what I hold to be the value of Freud's theory to medicine. Freud's theory of the unconscious should appeal to the physician in that it provides him with a definite working scheme of influences, which he has long known to be active in the causation of mental disorders and of the bodily disorders which are traceable to mental factors. The modern conception of such disorders is that they are not merely the result of some shock or strain, but are the outcome of the whole life-history of those who suffer, that they are the result of the totality of the individual experience of the patient as well as of that ancestral experience which we call heredity. Of this ancestral experience, and to a large extent of the individual experience, everyone will acknowledge that it is not accessible to the manifest consciousness of the patient and cannot be learnt from him by the ordinary methods of obtaining the history of the patient and his illness. The great merit of Freud is that he has provided us with a theory of the mechanism by which this experience, not readily and directly accessible to consciousness, produces its effects, while he and his followers have devised clinical methods by which these hidden factors in the causation of disease may be [p. 169] brought to light. For the physician who is not content to walk in the old ruts when in the presence of the greatest afflictions which can befall mankind, Freud has provided a working scheme of diagnosis and therapeutics to aid him in his attempts to discover the causes of mental disorder and to find means by which it may be remedied. My own standpoint is that Freud's psychology of the unconscious provides a consistent working hypothesis to aid us in our attempts to discover the rôle of unconscious experience in the production of disease. To me it is only such an hypothesis designed, like all hypotheses, to stimulate inquiry and help us in our practice, while we are groping our way towards the truth concerning the nature of mental disorder. We can be confident that the scheme as it stands before us now is only the partial truth and will suffer many modifications with further research, but that it takes us some way in the direction of the truth seems to me certain. If this value of Freud's theory were only a probability, or even only a possibility, are we justified in ignoring it as an instrument for the better understanding of disorders of which at present we know so little? Are we to reject a helping hand with contumely because it sometimes leads us to discover unpleasant aspects of human nature and because it comes from Vienna?

Footnotes

[1] A paper read at a meeting. of the Edinburgh Pathological Club, March 7, 1917; published in the Lancet, June 16, 1917.

[2] Cf. Sociological Review (1916), ix. 11.

A CASE OF CLAUSTROPHOBIA[1]

The case I am about to record is that of a medical man, aged thirty-one, who from childhood has suffered from a dread of being in an enclosed space, and especially of being under conditions which would interfere with his speedy escape into the open.

When I saw him first his earliest memory of this dread went back to the time when at the age of six he slept with his elder brother in what is known in Scotland as a box-bed. The bed stood in a recess with doors which could be closed so as to give the appearance of a sitting-room. The child slept on the inner side of the bed next to the wall, and he still vividly remembers his feat and the desire to get out of bed, which he did not satisfy for fear of waking his brother. He would lie in a state of terror, wondering if he would be able to get out if the need arose.

His next memory bearing on his phobia is of being taken to see some men descending the shaft of a coal-pit. There came to him at once the fear that were he going down something might happen to prevent his getting out. He remembers that whenever in childhood he was taken for a journey by train he dreaded the tunnels, and if by chance the train stopped in a tunnel he feared that there might be an accident and that he would not be able to get out. This fear of tunnels became worse as he grew older. He would not travel by the tube-railway, and remembers his horror when on one occasion he had to do so. When he began to go to the theatre or other [p. 171] crowded building he was always troubled unless be was near the door, and he was never happy unless he could see a clear and speedy made of exit. As long as he can remember he has felt an intense sympathy whenever he has read of prisoners being confined in a narrow cell, and be has always been greatly disturbed by tales of burial alive.

He was always nervous and excitable as a child and suffered from night-terrors. He has been liable, as long as he can remember, to worry without knowing why. When about twelve years old he began to stammer, ascribing its onset to the imitation of a school-fellow. It soon passed off, but ever since be has been liable to stammer when out of health.

During boyhood he had occasional attacks of sleeplessness, loss of appetite, and inability to work. When about twenty-two years of age he decided to go in for medicine, and while reading for the preliminary had an attack of this kind more severe than usual, which prevented his working for some time. A similar attack during the second year of his medical studies made him fear that he would have to give up medicine, but the leisure of a vacation restored him, and he completed his medical course. While serving as house-surgeon he again broke down in health, but managed to finish his period of office, and then did very light work for nine months.

About six years ago, while a medical student, he heard of a German, whom I will call A., who received patients into his house in order to cure them of stammering and other nervous ailments. He stayed with him for two weeks, the treatment consisting mainly of a variety of suggestion in which the patients were told to relax their muscles and concentrate their minds on the qualities they desired to attain. A. had recently become acquainted with the work of Freud, and had visited Vienna in order to learn something of his methods. Some time later the patient again put himself under the care of A. in order to undergo a course of psycho-analysis. The analyst in this case does not appear to have been acquainted with the method of free association, and after an unsuccessful attempt to carry out a series of word-associations the process of psycho-analysis [p. 172] resolved itself into an inquiry into dreams. In company with others the patient was instructed about Freud and his views. He was told that the cause of his trouble certainly lay in some forgotten experience of childhood of a sexual nature. When he related his dreams they were invariably interpreted by means of symbolism of a sexual character. Thus, if he had dreamed of water, he was told that this indicated a wish for sexual intercourse. It is a striking feature of the process of examination and treatment to which the patient was subjected that it failed to discover the special dread of closed spaces from which he suffered. At this time he had not realised that his dread was exceptional or was capable of treatment. He had supposed that everyone objected to conditions which were so trying to himself, and it was only on account of his stammering and his general nervousness that he had sought treatment. Consequently he told A. nothing about his dread and the process of "analysis" failed to detect it. Not only did the treatment lead the mind of the patient exclusively in a sexual direction, but it also failed to discover or remedy the claustrophobia.

This process of so-called psycho-analysis had no result which satisfied the patient. On the contrary, after two months of it his sleep became so disturbed and his general condition so the worse that he gave up the treatment and returned home. Nevertheless, he was left with the firm conviction, which he retained till he came under my care, that the root of his troubles lay in some forgotten sexual experience. This belief was so strong that he continued to search out for himself some forgotten experience of this kind, but without success, and shortly before the outbreak of the war he was thinking of going to Vienna to consult Freud and find whether the master himself might not succeed in discovering the lost memory.

The outbreak of the war interfered with this plan. At that time the patient was still suffering from the effects of his breakdown when a house-surgeon, but as soon as he had recovered sufficiently he joined the R.A.M.C. and went to France. When he reached the front he had to live and work in dugouts [p. 173] and was at once troubled by the dread of the limited space, and especially by the fear that he might not be able to get out if anything happened. His dread was greatly stimulated on his first day in a dug-out when, on asking the use of .spade and shovel, he was told that they were to be used in case he was buried. It was only when he found others living and working in comfort in dug-outs that for the first time he realised the exceptional nature of his dread, and recognised that he was the subject of an abnormal condition. After two attacks of trench-fever his dread was greatly accentuated and increased to such an extent as to make his life almost unendurable. He slept so badly that he had recourse to hypnotics and often spent a large part of the night walking about the trenches rather than remain in his dug-out. His health became so impaired that he was advised by his commanding-officer to consult the A.D.M.S., who sent him into hospital. He was there treated by rest and was given paraldehyde every night. He was told to keep his thoughts from war-experience and to dwell exclusively on pleasant topics such as beautiful scenery.

After three weeks in hospital in France he was sent to London where he was again treated by rest and hypnotics. When he came under my care he had been sleeping very badly in spite of the hypnotics. He had been having terrifying dreams of warfare from which he would awake sweating profusely and think that he was dying. These dreams had become less frequent but still occurred. He stammered very badly and was often depressed and restless. He found it difficult to read anything which required a mental effort and complained that his memory was defective, especially for recent occurrences. He had occasional frontal headache and suffered from pain and discomfort after food, which he ascribed to the paraldehyde he had taken, and he was liable to alternating constipation and diarrhœa. His deep reflexes were somewhat exaggerated.

In obtaining his history I learnt about his interest in Freud, and about the previous attempts to remedy his condition by means of psycho-analysis. It was only when I explained to [p. 174] him my views concerning the exaggerated interest in sex shown by Freud and his disciples that he learnt for the first time that forgotten experience of other than a sexual kind might take a part in the production of nervous states. It was agreed that "psycho-analysis" should be given a fresh trial from this point of view.

The next interview was devoted to a full inquiry into his previous experience in analysis, the results of which have already been given. As a preliminary to the following sitting I asked him to remember as fully as possible any dreams he might have in the interval, and to record any memories which came into his mind while thinking over the dreams. He was instructed to come to me at once if he had any dreams of interest. A few days later he dreamed of being in France, and of being chased by someone into a deep hole in which his pursuer killed a rabbit in place of himself and threw it into a pond covered with scum. The rabbit came to life again, and was swimming in the pond when a girl tried to kill it with a poleaxe, but only succeeded in making a gash in its back with the sharper end. The patient told her to kill it with the blunt limb and awoke. In the dream the rabbit was regarded as a ferocious animal which the patient feared would get away, and this fear continued for some time after he awoke..

While thinking over the dream in bed immediately after awaking, there came into the patient's mind an incident which had occurred soon after he had gone to live in the house with the box-bed. At this time his brother kept pet rabbits, and in order to annoy his brother after a quarrel the patient had struck one of the rabbits on the head and it had become unconscious. The brother became angry and was proceeding to "hammer" the patient when the rabbit came to life again. The incident had made a great impression at the time, but so far as the patient knew he had not thought of it since he was a boy. While telling me the dream on the following day another incident from the same period came into his mind. Near the house was a pond, and shortly after the incident with the rabbit the patient saw [p. 175] three boys trying to drown a dog. They threw it into the water with a brick tied round its neck, but as the animal was still able to swim the boys threw stones at it, injuring its eyes and mouth till it sank. Here again the patient had not thought of the incident for years, though he remembered that he could not visit the pond later without fear. This recollection was followed by another which occurred a year or two later. He and two other boys tried to drown a rat in a bucket at the house of one of the boys, but the animal was so strong that they could hardly keep it in. The patient remembered that he experienced definite fear at the thought that the animal would escape.

In the light of the incident which came to mind later the prominence of animals in these recollections of childhood may have been significant, and all the incidents are more or less connected with the emotion of fear, but they did not seem at the time to have any relation to the phobia. It is especially noteworthy that they were not thought by the patient himself to be significant as was the case with the recollection which occurred later. They were, however, very useful in convincing the patient of the possibility of recalling forgotten incidents of childhood, and showing him that incidents other than those of a sexual nature might be recalled. They suggested that the method he was following might, if persevered in, lead to memories more obviously related to his symptoms.

Three nights later he had another dream. As he lay in bed thinking over the dream, there came into his mind an incident dating back to three or four years of age which had so greatly affected him at the time that it now seemed to the patient almost incredible that it could ever have gone out of his mind, and yet it had so completely gone from his manifest memory that attempts prolonged over years had failed to resuscitate it. The incident was of a kind which convinced him at once that the long-sought memory had been found. Unfortunately his interest in the regained memory was so great that the dream which had suggested it was completely forgotten and all attempts to recall it were unavailing. [p. 176]

The incident which he remembered was a visit to an old rag-and-bone merchant who lived near the house which his parents then occupied. This old man was in the habit of giving boys a halfpenny when they took to him anything of value. The child had found something and had taken it alone to the house of the old man. He had been admitted through a dark narrow passage from which he entered the house by a turning about half-way along the passage. At the end of the passage was a brown spaniel. Having received his reward, the child came out alone to find the door shut. He was too small to open the door, and the dog at the other end of the passage began to growl. The child was terrified. His state of terror came back to him vividly as the incident returned to his mind after all the years of oblivion in which it had lain. The influence which the incident made on his mind is shown by his recollection that ever afterwards he was afraid to pass the house of the old man, and if forced to do so, always kept to the opposite side of the street.

Ten days later the patient dreamed that he visited Edinburgh for the purpose of taking the Diploma in Psychological Medicine. As he lay in bed thinking over his dream and its possible antecedents, he found that he was saying to himself over and over again the name "McCann." He could not at first remember that he knew anyone so called, but it suddenly flashed on his mind that it was the name of the old rag-and-bone merchant in whose house he had been terrified.

One thing was needed to make the story complete. It seemed possible that these thoughts, recalled in consequence of thinking over dreams, might be purely fictitious. It might be that in his intense desire to find some experience of childhood which would explain his dread, the patient might have dreamed, or thought of, purely imaginary incidents which had been mistaken for real-memories. Luckily the patient's parents are still alive, and on inquiry from them it was learnt that an old rag-and-bone merchant had lived in the neighbourhood in such a house as the patient remembered and that his name was McCann. Until they were told some twenty-seven years later they had no idea [p. 177] that their child knew anything of the old man entered his house.

I propose first to consider this case in so far as it affords evidence concerning the forgetting of unpleasant experience and the possibility of recalling such experience to manifest memory. It is well to distinguish this problem from the quite separate problems how far such forgotten experience acts as the basis of morbid states and how far the recalling of the forgotten experience to manifest consciousness is of value therapeutically.

The main facts of the case from the first of these three points of view is that by following a certain procedure there came back to the patient a memory from early childhood which had, so far as he knew, been completely absent from his manifest consciousness for about twenty-seven years. It had been so completely forgotten that even six years devoted to research into his infantile memories had failed to recall it. If it had not been for the independent confirmation of his parents the whole memory might have been dismissed as fictitious, but their evidence makes it clear that we have to do with the revival of a genuine memory.

It will be well here to consider the conditions which led to the recovery of this long-forgotten incident. The facts that it should have eluded observation although diligently sought for six years, and that it should have come so readily to light at a later time, suggest that there was something faulty in the process by which the search had been conducted before the patient came under my care. We may inquire why his previous attempts to discover the memory had failed when they succeeded so rapidly as soon as the subject was approached by a different method.

One cause of failure is undoubtedly to be found in the previous turning of the patient's thoughts exclusively in the direction of sex. He had been assured that the memory to be revived would be concerned with sexual experience. All his endeavours had been devoted to the end of finding such an experience. We could hardly have a better example of the obstruction placed in the path of knowledge by the exclusive preoccupation [p. 178] of the Freudian school with the problem of sex. In dealing with this subject on another occasion[2] I have dwelt on the part taken by the exaggerated, if not morbid, interest in sex in producing the widespread prejudice against Freud's psychology which undoubtedly exists. The case I now record shows that the evil goes much deeper, and that the exclusive interest in sex map actually obstruct the discovery of an infantile experience which furnishes as good an example as could be desired of unconscious experience and of the possibility of recalling it to manifest memory.

A second, and perhaps more important, cause of failure is that until the patient came under my care his attention had not been especially directed to his claustrophobia It was only when he recognised that his fear of being in a dug-out in France was not shared by others that he realised the specific character of his dread. It was only when he came under my care that for the first time the process or analysis started from and centred round the dread of closed spaces. Throughout all our conversations the attention of the patient was tuned in this direction, thus leading the dream-thoughts to occupy themselves with this topic until they reached and brought to the surface the memory which had lain dormant for twenty-seven years. The case well shows that the process of analysis by which forgotten experience is laid bare is not a loose method of examination which may start anywhere and be carried on anyhow, but, if it is to be successful, must be based on definite principles. It must start from some special symptom or other experience, and must be conducted with a definite relation to the experience it is desired to reach.

The previous failure of the patient to recover his infantile experience is to be explained, partly by the exclusively sexual direction of his interest, partly by the process of examination and inquiry having failed to start from the dread of closed spaces to which the infantile experience has so obvious a relation. A problem which remains for consideration is whether the later success was merely due to these two faults having been [p. 179] remedied, or whether there was any positive virtue in the special method which was then employed. This method is essentially that of free association as understood by Freud -- the method of "abstraction" of Morton Prince -- but starting from the incidents of a dream and carried out during the time immediately following the dream. In my own experience I have found this time especially favourable for the recovery of memories, the state of half-wakefulness seeming to be especially favourable to the freedom of association. The employment of free association under these conditions must, except under very special circumstances, be concluded in the main by the patient himself. The physician helps in the process by leading the waking thoughts of the patient in a direction calculated to arouse the desired experience, and he may also, as in the present case, help to elicit memories other than those which are recalled immediately after the dream, but the method is only suited to intelligent and well-instructed patients.

Thus far I have dealt only with the evidence provided by this case of claustrophobia in favour of the reality of unconscious experience and with the means by which it may again come to form part of the system of fully conscious memories. I have now to consider how far this case supports the contention that the forgetting of such experience acts as the basis of pathological states. In the case before us the pathological state is a definite example of a phobia. The problem for decision is whether the specific dread from which the patient suffered for so many years is the direct product of the forgotten experience of his childhood. The whole character of the infantile experience is one well calculated to produce such a fear as that from which the patient had so long suffered. The situation of a small child of four in a dark narrow passage with a strange growling dog as his sole companion is certainly one we might well expect to produce a lasting impression. The infantile experience accounts for the special feature of the claustrophobia that it is not so much a closed space itself which the patient dreads, but it is the fear that he may not be able to escape which especially haunts his mind. The inability of the child [p. 180] of four to open the door leading him from darkness and danger into light and safety seems to have been perpetuated in the special character of the claustrophobia afflicting the man of thirty. Throughout his life it has been when he sees no way of escape, whether at a distance from an exit, in a tunnel, or tube-railway, that the dread comes upon him, and when he went to France it was more especially the fear of being buried in his dug-out which drove him to leave conditions usually regarded as those of comparative safety to wander in the more dangerous trenches. This close correspondence between the infantile experience and the dread of later life can leave little doubt that the two are definitely related to one another, and that the infantile experience was the primary condition of the claustrophobia. It would seem probable that the phobia was accentuated and fixed later by his experience at the age of six, when night after night he lay in the box-bed, fearing to show any signs of fear owing to the presence of his brother. The process seems to have been one in which the great potentialities of an infantile impression were developed and fixed so that the emotional condition associated with the experience of the infant came to form part of the constitution of the boy and man. It is possibly owing to this later experience that the dread which was to occupy and often master the mind of the patient for nearly thirty years had as its object the narrow space rather than the dog which was the more immediate cause of the child's terror. So far as the patient remembers he has never had any fear of dogs, but it is possible that there was a period when the dread of the child was also directed to the animal, and that it was only the later and long-continued terror at the age of six which transferred the dread so completely to the other chief element of the earlier experience.

Another problem for consideration is how far his case supports Freud's special theory of "repression"[3] and active forgetting. What is needed here is some definite explanation of the process by which the acute and fully conscious terror of the child became converted into forgotten experience which was [p. 181] only restored to manifest consciousness after many years. What can have been the nature of the process by which the fully conscious mid vivid terror of the infant of four was converted into something unknown and unsuspected, working in subterranean fashion to reproduce .a vague state of dread or terror whenever the patient was exposed to conditions similar to those of his infantile experience? This topic belongs to the most difficult and obscure department of the subject. In the case of adults there is reason to believe that the process of active forgetting or suppression may in some cases take place more or less suddenly as the result of a shock or during a period of unconsciousness or delirium. On the other hand, it may be the result of a long-continued process of witting or half-witting exclusion from attention. It is difficult to imagine the latter kind of process taking place in a child of four or five. It seemed possible that it was the result of an illness in which the forgetting was assisted by some condition which produced an obvious modification of consciousness. I therefore asked my patient to make inquiries into the history of his early illnesses. He found that when between two and three years of age he had an attack of scarlet fever, so severe that the doctor despaired of his recovery. Between five and six he had enteric fever, which does not seem to have been especially severe. When about six or seven years old he had an abscess in the shoulder which lasted some months. Later he had pleurisy and was delirious, and there was again for a time little hope of his recovery. This was followed by an abscess in the foot which took some months to heal. The patient thus had a succession of severe illnesses both before and after the incident which seemed to have determined his claustrophobia The scarlet fever may have so weakened his health as to make him susceptible to suppression or to enhance an innate susceptibility in this direction, while one of the later illnesses may have provided an opportunity for conditions which would assist the process of suppression itself. I have now considered how far we can accept this case as evidence for the reality of unconscious experience and for the view that such experience is the basis of the pathological state [p. 182] of claustrophobia There still remains the question how far the case supports the contention of Freud that the bringing of unconscious experience to light is of therapeutical value. Two problems should be carefully distinguished. It is one problem whether the restoration of a forgotten experience to manifest memory relieves nervous morbid states, and it is a different problem to discover through what processes the "cure" works.

As regards the first problem, there is no doubt that the recovery of the forgotten experience of my patient had a great effect on his state. A few days after recalling the memory he sat without disturbance in the middle of a crowded picture-house under conditions which for years before would have given him the most serious discomfort and dread. The patient himself was so confident that he wished me to lock him in some subterranean chamber of the hospital, but I need hardly say that I declined to put him to, any such heroic test. He has since travelled in the tube-railway with no discomfort whatever, so that the ordinary conditions which had brought his phobia into activity for many years no longer have this effect. He has even been down a coal-mine, when be went for more than a mile along narrow underground passages, the mere thought of which would once have made him shrink in horror. A striking sequel of the recovery of his infantile memory is that terrifying dreams of being unable to escape from enclosed spaces from which he formerly suffered now trouble him no longer, and he had a dream, in which he found himself in a narrow cell in the company of a bloodhound, and was amazed in the dream that he should be so happy and comfortable in this situation.

The effect on the other symptoms from which he was suffering as the result of his war experience has been less satisfactory. His stammering improved to some extent, and still more striking than any objective improvement was the disappearance of a dread of stammering which had been a constant source of trouble since coming home from France, He became able to take plenty of physical and mental exercise, but he continued to sleep badly and be troubled by disturbing dreams of warfare. The continuance of these symptoms, however, is certainly due [p. 183] to the fact that though his claustrophobia had formed the starting-point of his general war-neurosis, the neurosis was kept active by other forms of anxiety.

In connection with his broken sleep and disturbing dreams of warfare one point may be considered. In entering upon the line of treatment which I have described in this paper I hesitated whether I was justified in possibly adding to his other causes of loss of sleep by asking him to attend to and think over his dreams. The progress of the case speedily removed any apprehensions of this kind. After his infantile memories had been discovered he continued to be interested in his dreams and their analysis, but did not find that the process interfered with his sleep. Even while on the search for forgotten memories he did not attempt any analysis of that class of dream, dealing with scenes of war, which especially disturbed his sleep.

The last problem I have to consider is concerned with the agency by which the recovery of the lost memory has so greatly relieved the claustrophobia of the patient according to the older views of Freud and his disciples the raising of suppressed experience to the surface is in itself sufficient to bring shout the disappearance of morbid states, and this curative action is often cited as evidence in favour of the general theory of suppression. The case before us might well be regarded as striking evidence in favour of their view. The recollection of the incident of his childhood has been followed by the disappearance of the dread which has been with him for so many years. It might seem at first sight evident that this disappearance has been the direct result of the reintegration of the forgotten and suppressed experience with his ordinary personality. Another possibility must, however, be considered.

The whole procedure of psycho-analysis is calculated to bring into play the agencies of faith and suggestion. Thus, the patient had been assured from his first attempt at psycho-analysis that the recovery of a forgotten experience of childhood would effect a cure. It was evident when he came under my care that in spite of previous failure his mind was still dominated by the belief that if the right experience could be found he [p. 184] would recover. When the memory of the passage and the dog came back to him his mind was filled with a sense of comfort as regards his illness such as he had not known for years.

I did nothing to enhance his confidence in the Freudian interpretation of the process by which the recovery of a lost memory produces a cure, but in spite of my own scepticism concerning the mechanism of recovery, I was careful to say nothing which would have disturbed his faith. This faith was so beat that it cannot be excluded as a factor in the therapeutic success of the revival of the forgotten experience. His case has one feature, however, which suggests, if it cannot be said to prove, that the recovery of the memory rather than the influence of faith and suggestion was the essential agent in producing the disappearance of his dread. For years the patient had believed that the recovery of the right memory would cure his stammering and get rid of his general nervousness. For reasons already considered, his faith had not had the state of claustrophobia as its object. Nevertheless, it was this symptom which was so greatly relieved, though we cannot yet say that it has been wholly cured.[4] The stammering and general nervousness, on. the other hand, which had throughout been the special objects round which his faith was working, though altered for the good, have been relieved in far less degree. The argument is not conclusive, because the direction of the patient's attention towards his claustrophobia, which was an essential element of my treatment, may have acted as an instrument by means of which the agencies of faith and suggestion already working in the patient's mind were turned towards his claustrophobia.

Footnotes

[1] Published in the Lancet, August 18, 1917.
[2] See p. 163.
[3] "Suppression" according to the terminology of this book.
[4] This was written in 1917. The patient has remained till the present time (May 1920) wholly free from any dread of confined space, and we can now say with some confidence that this morbid state was "cured" by the procedure adopted.

THE REPRESSION OF WAR EXPERIENCE[1]

I do not attempt to deal in this paper with the whole problem of the part taken by repression in the production and maintenance of the war-neuroses. Repression is so closely bound up with the pathology and treatment of these states that the full consideration of its rôle would amount to a complete study of neurosis in relation to the war. It is necessary at the outset to consider an ambiguity in the use of the term "repression" as it is now used by writers on the pathology of the mind and nervous system. The term is currently used in two senses which should be carefully distinguished from one another. It is used for the process whereby a person endeavours to thrust out of his memory some part of his mental content, and it is also used for the state which ensues when, either through this process or by some other means, part of the mental content has become inaccessible to manifest consciousness. In the second sense the word is used for a state which corresponds closely with that known as dissociation,[2] but it is useful to distinguish mere inaccessibility to memory from the special kind of separation from the rest of the mental content which is denoted by the term dissociation. The state of inaccessibility may therefore be called "suppression" in distinction from the process of repression. In this paper I use "repression" for the active or voluntary process by [p. 186] which it is attempted to remove some part of the mental content out of the held of attention with the aim of making it inaccessible to memory and producing the state of suppression.

Using the word in this sense, repression is not in itself a pathological process, nor is it necessarily the cause of pathological states. On the contrary, it is a necessary element in education and in ah social progress. It is not repression in itself which is harmful, but repression under conditions in which it fails to adapt the individual to his environment.

It is in times of special stress that these failures of adaptation are especially liable to occur, and it is not difficult to see why disorders due to this lack of adaptation should be so frequent at the present time. There are few, if any, aspects of life in which repression plays so prominent end so necessary a part as in the preparation for war. The training of a soldier is designed to adapt him to act calmly and methodically in the presence of events naturally calculated to arouse disturbing emotions. His training should be such that the energy arising out of these emotions is partly damped by familiarity, partly diverted into other channels. The most important feature of the present war in its relation to the production of neurosis is that the training in repression normally spread over years has had to be carried out in short spaces of time, while those thus incompletely trained have had to face strains such as have never previously been known in the history of mankind. Small wonder that the failures of adaptation should have been so numerous and so severe.

I do not now propose to consider this primary and fund mental problem of the part played by repression in the original production of the war-neuroses The process of repression does not cease when some shock or strain has removed the soldier from the scene of warfare, but it may take an active part in the maintenance of the neurosis New symptoms often arise in hospital or at home which are not the immediate and necessary consequence of war experience, but are due to repression of painful memories and thoughts, or of unpleasant affective states arising out of reflection concerning this experience. It [p. 187] is with the repression of the hospital and of the home rather than with the repression of the trenches that I deal in this paper. I propose to illustrate by a few sample eases some of the effects which may be produced by repression and the line of action by which these effects may be remedied. I hope to show that many of the most trying and distressing symptoms from which the subjects of war-neurosis suffer are not the necessary result of the strain and shocks to which they have been exposed is warfare, but are due to the attempt to banish from the mind distressing memories of warfare or painful affective states which have come into being as the result of their war experience.

Everyone who has had to treat cases of war-neurosis, and especially that form of neurosis dependent on anxiety, must have been faced by the problem what advice to give concerning the attitude the patient should adopt towards his war experience. It is natural to thrust aside painful memories just as it is natural to avoid dangerous or horrible scenes in actuality. This natural tendency to banish the distressing or the horrible is especially pronounced in those whose powers of resistance have been lowered by the long-continued strains of trench life, the shock of shell explosion, or other catastrophe of warfare. Even if patients were left to themselves, most would naturally strive to forget distressing memories and thoughts. They are, however, very far from being left to themselves, the natural tendency to repress being in my experience almost universally fostered by their relatives and friends, as well as by their medical advisers. Even when patients have themselves realised the impossibility of forgetting their war experiences and have recognised the hopeless and enervating character of the treatment by repression, they are often induced to attempt the task in obedience to medical orders. The advice which has usually been given to my patients in other hospitals is that they should endeavour to banish all thoughts of war from their minds. In some cases all conversation between patients, or with visitors, about the war is strictly forbidden, and the patients are instructed to lead [p. 188] their thoughts to other topics, to beautiful scenery and other pleasant aspects of experience.

To a certain extent this policy is perfectly sound. Nothing annoys a nervous patient more than the continual inquiries of his relatives and friends about his experiences at the Front, not only because it awakens painful memories, but also because of the obvious futility of most of the questions and the hopelessness of bringing the realities home to his hearers. Moreover, the assemblage together in a hospital of a number of men with little in common except their war experiences, naturally leads their conversation far too frequently to this topic, and even among those whose memories are not especially distressing it tends to enhance the state for which the term "fed up" seems to be the universal designation.

It is, however, one thing that those who are suffering from the shocks and strains of warfare should dwell continually on their war experience or be subjected to importunate inquiries; it is quite another matter to attempt to banish such experience from their minds altogether. The cases I am about to record illustrate the evil influence of this latter course of action and the good effects which follow its cessation.

The first case is that of a young officer who was sent home from France on account of a wound received just as he was extricating himself from a mass of earth in which he had been buried. When he reached hospital in England he was nervous and suffered from disturbed sleep and loss of appetite. When his wound had healed he was sent home on leave, where his nervous symptoms became more pronounced so that at his next board his leave was extended. He was for a time an out-patient at a London hospital and was then sent to a convalescent home in the country. Here he continued to sleep badly, with disturbing dreams of warfare, and became very anxious about himself and his prospects of recovery. Thinking he might improve if he rejoined his battalion, he made so light of his condition at his next medical board that he was on the point of being returned to duty when special inquiries about his sleep led to his being sent to Craiglockhart War Hospital [p. 189] for further observation and treatment. On admission he reported that it always took him long to get to sleep at night, and that when he succeeded he had vivid dreams of warfare. He could not sleep without a light in his room; because in the dark his attention was attracted by every sound. He had been advised by everyone he had consulted, whether medical or lay, that he ought to banish all unpleasant and disturbing thoughts from his mind. He had been occupying himself for every hour of the day in order to follow this advice and had succeeded in restraining his memories and anxieties during the day, but as soon as he went to bed they would crowd upon him and race through his mind hour after hour, so that every night he dreaded to go to bed.

When he had recounted his symptoms and told me about his method of dealing with his disturbing thoughts, I asked him to tell me candidly his own opinion concerning the possibility of keeping these obtrusive visitors from his mind. He said at once that it was obvious to him that memories such as those he had brought with him from the war could never be forgotten. Nevertheless, since he had been told by everyone that it was his duty to forget them, he had done his utmost in this direction. I then told the patient my own views concerning the nature and treatment of his state. I agreed with him that such memories could not be expected to disappear from the mind and advised him no longer to try to banish them, but I that he should see whether it was not possible to make them into tolerable, if not even pleasant, companions instead of evil influences which forced themselves upon his mind whenever the silence and inactivity of the night came round. The possibility of such a line of treatment had never previously occurred to him, but my plan seemed reasonable and he promised to give it a trial. We talked about his war experiences and his anxieties, and following this he had the best night he had had for five months. During the following week he had a good deal of difficulty in sleeping, but his sleeplessness no longer had the painful and distressing quality which had been previously given to it by the intrusion of painful thoughts of warfare. [p. 190] In so far as unpleasant thoughts came to him these were concerned with domestic anxieties rather than with the memories of war, and even these no longer gave rise to the dread which had previously troubled him. His general health improved; his power of sleeping gradually increased and he was able after a time to return to duty, not in the hope that this duty might help him to forget, but with some degree of confidence that he was really fit for it.

The case I have just narrated is a straightforward example of anxiety-neurosis which made no real progress as long as the patient tried to keep out of his mind the painful memories and anxieties which had been aroused in his mind by reflection on his past experience, his present state and the chance of his fitness for duty in the future. When in place of running away from these unpleasant thoughts he faced them boldly and allowed his mind to dwell upon them in the day, they no longer raced through his mind at night and disturbed his sleep by terrifying dreams of warfare.

The next case is that of an officer whose burial as the result of a shell-explosion had been followed by symptoms pointing to some degree of cerebral concussion. In spite of severe headache, vomiting and disorder of micturition, he remained on duty for more than two months. He then collapsed altogether after a very trying experience in which he had gone out to seek a fellow officer and had found his body blown into pieces with head and limbs lying separated from the trunk. From that time he had been haunted at night by the vision of his dead and mutilated friend. When he slept he had nightmares in which his friend appeared, sometimes as he had seen him mangled on the field, sometimes in the still more terrifying aspect of one whose limbs and features had been eaten away by leprosy. The mutilated or leprous officer of the dream would come nearer and nearer until the patient suddenly awoke pouring with sweat and in a state of the utmost terror. He dreaded to go to sleep, and spent each day looking forward in painful anticipation of the night. He had been advised to keep all thoughts of the war from his [p. 191] mind, but the experience which recurred so often at night was so insistent that he could not keep it wholly from his thoughts, much as he tried to do so. Nevertheless, there is no question but that he was striving by day to dispel memories only to bring them upon him with redoubled force and horror when he slept.

The problem before me in this case was to find some aspect of the painful experience which would allow the patient to dwell upon it in such a way as to relieve its horrible and terrifying character. The aspect to which I drew his attention was that the mangled state of the body of his friend was conclusive evidence that he had been killed outright, and had been spared the prolonged suffering which is too often the fate of those who sustain mortal wounds. He brightened at once, and said that this aspect of the case had never occurred to him, nor had it been suggested by any of those to whom he had previously related his story. He saw at once that this was an aspect of his experience upon which he could allow his thoughts to dwell. He said he would no longer attempt to banish thoughts and memories of his friend from his mind, but would think of the pain and suffering he had been spared.

For several nights he had no dreams at all, and then came a night in which he dreamt that he went out into No Man's Land to seek his friend, and saw his mangled body just as in other dreams, but without the horror which had always previously been present. He knelt beside his friend to save for the relatives any objects of value which were upon the body, a pious duty he had fulfilled in the actual scene, and as he was taking off the Sam Browne belt he woke, with none of the horror and terror of the past, but weeping gently, feeling only grief for the loss of a friend. Some nights later he had another dream in which he met his friend, still mangled, but no longer terrifying. They talked together, and the patient told the history of his illness and how he was now able to speak to him in comfort and without horror or undue distress. Once only during his stay in hospital did he again experience horror in connection with any dream of his friend. During the few [p. 192] days following his discharge from hospital the dream recurred once or twice with some degree of its former terrifying quality, but in his last report to me he had only had one unpleasant dream with a different content, and was regaining his normal health and strength.

In the two cases I have described there can be little question that the most distressing symptoms were being produced or kept in activity by reason of repression. The cessation of the repression was followed by the disappearance of the most distressing symptoms, sad great improvement in the general health. It is not always, however, that the line of treatment adopted in these cases is so successful. Sometimes the experience which a patient is striving to forget is so utterly horrible or disgusting so wholly free from any redeeming feature which can be used as a means of readjusting the attention, that it is difficult or impossible to find an aspect which will make its contemplation endurable. Such a case is that of a young officer who was flung down by the explosion of a shell so that his face struck the distended abdomen of a German several days dead, the impact of his fall rupturing the swollen corpse. Before he lost consciousness the patient had clearly realised his situation, and knew that the substance which filled his mouth and produced the most horrible sensations of taste and smell was derived from the decomposed entrails of an enemy. When he came to himself he vomited profusely, and was much shaken, but "carried on" for several days, vomiting frequently, and haunted by persistent images of taste and smell.

When he came under my care, several months later, suffering from horrible dreams, in which the events I have narrated were faithfully reproduced, he was striving by every means in his power to keep the disgusting and painful memory from his mind. His only period of relief had occurred when he had gone into the country, far from all that could remind him of the war.

This experience, combined with the horrible nature of his memory and images, not only made it difficult for him to discontinue the repression, but also made me hesitate to advise this measure with any confidence. During his stay in hospital [p. 193] the dream became less frequent and less terrible, but it still recurred, and it was thought best that he should leave the Army and seek the conditions which had previously given him relief.

A more frequent cause of failure or slight extent of improvement is met with in cases in which the repression has been allowed to continue for so long that it has become a habit. Such a case is that of an officer above the average age who, while looking at the destruction wrought by a shell explosion, lost consciousness, probably as the result of a shock caused by a second shell. He was so ill in France that he could tell little about his state there. When admitted to hospital in England he had lost power and sensation in his legs, and was suffering from severe headache, sleeplessness and terrifying dreams. He was treated by hypnotism and hypnotic drugs, and was advised neither to read the papers nor talk with anyone about the war. After being about two months in hospital he was given three months' leave. On going home he was so disturbed by remarks the about the war that he left his relatives and buried himself in the heart of the country, where he saw no one, read no papers, and resolutely kept his mind from all thoughts of war. With the aid of aspirin and bromides he slept better and had less headache, but when at the end of his period of leave he appeared before a medical board and the President asked a question about the trenches, he broke down completely and wept. He was given another two months' leave, and again repaired to the country to continue the treatment by isolation and repression. This went on until the order that all officers must be in hospital or on duty led to his being sent to an inland watering-place, where no inquiries were made about his anxieties or memories, but he was treated by baths, electricity and massage. He rapidly became worse; his sleep, which had improved, became as bad as ever, and he was transferred to Craiglockhart War Hospital. He was then very emaciated, with a constant expression of anxiety and dread. His legs were still weak, and he was able to take very little exercise or apply his mind or any time. His chief complaint was of sleeplessness and frequent [p. 194] dreams in which war scenes were reproduced, while all kinds of distressing thoughts connected with the war would crowd into his mind as he was trying to get to sleep.

He was advised to give up the practice of repression, to read the papers, talk occasionally about the war, and gradually accustom himself to thinking of, and hearing about, war experience. He did so, but in-a half-hearted manner, being convinced that the ideal treatment was that he had so long followed. He was reluctant to admit that the success of a mode of treatment which led him to break down and weep when-the war was mentioned was of a very superficial kind. Nevertheless, he improved distinctly and slept better. The reproduction of scenes of war in his dreams became less frequent, and were replaced by images the material of which was provided by scenes of home-life. He became able to read the papers without disturbance, but was loth to-acknowledge that his improvement was ;connected with this ability to face thoughts of war, saying that he had been as well when following his own treatment by isolation, and he evidently believed that he would have recovered if he had not been taken from his retreat and sent into hospital. It soon became obvious that the patient would be of no further service in the Army, and he relinquished his commission.

I cite this case not so much as an example of failure, or relative failure, of the treatment by removal of repression, for it is probable that such relaxation of repression as occurred was a definite factor in his improvement. I cite it rather as an example of the state produced by long-continued repression and of the difficulties which arise when the repression has had such apparent success as to make the patient believe in it.

In the cases I have just narrated there was no evidence that the process of repression had produced a state either of suppression or dissociation. The memories of the painful experience were at hand ready to be recalled or even to obtrude themselves upon consciousness at any moment. A state in which repressed elements of the mental content find their expression in dreams may perhaps be regarded as the first step towards suppression [p. 195] or dissociation, but if so, it forms a very early stage of the process.

There is no question that some people are more liable to become the subjects of dissociation or splitting of consciousness than others. In some persons there is probably an innate tendency in this direction; in others the liability arises through some shock or illness; while other persons become especially susceptible as the result of having been hypnotised.

Not only do shock and illness produce a liability to suppression, but these factors may also act as its immediate precursors and exciting causes. How far the process of voluntary repression can produce this state is more doubtful. It is probable that it only has this effect in persons who are especially prone to the occurrence of suppression. The great frequency of the process of voluntary repression in cases of war-neurosis might be expected to provide us with definite evidence on this head and there is little doubt that such evidence is present. As an example I may cite the case of a young officer who had done well in France until he had been deprived of consciousness by a shell, explosion. The next thing he remembered was being concluded by his servant towards the base, thoroughly broken down. On admission into hospital he suffered from fearful headaches and had hardly any sleep, and when he slept he had terrifying dreams of warfare. When he came under my care two months later his chief complaint was that whereas ordinarily he felt cheerful and keen on life, there would come upon him at times, with absolute suddenness, the most terrible depression, state of a kind absolutely different from an ordinary fit of "the blues," having a quality which he could only describe as "something quite on its own."

For some time he had no attack and seemed as if he had not care in the world. Ten days after admission he came to me one evening, pale and with a tense anxious expression which wholly altered his appearance. A few minutes earlier he had been writing a letter in his usual mood, when there descended upon him a state of deep depression and despair which seemed to have no reason. He had had a pleasant and not too tiring [p. 196] afternoon on some neighbouring hills, and there was nothing in the letter he was writing which could be supposed to have suggested anything painful or depressing. As we talked the depression cleared off and in about ten minutes he was nearly himself again. He had no further attack of depression for nine days, and then one afternoon, as he was standing looking idly from a window, there suddenly descended upon him the state of horrible dread. I happened to be away from the hospital and he had to fight it out alone. The attack was more severe than usual and lasted for several hours. It was so severe that he believed be would have shot himself if his revolver had been accessible. On my return to the hospital some hours after the onset of the attack he was better, but still looked pale and anxious. His state of reasonless dread had passed into one of depression and anxiety natural to one who recognises that he has been through an experience which has put his life in danger and is liable to recur.

The gusts of depression to which this patient was subject were of the kind which I was then inclined to ascribe to the hidden working of some forgotten yet active experience, and it seemed natural at first to think of some incident during the time which elapsed between the shell explosion which deprived him of consciousness and the moment when he came to himself walking back from the trenches. I considered whether this was not a case in which the lost memory might be recovered by means of hypnotism, but in the presence of the definite tendency to dissociation I did not like to employ this means of diagnosis, and less drastic methods of recovering any forgotten incident were without avail.

It occurred to me that the soldier who was accompanying the patient on his walk from the trenches might be able to supply a clue to some lost memory. While waiting for an answer to this inquiry I discovered that behind his apparent cheerfulness at ordinary times the patient was the subject of grave apprehensions about his fitness for further service in France, which he was not allowing himself to entertain owing to the idea that such thoughts were equivalent to cowardice, or might at any [p. 197] rate be so interpreted by others. It became evident that he had been practising a systematic process of repression of these thoughts and apprehensions, and the question arose whether this repression might not be the source of his attacks of depression rather than some forgotten experience. The patient had already become familiar with the idea that his gusts of depression might be due to the activity of some submerged experience and it was only necessary to consider whether we had not hitherto mistaken the repressed object. Disagreeable as was the situation in which he found himself, I advised him that it was one which it was best to face, and that it was of no avail to pretend that it did not exist. I pointed out that this procedure might produce some discomfort and unhappiness, but that it was far better to suffer so than continue in a course whereby painful thoughts were pushed into hidden recesses of his mind, only to accumulate such force as to make them well up and produce attacks of depression so severe as to put his life in danger from suicide. He agreed to face the situation and no longer to continue his attempt to banish his apprehensions. From this time he had only one transient attack of morbid depression following a minor surgical operation. He became less cheerful generally and his state acquired more closely the usual characters of anxiety-neurosis, and this was so persistent that he was finally passed by a medical board as unfit for military service.

In the cases I have recorded, the elements of the mental content which were the object of repression were chiefly distressing memories. In the case just quoted painful anticipations were prominent, and probably had a place among the objects of repression in other cases. Many other kinds of mental experience may be similarly repressed. Thus, after one of my patients had for long baffled all attempts to discover the source of his trouble, it finally appeared that he was attempting to banish from his mind feeling of shame due to his having broken down. Great improvement rapidly followed a line of action in which he faced this shame and thereby came to see how little cause there was for this emotion. In another case an officer had [p. 198] carried the repression of grief concerning the general loss of life and happiness through the war to the point of suppression, the suppressed emotion finding vent in attacks of weeping, which came on suddenly with no apparent cause. In this case the treatment was less successful, and I cite it only to illustrate the variety of experience which may become the object of repression.

I will conclude my record by a brief account of a case which is interesting in that it might well have occurred in civil practice. A young officer after more than two years' service bad failed to get to France, in spite of his urgent desires in that direction. Repeated disappointments in this respect, combined with anxieties connected with his work, had led to the development of a state in which he suffered from troubled sleep, with attacks of somnambulism by night and "fainting fits" by day. Some time after he came under my care I found that, acting under the advice of every doctor he had met, he had been systematically thrusting all thought of his work out of his mind, with the result that when he went to bed battalion orders and other features of his work as an adjutant raced in endless succession through his mind and kept him from sleeping. I advised him to think of his work by day, even to plan what he would do when he returned to his military duties. The troublesome night-thoughts soon went; he rapidly improved and returned to duty. When last he wrote his hopes of general service had at last been realised.

In the cases recorded in this paper the patients had been repressing certain painful elements of their mental content. They had been deliberately practising what we -must regard as a definite course of treatment, in nearly every case adopted on medical advice, in which they were either deliberately thrusting certain unpleasant memories or thoughts from their minds or were occupying every moment of the day in some activity in order that these thoughts might not come into the focus of attention. At the same time they were suffering from certain highly distressing symptoms which disappeared or altered in character when the process of repression ceased. Moreover, the symptoms by which they had been troubled were such as receive [p. 199] a natural, if not obvious, explanation as the result of the repression they had been practising. If unpleasant thoughts voluntarily repressed during the day, it is natural that they should rise into activity when the control of the waking state is removed by sleep or is weakened in the state which precedes and follows sleep and occupies its intervals. If the painful thoughts have been kept from the attention throughout the day by means of occupation, it is again natural that they should come into activity when the silence and isolation of the night make occupation no longer possible. It seems as if the thoughts repressed by day assume a painful quality when they come to the surface at night far more intense than is ever attained if they are allowed to occupy the attention during the day. It is as if the process of repression keeps the painful memories or thoughts under a kind of pressure during the day, accumulating such energy by the time night comes that they race through the mind with abnormal speed and violence when the patient is wakeful, or take the most vivid and painful forms when expressed by the imagery of dreams.

When such distressing, if not terrible, symptoms disappear or alter in character as soon as repression ceases, it is natural to conclude that the two processes stand to one another in the relation of cause and effect, but so great is the complexity of the conditions with which we are dealing in the medicine of the mind that it is necessary to consider certain alternative explanations.

The disappearance or improvement of symptoms on the cessation of voluntary repression may be regarded as due to the action of one form of the principle of catharsis. This term is generally used for the agency which is operative when a suppressed or dissociated body of experience is brought to the surface so that it again becomes reintegrated with the ordinary personality. It is no great step from this to the mode of action recorded in this paper, in which experience on its way towards suppression has undergone a similar, though necessarily less extensive, process of reintegration.

There is, however, another form of catharsis which may have [p. 200] been operative in some of the cases I have described. It often happens in cases of war-neurosis, as in neurosis in general, that the sufferers do not suppress their painful thoughts, but brood over them constantly until their experience assumes vastly exaggerated and often; distorted importance and significance. In such cases the greatest relief is afforded by the mere communication of these troubles to another. This form of catharsis may have been operative in relation to certain- kinds of experience in some of my cases, and this complicates our estimation of the therapeutic value of the cessation of repression. I have, however, carefully chosen for' record on this occasion cases in which the second form of catharsis, if present at all, formed an agency altogether subsidiary to that afforded by the cessation of repression.

Another complicating factor which may have entered into the therapeutic process in some of the cases is re-education. This certainly came into play in the case of the patient who bad the terrifying dreams of his mangled friend. In his case the cessation of repression was accompanied by the direction of the attention of the patient to an aspect of his painful memories which he had hitherto completely ignored. The process by which his attention was thus directed to a neglected aspect of his experience introduced a factor which must be distinguished from the removal of repression itself. The two processes are intimately associated, for it was largely, if not altogether, the new view of his experience which made it possible for the patient to dwell upon his painful memories. In some of the other cases this factor of re-education undoubtedly played a part, not merely in making possible the cessation of repression, but also in helping the patient to adjust himself to the situation with which he was faced, thus contributing positively to the recovery or improvement which followed the cessation of repression.

A more difficult and more contentious problem arises when we consider how far the success which attended the cessation of repression may have been, wholly or in part, due to faith and suggestion. Here, as in every branch of therapeutics, whether [p. 201] it be treatment by drugs, diet, baths, electricity, persuasion, re-education or psyche-analysis, we come up against the difficulty raised by the pervasive and subtle influence of these agencies working behind the scenes. In the subject before us, as in every other kind of medical treatment, we have to consider whether the changes which occurred may have been due, not to the agency which lay on the surface and was the motive of the treatment, but at any rate, in part, to the influence, so difficult to exclude, of faith and suggestion. In my later work I have come to believe so thoroughly in the injurious action of repression, and have acquired so lively a faith in the efficacy of my mode of treatment, that this agency cannot be excluded as a factor in any success I may have. In my earlier work, however, I certainly had no such faith, and advised the discontinuance of repression with the utmost diffidence. Faith on the part of the patient may, however, be present even when the physician is diffident. It is of more importance that several of the patients had been under my care for some time without improvement until it was discovered that they were repressing painful experience. It was only when the repression ceased that improvement began.

Definite evidence against the influence of suggestion is provided by the case in which the dream of the mangled friend came to lose its horror, this state being replaced by the far more bearable emotion of grief. The change which followed the cessation of repression in this case could not have been suggested by me, for its possibility had not, so far as I am aware, entered my mind. So far as suggestions, witting or unwitting, were given, these would have had the form that the nightmares would cease altogether, and the change in the affective character of the dream, not having been anticipated by myself, can hardly have been communicated to the patient. It is, of course, possible that my own belief in the improvement which would follow the adoption of my advice acted in a general manner by bringing the agencies of faith and suggestion into action, but these agencies can hardly have produced the specific and definite form which the improvement took. In other of the cases I have recorded, faith and suggestion probably played some part, [p. 202] that of the officer with the sudden and overwhelming attacks of depression being especially open to the possibility of these influences.

Such complicating factors as I have just considered can no more be excluded in this than in any other branch of therapeutics, but I am confident that their part is small beside that due to stopping a course of action whereby patients were striving to carry out an impossible task. In some cases faith and suggestion, reeducation and sharing troubles with another, undoubtedly form the chief agents in the removal or amendment of the symptoms of neurosis, but in the cases I have recorded there can be little doubt that they contributed only in a minor degree to the success which attended the giving up of repression.

Before I conclude, a few words must be said about an aspect of my subject to which I have not so far referred. When treating officers or men suffering from war-neurosis, we have not only to think of the restoration of the patient to health, we have also to consider the question of fitness for military service. It is necessary to consider briefly the relation of the prescription of repression to this aspect of military medical practice.

When I find that a soldier is definitely practising repression, I am accustomed to ask him what he thinks is likely to happen if one who has sedulously kept his mind from all thoughts of war, or from special memories of warfare, should be confronted with the reality, or even with such continual reminders of its existence as must inevitably accompany any form of military service at home. If, as often happens in the case of officers, the patient is keenly anxious to remain in the Army, the question at once brings home to him the futility of the course of action he has been pursuing. The deliberate and systematic repression of all thoughts and memories of war by a soldier can have but one result when he is again faced by the realities of warfare.

Several of the officers whose cases I have described or mentioned in this paper were enabled to return to some form of military duty with a degree of success very unlikely if they had persisted in the process of repression. In other cases, either because the repression had been so long continued or for [p. 203] some other reason, return to military duty was deemed inexpedient. Except in one of these cases, no other result could have been expected with any form of treatment. The exception to which I refer is that of the patient who had the sudden attacks of reasonless depression. This officer had a healthy appearance, and would have made light of his disabilities at a Medical Board. He would certainly have been returned to duty and sent to France. The result of my line of treatment was to produce a state of anxiety which led to his leaving the Army. This result, however, is far more satisfactory than that which would have followed his return to active service, for he would inevitably have broken down under the first stress of warfare, and might have produced some disaster by failure in a critical situation or lowered the morale of his unit by committing suicide.

In conclusion, I must again mention a point to which reference was made at the beginning of this paper. Because I advocate the facing of painful memories, and deprecate the ostrich-like policy of attempting to banish them from the mind, it must not be thought that I recommend concentration of the thoughts on such memories. On the contrary, in my opinion it is just as harmful to dwell persistently upon painful memories or anticipations, and brood upon feelings of regret and shame, as to attempt to banish them wholly from the mind. It is necessary to be explicit on this matter when dealing with patients. In a recent case in which I neglected to do so, the absence of any improvement led me to inquire into the patient's method of following my advice, and I found that, thinking he could not have too much of a good thing, he had substituted for the system of repression he had followed before coming under my care, one in which he spent the whole day talking, reading, and thinking of war. He even spent the interval between dinner and going to bed in reading a book dealing with warfare.

There are also some victims of neurosis, especially the very young, for whom the horrors of warfare seem to have a peculiar fascination, so that when the opportunity presents itself they cannot refrain from talking by the hour about war experiences, [p. 204] although they know quite well that it is bad for them to do so. Here, as in so many other aspects of the treatment of neurosis, we have to steer a middle course. Just as we prescribe moderation in exercise, moderation at work and play, moderation in eating, drinking, and smoking, so is moderation necessary in talking, reading, and thinking about war experience. Moreover, we must not be content merely to advise our patients to give up repression, we must help them by every means in our power to put this advice into practice. We must show them how to overcome the difficulties which are put in their way by enfeebled volition, and by the distortion of their experience due to its having for long been seen exclusively from some one point of view. It is only by a process of prolonged re-education that it becomes possible for the patient to give up the practice of repressing war experience.

Footnotes

[1] Read at a meeting of the Section of Psychiatry, Royal Society of Medicine, December 4, 1917; published in the Proceedings of the Royal Society of Medicine, 1918, vol. xi. (Section of Psychiatry), pp. 1-17. See also Lancet, vol. 194 (1918), p. 173.

[2] This term is used here in a wider sense than that adopted in this book.

WAR-NEUROSIS AND MILITARY TRAINING[1]

Discussions concerning the causation of the war-neuroses usually deal with two main topics. Either they consider the predisposition to nervous disorder of those who have broken down under the shocks and strains of warfare, or they are concerned with the relative shares taken by physical and mental factors as the immediate antecedents of these failures. In connection with the first topic, various writers have discussed the part taken by congenital or acquired tendencies to nervous or mental instability as shown either by family history or by the occurrence of nervous troubles before joining the army. Under the second heading have been considered especially the part taken by exhaustion, concussion or emotional shock as the immediate precursors of a nervous or mental collapse, or by conditions of strain and anxiety which have lowered the resistance of the soldier to the shock or illness which was the immediate antecedent of his failure.

These two topics do not exhaust the causes of war-neurosis. Between the time that a man joins the army and that at which he breaks down, he passes through a special experience, very different from that of any form of civilian life. He is first subjected to a special training, and when this training has reached a certain degree of perfection he meets another set of experiences, perhaps even more remote from those of civil life, in which he has to perform the military duties he has learned during his training.

Two separate problems must be distinguished: one, the relation of military training and the nature of military duties to [p. 206] the occurrence of neurosis; the other, the part taken by these factors in determining the special form which the neurosis takes. There is little question that one of the chief causes of the great prevalence of nervous disorders in the war is that vast numbers of men have been called upon to endure hardships and dangers of unprecedented severity with a quite insufficient training. There is equally little doubt that the special nature of the duties involved in trench warfare has taken a large part in determining the great frequency of neurosis.

It is not, however, the purpose of this report to deal with the problem of the part taken by military training and military duties in the causation of neurosis in general. Its aim is to deal only with the second of the two problems stated above. For this purpose it is necessary to consider briefly the varieties of war-neurosis, the main headings under which the almost infinite variety of its symptoms can be classified.

Excluding from the category of neurosis cases of simple exhaustion or concussion and disorders of circulation or digestion due to infection, and excluding also definite psychoses, cases of war-neurosis fall into three main groups, though intermediate and mixed examples are of frequent occurrence. The first group comprises cases in which the disorder finds expression in some definite physical form, such as paralysis, mutism, contracture, blindness, deafness, or other anæsthesia. The characteristic common to all these symptoms is that they are such as can be readily produced in hypnotism or other state in which suggestion is especially potent. I propose later to consider how far the considerations to be brought forward in this report help us towards a satisfactory nomenclature. In the meantime I shall be content to speak of this group as hysteria, the term by which it was generally known before the war and one which, in spite of its unsatisfactory character, is still widely used.

The second group consists of cases in which the disorder shows itself especially in lack of physical and mental energy, in disorders of sleep and of the circulatory, digestive, and urogenital systems. On the mental side there is usually depression, restlessness, [p. 207] irritability and enfeeblement of memory, and on the physical side tremors, ties, or disorders of speech. This group is usually known as neurasthenia in this country, but in this case I shall anticipate the results of my later discussion and speak of it by the term anxiety-neurosis.

The third group, with which I shall have little to do in this report, is characterised by the definitely psychical form of its manifestations. This group comprises a number of different varieties. In some cases the most obvious symptom is mental instability and restlessness with alternations of depression and excitement or exaltation, similar to those of manic-depressive insanity. In other cases there are morbid impulses of various kinds, including those towards suicide or homicide. In some the chief symptoms are obsessions or phobias, while others suffer from hallucinations or delusions. The special feature of all these cases is that the symptoms resemble in kind those of the definite psychoses, but have neither the severity nor the fixity which makes the seclusion of the patient or any legal restriction in the management of his affairs necessary.

There is no evidence that the psycho-neuroses of the third group are especially liable to affect either officers or men, but the other two groups show a remarkable difference in this respect which I propose to take as my guide in the treatment of the subject. The group which I have provisionally labelled hysteria is especially apt to affect the private soldier, Pure cases of this kind are rare among officers who, as a rule, only suffer from this form of disorder as complications of states of anxiety, or when there is some definite, physical injury to act as a continuous source of suggestion. Anxiety-neurosis is not similarly limited to officers, but affects them more frequently, and usually more profoundly, than the private soldier.

I propose to take this difference in the incidence of the two chief forms of neurosis as a clue to the better understanding of the nature of these states. I hope to show that this difference can be largely explained by differences in the character and effects of military training and - military duties. For this purpose it will be necessary first to state the general theory of the [p. 208] neuroses of warfare upon which my treatment of the subject will he based. This theory is that the neuroses of war depend upon a conflict between the instinct of self-preservation and certain social standards of thought mid conduct, according to which fear and its expression are regarded as reprehensible. From infancy the influence of parents and teachers is directed to bring about the repression of any manifestation of fear, and since the ordinary life of the modern civilised adult rarely presents any features which come into conflict with the instinct of self-preservation, this repression meets with little opposition and rarely produces any serious conflict. The child has many experiences which tend to call forth the emotion of fear in its cruder forms, but once adult age is reached, occasions which tend to produce fear rarely occur, and there is little in the ordinary life of the modern civilised man which tends to set up any conflict between the instinct of self-preservation and acquired social standards.

The business of the soldier, on the other hand, is one which necessarily brings its follower into the presence of danger, and as we shall see, one of the chief objects of military-training is to fit the soldier to meet the special assaults upon the instinct of self-preservation to which his calling will expose him. In one of the two chief forms of war-neurosis the conflict is solved by the occurrence of some disability-paralysis, contracture, mutism or anæsesthesia -- which, so long as it exists, incapacitates the patient from further participation in warfare and thus removes all immediate necessity for conflict between instinct and duty. Anxiety-neurosis, on the other hand, is a state or process in which the conflict has not been solved but is unduly active, the controlling social factors having been weakened by exhaustion, illness, strain or shock, so that the motives arising out of the instinct of self-preservation have gained in power, while in many cases the social factors have produced new conflicts and causes of anxiety which may be as potent as the primary conflict with the instinct of self-preservation.

The object of this report is to consider the part taken in this conflict by the processes of military training and military [p. 209] duties, but before considering this, it will be well to inquire whether the life of officer and man before the war provides any reason why the two should be affected in different ways by the strains and shocks of warfare.

One possible cause may be found in difference of general education. On the whole the officer is more widely educated than the private soldier; his mental life is more complex and varied, and he is therefore less likely to be content with the crude solution d the conflict between instinct and duty which is provided by such disabilities as dumbness or the helplessness of a limb. The histories of officers suffering from anxiety-neurosis often show the existence of temporary mutism, paralysis or other functional disability in the early stages of their illness, but these solutions of their conflict do not satisfy them and their disabilities speedily disappear, to be replaced sooner or later by symptoms directly dependent on anxiety.

Another possible cause is to be found in the quality of the education, and especially the school education of officer and man. Fear and its expression are especially abhorrent to the moral standards of the public schools at which the majority of officers have been educated. The games and contests which make up so large a part of the school curriculum are all directed to enable the boy to meet without manifestation of fear any occasion likely to call forth that emotion. The public school boy enters the army with along course of training behind him which enables him successfully to repress, not only expressions of fear, but also the emotion itself. A similar schooling forms part of the education of the primary schools whence the majority of private soldiers have come, but it has been less extensive and less systematic than in the public boarding schools, though it is probable that the popularity of certain games has done much to lessen the difference in recent years.

If the behaviour of the officer and private soldier after they have become the victims of neurosis is any guide to their standards before the war, the private soldier has far fewer scruples about giving expression to his fears, this expression being both more explicit and less subject to repression. [p. 210]

These differences must only be taken in the rough and as applicable on a large scale, but there is little doubt that the average private enters upon his military training with less aversion from the expression of fear than the average officer, and that his simpler mental training makes him more easily content than the officer with the crude solution of the conflict between instinctive and acquired motives which is provided by some bodily disability.

The liability of officers and men to different forms of war-neurosis is thus partly capable of explanation by differences in the conditions to which they have been exposed before the war. It is the object of this report to show that these or any other conditions[2] existing before the soldier joins the army are greatly assisted by differences in the nature of the training of officers and men and of the duties which fall to their lot. I will begin by considering the general aims and character of military training. Its two chief aims are to fit each individual soldier to ad in harmony with his fellows, and to enable him to withstand the stresses and trials of warfare. Military training is designed to enable the soldier to act calmly and methodically in situations which would naturally tend to upset the balance of his conduct and in the face of dangers which would arouse the instinct of self-preservation. Its aim is to free the soldier, not merely from the danger of succumbing to the collapse of terror or the blind flight of panic, but also from those minor disturbances of efficiency which are due to apprehensions or to doubts concerning the issue of a combat. The ideal military training should bring the soldier into such a state that even the utmost horrors and rigours of warfare are hardly noticed, so inured is he to their presence and so absorbed in the immediate task presented by his military duties.

In carrying out the two chief aims of military training certain definite agencies are called into play. In fulfilling the first aim of adapting the soldier to act as one of an aggregate in complete harmony with its other members, one agency is habituation. [p. 211] The elementary drill of a soldier consists of processes in which this agency plays a most important part. The soldier is thoroughly drilled in certain relatively simple evolutions until he has acquired the habit of immediate and unreflecting response to a command by means of which his reactions correspond with those of all the other members of the aggregate; all act together as if there were one mind in common to the whole. The individual soldier has to sink his individuality in order to act without hesitation or reflection as one of a section, platoon, company, battalion, or still larger group. The requirements of modern warfare are leading to some modification of this mechanical aspect of military training, but such modification only begins after the soldier has been subjected to a prolonged course of drill designed to adapt him to act as one of an aggregate.

An agency working with habituation, and one far more important from our present point of view, is suggestion.[3] The process by which an individual comes to act promptly and harmoniously as one of an aggregate is simply one variety of the process by which individuals come to act as members of social aggregates in general. A person who is being drilled is taken from our highly individualistic community, in which spontaneity and independence are encouraged, and is subjected to a course of training calculated to produce a state allied to that of existing communistic peoples or of animals which are accustomed to act in herds: One result of such a training, if it be not indeed also its chief aim, is to enhance the responsiveness of each individual to the influence of his fellows, and the form which is taken by military training is especially designed to enhance his responsiveness to those who are immediately above him in the military hierarchy. From one point of view the most successful training is one which attains such perfection of this responsiveness that each individual soldier not merely reacts at once to the expressed command of his superior, but is able to divine the nature of a command before it is given and [p. 212] acts as a member of the group immediately and correctly, even when the conditions of warfare might produce uncertainty if he relied entirely on the actual words or definite gestures of command. The process by which a capacity for such immediate response comes into being resembles very closely, if it be not actually identical with, the process we call suggestion. In the hypnotic state, in which the power and efficacy of suggestion reach their acme, the individual responds immediately and without question or hesitation, not merely to the command of his hypnotiser, but even to a desire or impulse of the hypnotiser's mind which is not expressed by speech or obvious gesture. The resemblance between the two states is so close that there is little doubt that one result of military training, and especially that of the more elementary forms of drill, is to enhance the suggestibility of those who are subjected to the process. It produces a modification of character which makes the soldier more immediately responsive to suggestion, whether this emanate from an individual officer or from the general body of the group, whether platoon, working-party, company or other body which forms the aggregate of which he is a member at the moment.

This enhanced responsiveness is well exemplified in certain well-known incidents occurring in the army which has carried the more mechanical aspects of military training to an extreme length.[4] The success of the Captain of Koepenick could only be possible in an army whose members had through a special course of training reached such a pitch of responsiveness to the commands of one in uniform that they obeyed without question the ludicrous orders of a cobbler.

The other aim of military training, which especially touches the liability to different forms of neurosis, is to fit the soldier to withstand the trials and stresses of warfare. One of the chief instruments by which this aim is met is that already considered, [p. 213] which makes the individual soldier act as a member of the aggregate to which be belongs in a closer sense than holds good in civil life. This does away with or diminishes greatly the tendency of any one individual in the group to react to fear or other emotional state in a way which would interfere with his military competence. In carrying out the aim of adapting the individual soldier to withstand the dangers of warfare, the first instrument is identical with that by which his actions come to be performed with the requisite immediacy and harmony. I have now to consider the other processes by which the soldier collectively is assisted to withstand the stresses of warfare. These processes bring into action two chief agencies, repression and sublimation.

In considering the process of repression in its relation to military training, two varieties must be distinguished. In the first variety an attempt is made to thrust some part of the mental content, some feeling, thought, memory or sentiment, from consciousness. In the second variety the effort is directed rather to the repression of the outward expression of some mental state, especially of feeling or emotion. There is no hard and fast line between these two forms. One who endeavours to control the expression of an emotion will also try to banish from his mind thoughts or memories likely to call the emotion forth. Since, however, it is the expression of an emotion which is appreciated by others, the repression of the outward manifestation bulks more largely in the process in so far as it is a feature of military training. There are probably great individual differences in the way in which different persons treat the conscious elements of the mental content in their efforts to subdue their outward expression. As I have pointed out elsewhere,[5] repression forms a necessary part of all education and adaptation to social life. Perhaps the most important feature on the repression of military training is the relatively late period of life at which it takes place. The older a person is, the more difficult it becomes for him to give up habitual modes of thought and action. It is where repression is [p. 214] incomplete and is the source of persistent mental conflict that it becomes a factor in the production and maintenance of neurosis. If the repression which forms part of military training is complete, it probably helps greatly towards the success of the repression which will become necessary when the soldier enters upon active service, but if it is incomplete, so that the soldier enters upon active service accompanied by the active conflicts so aroused, his success in the necessary repression of warfare will be prejudiced.

During military training much may be done, especially by means of games, to exercise the repression of fear and its expression, but during this part of his training other kinds of repression are more in evidence. In order to act as one of the aggregate to which he now belongs, the recruit has to repress any tendencies to individual action which would interfere, or are supposed by military tradition to interfere, with efficiency, and failure of these repressions has much to do with the production of war-neurosis. Thus, a frequent factor in the production of war-neurosis is the necessity for the restraint of the expression of sentiments of dislike or disrespect for those of superior rank, and these restraints become particularly trying when-those who are disliked or despised are the instruments by which the many restrictions of military life are imposed or enforced.

When the soldier is brought into contact with actual warfare, a new set of repressions come into action. It may become necessary to control and inhibit the expressions of emotion consequent upon the dangers of warfare. In some persons, especially those already well schooled in such repression, this process seems to take place with no obvious conflict, but in many cases the necessity for such repression is continually present, while in a far larger number this necessity comes into existence as the result of strain, the presence of a conflict in this respect being in many cases the first symptom of his abnormal state that the soldier notices. He may notice that whereas at one time he was hardly aware of shelling or other incident of warfare, he now tends to duck his head or [p. 215] perform some other involuntary movement whenever the noise of a shell is heard, thus betraying the presence of a conflict. A state in which such a tendency persists and requires continual repression is one of the most frequent forms taken by the early stage of war-neurosis.

When the soldier has been in the trenches for some time, a new necessity for repression may arise and may affect those who have not previously found it necessary to repress fears or apprehension, or in whom such repression, in so far as it has been present, has aroused no conflict. The soldier may undergo some particularly trying experience; some disgusting sight, or the death and mutilation of a friend, or other experience may be so painful that it continually intrudes itself upon him while he unavailingly strives to banish it from his mind.

The last agency to be considered is that made up by sublimation and side-tracking. To the soldier these words may be strange, but not so the processes which they denote. By sublimation is meant a process in which an instinctive tendency, more or less fostered by experience, which would normally find expression in some kind of undesirable conduct, has its energy directed into a channel in which it comes to have a positive social value. By side-tracking we mean a process in which the energy so diverted acquires no special social value, but is altogether harmless, or at any rate less harmful to the welfare of the individual and community than that expression in which the energy would otherwise find its outlet.

One of the simplest and most frequent forms of side-tracking is the oath. The "strange oaths" or other forms of lurid language of the soldier are nothing but the relatively innocent means by which an outlet is given to superfluous energy. The form of energy which is perhaps most frequently thus released is that arising out of the repressions which form part of military training. Another form of side-tracking is to be found in the conviviality and relative freedom from restraint in certain directions which form so frequent an accompaniment to the life of the soldier.

One of the chief means of diverting spare energy, however [p. 216] this may be produced, takes the form of games and athletic competitions. Since these are of definite military value, they must be regarded as a means of sublimation. These exercises do not merely train the mind and body and thus add to the efficiency of the soldier, but they also have the most important function of utilising spare energy, whether derived from the activity of suppressed complexes or the product of some more healthy process.

A most important instrument of sublimation is to be found in the development of esprit de corps. There is thus produced a body of sentiments which contribute greatly to military efficiency, while at the same time they provide a most valuable means of sublimating energy which might otherwise work in the opposite direction.

In the old army the chief vehicle of esprit de corps was the regiment. The regular British soldier of the days before the war was above everything a member of the regiment. The honour and welfare of his regiment formed one of his chief interests, and the desire that he might do nothing to tarnish this honour or prejudice this welfare stood forth prominently among the means which enabled him to withstand trials and dangers.

This esprit de corps of the old army was chiefly bound up with the institution of "long service." A soldier spent years, including the most impressionable of his life, in one regiment, with the other members of which he came to have relations of comradeship which were even more. efficacious as a protective against fear or other emotion than motives arising out of the more abstract sentiments of honour and duty.

These features of the process of military sublimation have been much changed in the more recent history of the British army, especially during the war, but these changes have only modified the process and have not changed its essential character. They have affected the nature of the unit with which the esprit de corps is associated, the spirit embodied in the regiment or the company being now attached to the battalion or platoon, or other unit which has been brought into existence by the [p. 217] exigencies of warfare. The old spirit based on long years of comradeship has during the present war been replaced by one based on the sharing of common hardships and dangers.

More important than either esprit de corps in the strict sense or the camaraderie which is so closely associated with it, is the special relation existing between officers and men. Anyone having much to do with those who have taken part in the fighting of the war must have been struck by the extraordinary manner in which an officer, perhaps only just fresh from school, has come to stand in a relation to his men more nearly resembling that of father and son than any other kind of relationship. It seems dear that different battalions show the incidence of neurosis in very different degrees, and this is probably due more than anything else to the nature of the relations between officers and men by which the private soldier acquires towards his officer sentiments of duty and trust, while the officer is actuated, it may be dominated, by interest which could not be greater if those under his command were his own children.

This brief sketch of the aims and methods of military training has led me to distinguish three main processes -- suggestion, repression and sublimation, while others of less importance in relation to neurosis are habituation and side-tracking. I can now consider how those different factors will affect officers and men respectively. The heightening of suggestibility, though probably an inevitable result of any kind of military training, is pre-eminently one which affects the private soldier. It is the private soldier especially who is submitted to prolonged mechanical drill and is continually subject to the commands of others, while the officer is not only less fully drilled, but the periods in which he is subject to the commands of others are relieved by other periods in which he is the dispenser of commands and orders.

Sublimation, on the other hand, has more effect on the officer. It is doubtful how far the honour and welfare of the regiment or other unit appeals to the private soldier in general, though it is perhaps almost, if not quite, as definite among the non-commissioned as among the commissioned officers of the old army. In [p. 218] the new army, it probably means little or nothing to the ordinary soldier, in whose case any sublimation due to military training has its source in comradeship or in his feeling of respect and duty towards his officers, and especially towards either his platoon- or company-commander. It is because the aggregate with which he acts is composed of men with whom he has shared hardships and dangers with many of whom he has become comrade and friend, that this aggregate comes to have an influence upon him, while in other cases the relation towards his officer is more important. In each case, however, the result is the production of a state of dependence which works in the same direction as the factor of suggestibility already considered. The point of especial importance in relation to the incidence of neurosis is that the fact of comradeship to some extent, and far more the state of dependence on his officer, diminish the sentiment of responsibility and thus tend to enhance suggestibility or, perhaps more correctly, work in the same direction as suggestibility. In the case of the officer, on the other hand, the relation towards his men brings with it responsibilities which are perhaps more potent than any other element of his experience in determining the form taken by his nervous disorder, if he should break down. It is these responsibilities and other conditions associated with them which lead to his being so especially prone to suffer from the state of anxiety-neurosis.

The third main factor, repression, is very important in relation to the incidence of different forms of neurosis in officers and men. The officer is driven by his position to repress the expression of emotion far more persistently than the private soldier. It is the special duty of the junior officer to set an example in this respect to his men, to encourage those who show signs of giving way. In the proper performance of this duty, it is essential that the officer shall appear calm and unconcerned in the midst of danger. The difficulty of keeping up this appearance after long-continued strain or after some shock of warfare has lessened the power of control, produces a state of persistent anxiety which is the most frequent and potent factor in the [p. 219] production of neurosis, and is especially important in determining the special form it takes. The private soldier has to think only or chiefly of himself; he has not to bear with him continually the thought that the lives of forty or fifty men are immediately, and of many more remotely, dependent on his success in controlling any expression of fear or apprehension.

A factor of minor importance, but one which is nevertheless worth mentioning here, is that the officer is less free to employ instruments by which the Tommy finds a safety valve for repressed emotion.

The preceding argument has led us to the conclusions that of the three main agencies upon which the success of military training depends, one, suggestion, is especially potent and prominent in the case of the private, while the other two, sublimation and repression, have by far the greatest effect in the case of the officer. One of the chief results of military training is to increase the suggestibility of the private, and this increased tendency in one direction is but little counteracted by sublimation or complicated by the necessity for vigorous repression. The factor of sublimation may even tend to enhance his dependence and suggestibility. In the case of the officer, any increase of suggestibility produced by his training is largely compensated by the necessity for individual and spontaneous action, while the esprit de corps and other means of sublimation only tend in many cases to heighten his sense of responsibility and thus add still another cause for his anxieties. There are many officers, both commissioned and non-commissioned, to whom the honour of the regiment or battalion is quite as potent as responsibility for the lives of others' in producing the state of anxiety which forms the essential element in the production of their neurosis.

I have now considered how far the different forms of war-neurosis can be traced to the influence of military training and the nature of military duties. It is gradually becoming apparent, however, that the conditions of military training and active service are very far from exhausting the factors by which war-neurosis [p. 220] is produced. A large part, perhaps even a majority of the prolonged cases of functional nervous disorders which fill our hospitals, can be traced directly to circumstances which have come into being after some shock, illness, or perhaps only the ordinary process of leave, has removed the soldier from the actual scene of warfare. I have now to inquire how far the influence of military training and the nature of military duties assist in producing the neurosis of the hospital and the home.

Histories of cases of war-neurosis show that officers after some shock or illness often suffer for a time from those symptoms which I have ascribed to suggestion, but whether owing to treatment or spontaneous change, these symptoms soon disappear. It may be that the failure to be content with a simple but crude solution of a conflict which satisfies the private soldier is due to superior education, but the nature of his training and duties also contribute to this result. If the disability were the unwitting outcome of a conflict between the instinct of self-preservation and a simple conception of military duty, it might suffice to be paralysed or mute, but if the morbid state depends primarily upon sentiments of responsibility towards his military unit or his comrades, such a solution is not likely to satisfy his nature long. His conflict differs from that of the private soldier in that it is founded largely upon acquired experience rather than upon instinctive trends. It is more actively conscious than the process which has produced a paralysis or mutism. These disabilities fail altogether to touch the special anxieties which have taken the foremost place in the production of his illness.

In the state of weakened volition produced by shock or exhaustion it seems to the officer impossible that he will ever again be able to exert the vigour of control and initiative which alone enabled him to maintain the upper hand in the conflict of the trenches, and with this realisation, the former conflict is replaced by one still more painful and enervating, in which sentiments of duty struggle ineffectually against a conviction of unfitness.

In this conflict military training and duty take a most [p. 221] important place. There are many officers whose conflict would be solved, or would never have existed, if it were merely a matter of personal safety. It is the knowledge, born of long experience, that the honour of their military unit and the safety of their comrades depend on their efficiency which forms by far the most potent factor in the production or maintenance of anxiety states. To the private soldier, devoid of such responsibilities, the mere solicitude about his safety forms a less potent motive for conflict, and one which is more easily solved. Once the disability due to suggestion has disappeared spontaneously or by treatment, there may be no obvious conflict left. The instinct of self-preservation, to which his disability has been essentially due, will of course still be there ready to reassert itself if the occasion arise, but any conscious conflict is so readily solved in accordance with obvious standards of social conduct that there is no opening for the occurrence of a state of anxiety sufficiently profound to act as the basis of neurosis.

The conclusion reached in the preceding pages is that the private soldier is especially apt to succumb to that form of neurosis which closely resembles the effects produced by hypnotism or other form of suggestion, because his military training has been of a kind to enhance his suggestibility. The officer, on the other hand, is less prone to this form of neurosis and falls a victim to it only when there is some organic injury which acts as a continuous source of suggestion. On the other hand the officer is especially liable to anxiety-neurosis, because the nature of his duties especially puts him into positions of responsibility which produce or accentuate mental conflicts set up by repression, thus producing states of anxiety, the form taken by his nervous disorder. It will now be well to inquire whether this relation of military training and duties to the form of neurosis points the way to any practical conclusions. Several aspects may be considered here: nomenclature, prophylaxis, and treatment.

The nomenclature of functional nervous disorders is at present in a very unsatisfactory state. Cases of paralysis, contracture, anæsthesia or convulsive seizures, which provide the most striking [p. 222] manifestations of functional nervous disorder, were once universally known under the name of hysteria, because they seemed to be- especially apt to affect women. The words "hysteria" and "hysterical" acquired a meaning which made their use inconvenient for many purposes, and they were gradually replaced in practice by the term "functional," at any rate in this country. This term, however, has so wide an application as to make it of little scientific or practical value. Used originally as a means of avoiding the word "hysteria" it has become a label for a large number of morbid states differing widely from one another in nature, and calling for very different forms of treatment.

Another functional syndrome which is widely recognised is neurasthenia. Even before the war, however, this term was being used in so wide a sense that it was becoming every year of less value, and it has now lost the last remnants of ally scientific value it once possessed by its adoption as the official designation of the army for all forms of functional nervous disorder. A third term, psychasthenia, has been used in most textbooks of medicine, but in a very unsatisfactory sense. The cases usually called neurasthenia present signs of mental as well as of bodily enfeeblement, and if the term "psychasthenia" had been used for those cases in which mental exhaustion is especially prominent, there might have been some sense in its use. The term has been used, however, for cases of obsession, phobia and compulsion in which there is often no sign of general mental exhaustion, cases differing from the so-called neurasthenia in the special direction taken by mental energy rather than in any defect in its amount. All the old terms being thus unsatisfactory for one reason or another, it becomes necessary to find a wholly new nomenclature.

Babinski[6] has recently proposed pithiatism, a word derived from the Greek term for persuasion, as a substitute for hysteria. This term has been especially chosen to distinguish the cases formerly called hysteria from other similar states on which persuasion [p. 223] has no effect. Babinski has been influenced in his choice of the word by the need for a term to distinguish functional from organic paralyses, especially from the reflex, paralysis in which Babinski is especially interested. Through this special interest he has been led to ignore the large group of functional nervous disorders which are especially open to the influence of persuasion, but yet differ fundamentally in nature from the cases which the term pithiatism is especially intended to denote. It is also unusual, and hardly satisfactory, to denote a disease on the basis of a feature of its therapy. It will be much more satisfactory if it is possible to find a term based on the ætiological rather than the therapeutical aspect of the syndrome.

One term of this kind which has been used by Freud and his followers is "conversion-neurosis," The use of this term is based on a definite theory, according to which the paralysis or other affection is held to be the outward manifestation of some underlying unconscious tendency which thus finds a more or less dramatic expression. The paralysis, contracture or convulsive seizure is regarded as the product of a process of conversion whereby the energy of some unconscious process is transformed into, and finds expression in, one or more of these symptoms. Partly because the term implies a theory which all will not be ready to accept, but still more because there are other pathological states to which the term would be equally appropriate, it is improbable that this term will find general acceptance. Since it is generally conceded that these functional paralyses, contractures and other manifestations closely resemble, if they be not identical with, the products of suggestion, it would seem that suggestion-neurosis[7] might be an appropriate term. If I am right in my view that the special prevalence of these states in the private soldier is due to his enhanced suggestibility, this term becomes still more appropriate. The term has the advantage that its meaning is at once obvious and does not require recourse to the dictionary. Suggestion, being a common English [p. 224] word, is very unlikely to acquire the inconvenient associations which have become attached to hysteria. Suggestion-neurosis not only carries its meaning on the surface, but this meaning is one which points directly to an essential feature of the state it denotes.

For the other chief form of functional nervous disorder no more appropriate term can be found than that which I have used in this report. The meaning of anxiety-neurosis is also at once apparent. It indicates in direct fashion that anxiety is both the main factor in causation and at the same time one of the leading symptoms. The only disadvantage of the term is that it has been used by Freud and his followers in a somewhat narrower sense than that given to it in this report and in the work of MacCurdy[8] and other writers on war-neurosis. The Freudian usage has, however, had so little effect on the general body of medical practice that this disadvantage is not very great, and the usage now proposed only involves such widening of the connotation of the term as we might expect to be the result of the experience derived from the war.

Anxiety-neurosis is so often accompanied by repression, and so many of its symptoms can be ascribed to this ætiological factor, that repression-neurosis might seem to afford an alternative term. There are, however, many cases of anxiety-neurosis in which repression is not present or is of little importance. In many cases even the opposed process of dwelling too exclusively on the causes of anxiety is in action, so that the use of repression-neurosis would make still another term necessary. It will therefore be more convenient to speak of anxiety-neurosis with or without repression, although in some cases repression is so prominent as to make repression-neurosis a useful term. If-this term is used, however, it must be remembered that the state denoted is only one variety of anxiety-neurosis.

If there is any truth in the foregoing scheme of the influence of military training and duties in the production of the different forms of war-neurosis, it is evident that much might be done in [p. 225] the way of prevention. If the special tendency of the private soldier to suffer from suggestion-neurosis is due to the effect of military training in heightening his suggestibility, it will follow that this training should be carefully reviewed with the aim of modifying those of its features which tend especially to produce this result. It is probable that the necessary changes would correspond closely with those already made necessary by the nature of modern warfare. The encouragement of independence and the less mechanical training which is following the multiplication of the means of warfare should have as one of their consequences a lessening of the tendency to heighten suggestibility, and should therefore diminish the occurrence of suggestion-neurosis.

Much could be done in the prevention of anxiety-neurosis if the commanding officer and the battalion medical officer were alive to the conditions upon which this state depends. If they worked together to utilise this knowledge, many a young subaltern and non-commissioned officer would be saved during the early stages of his disorder by rest or appropriate change of occupation and brought back to health and peace of mind. Such measures are adopted at the present time, but often not until anxiety has produced a state of obvious unfitness, so that the period of rest or change prescribed is quite inadequate to restore stability. If the nature and causation of anxiety-neurosis were more fully understood, it would be possible to intervene at an earlier stage and save many a valuable career, for the victims of this form of neurosis often suffer through excess of zeal and too heavy a sense of responsibility and are likely to be the most valuable officers.

Another line in which much might be done towards the prevention of anxiety-neurosis is suggested by the part which repression takes in the production of this state. If the soldier were taught the dangers of repression from the outset of his postpone a breakdown to make it far more severe whenever it comes. The influence of repression in the production and maintenance of anxiety-neurosis suggests that from the beginning [p. 226] of his training the soldier should be encouraged boldly to face in imagination the dangers and horrors which lie before him. A most successful officer has told me how in the early days of the war he encouraged his men to "think horribly," to accustom themselves in imagination to the utmost rigours and horrors of warfare, with the result that they were highly successful in bearing the exceptional trials of the Gallipoli campaign. It is difficult to gauge how far this success was due to the course advised and how far to other conditions arising out of the personality of the officer who advised it, but the experience suggests that much might be done in this direction. We can at least be sure that a soldier who steadfastly refuses to face in imagination the trials that lie before him is very unlikely to cope successfully with the reality. Many of those who pass unscathed through modern warfare do so because of the sluggishness of their imaginations, but if imagination is active and powerful, it is probably far better to allow it to play around the trials and dangers of warfare than to carry out a prolonged system of repression by which morbid energy may be stored so as to form a kind of dump ready to explode on the occurrence of some mental shock or bodily illness.

If the argument of this report is sound, that the cases of functional nervous disorder hitherto labelled hysteria are largely due to suggestion and depend on the enhanced suggestibility of the private soldier, it might seem at first sight the obvious course to make use of this heightened suggestibility in the treatment, and to use suggestion, either with or without the production of hypnotic state. If, however, suggestion be used in the ordinary crude way to remove symptoms, this line of treatment will only tend still further to heighten the suggestibility of the patient and to increase the tendency to similar disorders whenever he returns to the field. If at the time that the symptoms are removed, suggestions are given against the occurrence of similar disabilities in the future, more could be said for this line of treatment, but this of course would not affect the heightened suggestibility which is the root of the evil.

The argument of this report points rather to a course in [p. 227] which treatment should be directed to lessen the suggestibility by a process of re-education. This process should be so designed as to make the soldier understand the nature of the disorder which has afflicted him. He should be made to realise the essentially mental basis of his trouble and be thus put into a position in which, even if the disability recurs, he will not long be satisfied with it as a solution of the situation. This line of treatment has the disadvantage that it sometimes succeeds in doing away with the paralysis or other symptoms only to replace the physical disability by a state of anxiety; but a soldier in whom the conflict between the instinct of self-preservation and duty is so pronounced as to lead to this result is very unlikely to show any more real success if treated by suggestion. Here, however, as in so many other departments of psychotherapy in connection with the war, we are hampered by our almost total ignorance concerning the after-history of soldiers who have been subjected to different modes of treatment. It is possible that there are sufferers from suggestion-neurosis who are capable of long and valuable service if the symptoms due to suggestion are treated by means similar to those by which they have been produced.

In cases of anxiety-neurosis the lines of causation considered in this report offer less help in treatment than in prevention. The knowledge of the process by which his state has been produced often greatly helps a patient, especially in removing or diminishing depression, or even shame, consequent upon failure. If he can be brought to see that his illness is the outcome of definite agencies over which he has had no control, or has been due to excess rather than defect in certain good qualities, the symptoms may be greatly relieved and the patient set upon a path which, if the exigencies of military service allow, may enable him again to perform his military duties. The knowledge of causation set forth in this report is useful in thus providing a groundwork for the process of re-education.

Footnotes

[1] A report to the Medical Research Committee, London. Published in Mental Hygiene,

vol. ii, No. 4, pp. 513-533, October 1918.

[2] Among other possible conditions, those arising out of the influence of heredity should not be neglected.

[3] Another process or agency which might be considered here is imitation, but this process is probably only important in military training in so far as it depends upon suggestion.

[4] Ferenczi (see Contributions to Psycho-Analysis, Boston Badger, 1916, p. 58) has incidentally alluded to the similarity between he command of an officer and the suggestion of a hypnotist. He records how during his military service he saw an infantryman instantaneously fall asleep at his lieutenant's command.

[5] See Appendix III.

[6] See J. Babinski - and J. Froment, Hysteria or Pithiatism, and Reflex Nervous Disorders. London: University of London Press, 1918.

[7] I leave this proposal in the text of this Appendix, though I prefer the term "substitution-neurosis," founded on the pathology of the state which I have put forward in Chapter XVI.

[8] War Neuroses, Cambridge, 1918.

According to Freud, the unconscious is guarded by an entity working within the region of the unconscious, upon which it exerts a controlling and selective action. It checks those elements of unconscious experience which by their unpleasant nature would disturb their possessor if they were allowed to reach his consciousness, and if it permits these to pass, sees that they- appear in such a guise that their nature will not be recognised.

In sleep, according to Freud, this censorship allows much to reach the sleeping consciousness, but as a rule distorts it so that it appears only in a symbolic form and with so apparently meaningless a character that the comfort of the sleeper is not affected. Or, the process may perhaps be more correctly expressed as a selective action which only allows experience to pass when it has assumed this guise.

In the waking state the censorship is held to be even more active, or rather more efficient. It only allows unconscious experience to escape in the form of slips of the tongue or pen or to show its influence in apparently motiveless acts which, owing to the complete failure of the agent to recognise their nature, in no way interfere with the efficiency of the censorship.

There is no question that this concept of a censorship, acting as a guardian of a person against such elements of unconscious experience as would disturb the harmony of his life, is one which helps us to understand many of the more mysterious aspects of the mind. Such a process of censorship would account for a number of experiences which at first sight seem so strange and [p. 229] irrational that most students have been content to regard them as the products of chance, and as altogether inexplicable. It is only his thoroughgoing belief in determinism as applied to the sphere of mind which has not allowed Freud to be content with such explanation, or negation of explanation, and has led him to his concept of the censorship.

There are many, however, prepared to go far with Freud in their adherence to his scheme of psychology, who yet find it difficult to accept a concept which involves the working within the unconscious of an agency so wholly in the pattern of the conscious as is the case with Freud's censorship. The concept is based on analogy with a highly complex and specialised social institution, the endopsychic censorship being supposed to act in the same way as the official whose business it is to control the press and allow nothing to reach the community which will, in his opinion, disturb the harmony of its existence.

It would be more satisfactory if the controlling agency which the facts need could be expressed in some other form; Since the process which has to be explained takes place within the region of unconscious experience, or at least on its confines, we might expect to find the appropriate mode of expression in a physiological rather than a sociological parallel. It is to physiology rather than to sociology that we should look for the clue to the nature of the process by which a person is guarded from such elements of his unconscious experience as might disturb the harmony of his existence.

It is now generally admitted that the nervous system, in so far as function is concerned, is arranged in a number of levels, one above another, forming a hierarchy in which each level controls those beneath it and is itself controlled by those above. If we assume a similar organisation of unconscious experience, we should have a number of levels in which experience belonging to adult life would occupy a position higher than that taken by the experience of youth, and this again would stand above the experience of childhood and infancy. A level of more recently acquired experience would control one going back to an earlier period of life, and any intermediate level would central and be [p. 230] controlled according to its place in the time-order in which it came into existence.

Moreover, the levels would not merely differ in the nature of the material of which they are composed, the lowest level[1] being a storehouse of the experience of infancy, the next of the experience of childhood, and so on.[2] Much more important would be that character of the hierarchy according to which each level preserves in its mode of action the characteristics of the mentality in which it has its origin. Thus, the level of infamy would preserve the infantile methods of feeling, thinking and acting, and when this level became active in sleeping or waking life, its manifestations would take the special form characteristic of infancy. Similarly, the level recording the forgotten experience of youth would, when it found expression, reveal any special modes of mentality which belong to youth.

I have now to inquire how far this concept that higher levels of adult experience, acting according to the manner of adult life, control lower levels of infantile and youthful experience, acting according to the manner of infancy and youth, is capable of forming the basis of a scheme by means of which we may explain those facts of the sleeping and waking life which Freud refers to the action of his endopsychic censorship.

I will begin by considering dreams, the special form in which experience becomes manifest in sleep. There is much reason to believe that the dream has, the characters of infancy; not so much that its material is derived from the experience of infancy, but rather that any experience which finds expression, in the dream is moulded according to the forms of feeling, thought and action proper to infancy. This character of the dream finds a natural explanation if its appearance in consciousness is simply-due to the removal in sleep of higher controlling levels, so that the lower levels with their infantile modes of expression [p. 231] come to the surface and are allowed to manifest themselves in their natural guise. The phantastic and irrational character of the dream would not be due to any elaborate process of distortion, carried out by all agency partaking of a demonic character. It would be rather the direct consequence of the coming into activity of modes of behaviour which in the ordinary state me held in check by levels embodying the experience of later life.

It will be well at this stage of the argument to state as exactly as possible how the view I now put forward differs from that of Freud. This writer supposes that his "censorship" is a process which has come into being as a means of protecting a sleeper from influences which would awake him. So far as I understand Freud, the distortion of the latent content of the dream is a result of the activity of the censorship. It is a transformation designed to elude this activity. I suppose, on the other hand, that the form in which the latent content of the dream manifests itself depends on something inherent in the experience which forms this latent content or inherent in the mode of activity by which it is expressed. If the controlling influences derived from the experience of later life are removed, the experience finding expression in the dream must take the form proper to it, and would do so quite regardless of its influence upon the comfort .f the sleeper and the duration of his sleep. I do not deny that the infantile form in which unconscious or subconscious experience reveals itself in dreams may be useful in promoting or maintaining sleep, But if there be such utility, it is a secondary aspect of the process. It is even possible that this protective and defensive function may be a factor which has assisted the survival of the dream as a feature of mental activity, but the character of the dream is primarily the result of the way in which the mind has been built up. It is a consequence of the fact that early modes of mental functioning have not been scrapped when more efficient modes have come into existence, but have been utilised in so far as they are of service, and suppressed in so far as they are useless.[3] suppose[sic] that the general mode in which the mind has developed is of the same order as that now generally acknowledged to have characterised the development of the nervous system, and that the special character of the dream is the direct result of that mode of development. As a by-product of this special development the dream may have acquired a useful function in protecting the sleeper from experience by which he would be disturbed, but in his concept of the censorship, Freud has unduly emphasised this Protective function. His view of the endopsychic censorship with its highly anthropomorphic colouring tends to obscure the essential character of the dream as a product of a general principle of the development of mind.

I can now pass to other activities ascribed to the censorship by Freud. The phenomena of the waking life which need consideration are of two chief kinds. First, slips of the tongue or pen, apparently inexplicable examples of forgetting, and other similar processes which have been considered by Freud in his book on The Psychopathology of Everyday Life. The other group which needs explanation is made up of those definitely pathological processes which occur in the psycho-neuroses, for the explanation of which Freud has called upon his concept of the censorship.

I propose on this occasion to accept, without discussion, Freud's view that much processes as slips of the tongue or pen are the expression of tendencies lying beneath the ordinary level of waking consciousness. My object is not to dispute this part of his scheme of the unconscious, but to inquire whether such a scheme as I have suggested may not explain these slips in a way more satisfactory than one according to which they occur, owing to momentary lapses of vigilance on the part of a guard an watching at the threshold of consciousness.

The special character of slips of the tongue or pen is that a word which would be appropriate as the expression of some unconscious or subconscious trend of thought intrudes into a sentence expressing a thought with which it has no obvious connection, thus producing an irrational and nonsensical character similar to that of the dream. If it is true, and that it is so [p. 233] seems to me to stand beyond all doubt, that underlying orderly and logical trains of thought which make up our manifest consciousness, there are systems of organised experience embodying early phases of thought, and still earlier mental constructions which hardly deserve the name of thought, it is necessary that these lower strata should be held in some kind of check. Consistent thought and action would be impossible if there were continual and open conflict between the latest developments of our thought and earlier phases, phases, for instance, belonging to a time when, through the influence of parents and teachers, opinions were held directly contrary to those reached by the individual experience of later life. The earlier systems may and do influence the later thoughts, but the orderly expression of these later thoughts in speech, spoken or written, would be impossible unless the earlier systems were under some sort of control.

In so far as they are explicable on Freudian lines, slips of the tongue or pen seem to depend on two main factors; one, the excitation in some way of the suppressed or repressed body of experience which finds expression in the slip; the other, weakening of control by fatigue or impaired health of the speaker or writer. A suppressed body of experience ("complex") is especially, or perhaps only, liable to intrude into the speech by which other thoughts are being expressed when there has been some recent experience tending to call into activity the buried memory, while this expression is definitely assisted by weakening of the inhibiting factors due to fatigue or illness.

Such a process is perfectly natural as a simple failure of balance between controlled and controlling systems of experience, the temporary success of the controlled system being due either to increase of its activity, or weakening of the controlling forces, or both combined. It is not so clear that it accords with the protective influence ascribed by Freud to the censorship. The slips of tongue or pen may be quite as trying and annoying as the suppressed experience out of which they arise. There is no such useful function as the guardianship of sleep, which is ascribed by Freud to the censorship of the dream. [p. 234]

Another kind of experience fits better with Freud's concept of the censorship. The forgetting of experience when it is unpleasant or is a condition of some dreaded activity, of which such striking examples have been given by Freud,[4] definitely protects the comfort, at any rate the immediate comfort, of the person who forgets. The examples seem capable of explanation by the concept of a guardian watching at -the threshold of consciousness. At the same time they are not immediately explicable as a result of a mechanism by which more lately acquired control more ancient; systems of experience. They seem to involve a definite activity on the part of the controlling mechanism, which is not inaptly designated by the simile of a censorship. In the case of the dream I have pointed out that, if the scheme I propose be a true expression of the facts, we should expect that the controlling factors would sometimes acquire a useful function. This useful function need not be inherent in the process of development which brought the mechanism of control into existence. Just as there are certain features of the dream and certain kinds of dream which lend definite support to Freud's concept of the censorship, so the forgetting of experience which would lead to unpleasant action is a phenomenon which might be explained by the activity of a process similar to a censorship. Such a concept as that of the censorship, however, should explain and bring into relation with one another all the facts. If it only explains some of the facts, it becomes probable that the process of censorship is a secondary process, a later addition to one which has a more deeply-seated origin.

The other group of phenomena of the waking life, for the explanation of which Freud has had recourse to the concept of the censorship, consists of the psycho-neuroses, and especially that characterised by the mimetic representation of morbid states which is generally known as hysteria. A sufferer from this disease is one who, being troubled by some mental conflict, finds relief in a situation where the conflict is solved by the occurrence of some disability, such as paralysis, contracture, or [p. 235] mutism, a disability which makes it impossible for him to perform acts which a more healthy solution of his conflict would involve. The mimetic character of hysteria is definite, and the school of Freud has recognised the resemblance of the pathological process underlying it to the dramatisation and symbolisation of the dream. The disease is regarded as a means of manifesting motives belonging to the unconscious in such a manner that the sufferer does not recognise their nature and is content with the solution of the difficulty which the hysterical symptoms provide. According to Freud, the rôle of the censorship in this case is to distort the process by which the unconscious or subconscious manifests itself so that its nature shall not be recognised by the patient. This process is so successful that as a rule the patient not only succeeds in deceiving himself, but also those with whom he is associated. On the lines suggested in this paper, the concept of a censorship is in this case even less appropriate than it might seem to be in the case of the dream. The hysterical disability is amply explained by a process in which the higher levels are put in abeyance so that the lower levels are enabled to find expression. The state out of which the hysterical symptoms arise is one in which there is a conflict between a higher and more recently developed set of motives, which may be summed up under the heading of duty, and a lower and earlier set of motives provided by instinctive tendencies, The solution of the conflict reached by the hysteric is one in which the upper levels go out of action, while the lower levels find expression in that mimetic or symbolic form which is natural to the infantile stages of human development, whether individual or collective. The hysteric is satisfied with a mimetic representation as refuge from his conflict, just as the child or the savage is content with a mimetic representation of some wish which fulfils for him all the purposes of reality.

The infantile character of the process is still apparent if we turn to the process by which the higher levels of experience pass into abeyance. It is generally recognised that the abrogation of control which takes place in hysteria is closely connected with [p. 236] the process of suggestion. We know little of the nature of this process of suggestion, but there is reason to believe that it is one which takes a most important place in the earlier stages of mental development. If existing savage peoples afford any index of primitive mentality, this conclusion receives strong support, for among them the power of suggestion is so strong that it goes far beyond the production of paralyses, mutisms and anæsthesias, and is capable of producing the supreme disability of death.

This susceptibility to suggestion is to be connected with the gregariousness of Man in the early stages of the development of human culture. If animals are to act together as a body, it is essential that they shall possess some kind of instinct which makes them especially responsive to the influence of one another, one which will lead to the rapid adoption of any line of conduct which a prominent member of the group may take. In the presence of any emergency, it is essential that each member of a group shall be capable of losing at once the, conative tendencies set up by his individual appetites, and shall wholly subordinate these to the immediate needs of the group. Animals possessing this power by which the higher and more lately developed tendencies are inhibited by the collective needs set up by danger will naturally survive in the struggle for existence. If, as there can be little doubt, Man in the earlier stages of his cultural development was such an animal, we have an ample motive for his suggestibility, and for the greater strength of this character in the earlier levels of experience. According to-this point of view hysteria is the coming into activity of an early form of reaction to a dangerous or difficult situation. The protection against the danger or difficulty so provided is the direct consequence of the nature of the early form of reaction, and the concept of a censorship making it necessary that the manifestations shall take this form is artificial aid unnecessary.

The argument thus far set forth is that the phenomena, both of waking and- sleeping experience, which have led Freud to his concept of the censorship are explicable as the result of [p. 237] an arrangement of mental levels exactly comparable with that now generally recognised to exist in the nervous system, an arrangement by which more recently developed or acquired systems control the more ancient. The special characters of the manifestations which Freud has explained by his concept of his censorship have been regarded as inherent in the experience which finds expression when the more recently acquired and controlling factors have been weakened or removed.

The concept which I here put forward in place of the Freudian censorship is borrowed from the physiology of the nervous system. I propose now to consider briefly some facts usually regarded as strictly neurological and to discuss how they fit ill with the two concepts. In the case of the nervous system two chief classes of failure of control can be recognised -- one occasional and the other more or less persistent, at any rate for considerable periods. If the relations between the conscious and the unconscious are of the same order as those existing between the higher and lower levels of the nervous system, we may expect to find manifestations of nervous activity similar to those which Freud explains by his concept of the censorship.

Good examples of occasional lapses of control in the sphere of motor activity are provided by false strokes in work or play. The craftsman who makes a false stroke with his chisel or hammer, or the billiard player who misses his stroke, show examples of behaviour strictly comparable with slips of tongue or pen. From the point of view put forward in this paper, both kinds of occurrence are due to the failure of a highly complex and delicately balanced adjustment between controlling and controlled processes. If we could go into the causes of false strokes in work or play, we should doubtless find that each has its antecedents, and that the false stroke often has a more or less definite meaning and is the expression of some trend which does not lie on the surface. Such occurrences are readily explicable as failures of adjustment due either to weakening of control or disturbances in the controlled tendencies to movement. In the vast majority of cases, however, [p. 238] it would be very difficult, if not impossible, to force these into a scheme by which they rue due to the activity of a guardian who allows or encourages the occurrence of the false stroke in order to cover and disguise some more discomforting experience.

A definitely morbid disorder of movement, which may be taken as an example of the more persistent class of failures in control, is that known as tic, a spasmodic movement having a more or less purposive character. This disorder is definitely due to a weakening of-nervous control, and is most naturally explained as a dramatisation of some instinctive tendency called into action by a shock or strain. Thus, the ties of sufferers from war-neurosis may be regarded as symbols or dramatisations of some tendency which would be called into activity by danger, and the movements me often of such a kind as would avert or minimise the danger. The concept of a censorship is here not only unnecessary, but quite inappropriate. The form taken by the tic is that natural to an instinctive movement, but the tic depends essentially on weakening of the controlling forces normally in action. Its existence like that of hysteria, or perhaps more correctly like that of other hysterical manifestations, may act, or seem to the patient to act, as a protection against prospective danger or discomfort, but it is probable that such a function is secondary. It is an example of the utilisation by the organism of a reaction, the nature of which is determined by instinctive tendencies, and in no we requires the concept of a guardian watching at the threshold of consciousness, or at the threshold of activities normally associated with consciousness.

I will conclude this paper by considering how far the process which I propose to substitute for Freud's censorship has any parallels in human culture, for since the control of one level by another runs through the whole activity of the nervous system as well as through the whole of experience, we should expect to find it exemplified both in civilised and savage culture.

Every kind of human society reveals a hierarchical arrangement in which higher ranks control the lower, and inhibit or [p. 239] suppress activities belonging to earlier phases of culture. In certain cases this process of control includes the activity of a censorship by which activities seeking to find expression are consciously and deliberately held in check or suppressed. But this process of censorship forms only a very small part of the total mass of inhibiting forces by which more recently developed social groups control tendencies belonging to an older social order. When in time of stress the control exerted by more recent developments of social activity is weakened, the earlier levels reveal themselves in symbolic forms, well exemplified by the Sansculottism of the French Revolution and the red flag of the present day, but these symbolic or dramatic forms of expression are not in any way due to the activity of a censorship. They are rather manifestations characteristic of early forms of thought by means of which repressed tendencies find expression when the control of higher social levels is removed. They are not distortions produced or even allowed by the social censorship, but are manifestations proper to early forms of mental activity which occur in direct opposition to the censorship. Censorship is a wholly inappropriate expression for the social processes corresponding most closely with the features of dream or disease for the explanation of which this social metaphor has been used by Freud.

In a lecture on "Dreams and Primitive Culture"[5] I have described certain aspects of rude society which seem to show modes of social behaviour very similar to those qualities of the dream which Freud explains by the action of a censorship. I now suggest that these, like the censorship of civilised peoples, are not necessary products of social activity, something inherent in the social order, but are special developments. They seem to be specialised forms taken by the general process of control in order to meet special needs. It has been seen that the concept of an endopsychic censorship is capable of explaining certain more or less morbid occurrences in the waking life. A good case could be made for the view that [p. 240] the social censorship has in it something of the morbid, and that its existence points to something unhealthy in the social order. Whether it be the censorship of the Press of highly civilised societies, or the disguise of the truth found in the ritual of a Melanesian secret fraternity, the processes of suppression and distortion point to some fault in the social order, to some interference with the harmony and unity which should characterise the acts of a perfectly organised society.

Footnotes

[1] I leave on one side for the present the possibility that there may be a still lower level derived from inherited experience of the race. If there be such a level, we must suppose that this is controlled by the acquired experience of the individual.

[2] It must be noted that these levels, like those of the nervous system, are not discontinuous, but pass into one another by insensible gradations.

[3] Cf. Brit. Journ. Psych., vol. ix. (1918), p. 242.

[4] Psychopathology of Everyday Life.

[5] Manchester University Press, 1918. Reprinted from the Bulletin of the John Rylands Library, vol. iv. (1918), p. 387.

"WIND-UP"[1]

The expression "wind-up" was probably used originally for any state of mingled excitement and apprehension called into being by an unusual occurrence, and especially the prospect or actual presence of danger. It has, however, gradually come to be used in the army as a means of expressing fear in one or other of its forms, an expression by means of which a soldier will talk about fear without explicitly acknowledging the presence of this emotion. I propose here to use the word as a definite expression for fear.

Fear is the emotional or affective aspect of the instinctive process called into activity by danger. It is the modification of consciousness which accompanies certain instinctive forms of action in response to danger, and especially the response by flight. It is especially intense when there is interference with this or any other form of reaction to danger.

It is only in Man that we are able to study by means of introspection the various forms of fear. The first distinction to be made is between the emotional state or states accompanying the actual presence of danger and the various forms of fear which arise when there is only the prospect of danger, while in pathological states a large group of fears or states allied to fear occur independently of either actual or prospective danger.

Reaction to actual danger. -- The most frequent reaction to danger in Man is one of heightened capacity for the activities by which the danger may be met without any trace of the fear which, if present, would inevitably interfere with this capacity. A man in the presence of danger will carry but with the utmost coolness, and often with a degree of skill surpassing that which he usually shows, the measures necessary for the aversion of the [p. 242] danger or his escape from it. In such a case there is complete suppression of the emotion of fear which the danger might be expected to produce, and this suppression is nearly always accompanied by suppression of pain, so that an injury the dangerous object, or from any other source, is not perceived.

A second mode of reaction is the assumption of an aggressive attitude towards the source of danger with the accompaniment of the affective state of anger. In this case there is not a simple suppression of fear, but its place is taken by another emotion belonging to the instinct of aggression. If these lines of action fail, if the serviceable activity which would lead to escape from the danger is interfered with or becomes impossible to carry out, or if the aggressive reaction does not succeed, fear supervenes as an accompaniment either of flight or of the collapse which is apt to occur when the more normal and serviceable reactions fail. In some cases, however, the suppression of fear is so well established that this emotion remains completely absent even when the danger is so insistent and unavoidable that death or violent injury is inevitable. Thus, the emotion of fear may be completely absent during the fall and crash of an aeroplane in which death seems certain, being replaced by an interest such as might be taken by the mere witness of a spectacle, or by some apparently trivial line of thought. It is when some line of action is still possible, but this action is recognised to be fruitless and in vain, that fear, often in the acute form we call terror, is likely to supervene.

Reactions to prospective danger. -- The state most commonly produced by prospective danger is one of that degree of fear which we call apprehension. This may be so intense as to become indistinguishable from the fear which accompanies the actual presence of danger, but it is more usually a vague discomfort, with minor degrees of the tremor and muscular weakness which accompany fear.

This state of apprehension may occur, often in a relatively intense form, in men who become perfectly cool and collected as soon as the danger becomes actual, when the state of apprehension [p. 243] completely disappears so that there is no interference with the activity by which the danger may be averted The apprehension preceding the occurrence of danger is of exactly the same order as stage-fright or the fright preceding any other public performance, and just as the best actors and orators are liable to stage-fright, so may those who show the utmost coolness and bravery in the actual presence of danger be liable to apprehensions while the danger is still only in prospect.

In other cases the apprehensions at the prospect of danger are so acute, and so accompanied by physical manifestations which make appropriate action impossible, that the actual occurrence of danger only serves to bring about complete collapse.

Pathological fears. -- Fear is a very frequent accompaniment of pathological .states, and many of its more extreme forms only occur in adult Man as part of such states.

The most frequent form in which such intense fears arise is the nightmare or the night-terror of the half-waking state. These are especially characteristic of childhood, but they may occur in adult life in those who seem otherwise healthy, while they have recently become familiar as the most prominent symptom of states of anxiety arising out of the war.

Similar intense fears may occur in the first stage or following the administration of an anaesthetic, or attacks of terror may occur in the waking state as part of an anxiety-neurosis. Another pathological form taken by fear is shown by the various phobias, in each of which some special stimulus may arouse fear in one who otherwise may not know what fear means. The stimulus, which thus arouses fear, often in a very intense form, may be one which in other persons not only wholly fails to arouse this emotion, but may be a source of definite pleasure. Thus, a man who does not know fear in the presence of actual danger to life or limb, may suffer from acute fear at the sight of a cat or harmless snake, or an airman who is only stimulated by the utmost dangers of aerial warfare may suffer from acute apprehension in a lift or on a ladder only a few feet from the ground. These highly-specialised fears also occur in relation to definite sources of danger; thus, one who is undisturbed by most [p. 244] of the dangerous situations of warfare may have some special fear, whether of searchlights, sniping, or some special kind of shell.

Still another form of fear is the more or less persistent state of anxiety which forms so prominent a feature of the functional nervous disorder arising out of warfare that it has been adopted in the nomenclature of one of the most frequent forms taken by these disorders. In the healthy person anxiety is a state which comes into existence in consequence of some prospective misfortune or danger, but in morbid conditions it shows itself in the form of more or less continuous apprehension colouring the whole mental life, so that even the most ordinary occurrence are seen in the blackest light as sources of trouble or danger.

Suppression and repression in relation to fear. -- In the form of reaction to danger which seems to be characteristic of the normal healthy man, there is a complete absence of fear. No effort is needed to keep this emotion out of the mind for it shows no tendency to appear in consciousness. Fear in the presence of danger is, however, so necessary a part of the mental equipment of animals and is so frequently manifested in childhood, that we can confidently assume this emotion to be potentially present, but in a state of suppression. This assumption is supported by several lines of evidence. A man who when exposed to danger experiences no trace of fear, and behaves with the utmost coolness and bravery, may yet suffer: subsequently from acute fear in his dreams. If, as there is much reason to believe, suppressed affective states find expression in dreams owing to the weakening of control normally exerted in the waking state, the occurrence of fear in dreams following a dangerous experience would be a natural consequence of its ordinary existence in a state of suppression.

Still more important and conclusive is the occurrence of fear as the result of shock or long-continued strain and fatigue which lower the efficiency of the higher controlling levels of mental activity. Thus, one of the earliest signs of the strain of warfare is the occurrence of apprehensions in one who until then has passed through the dangers of warfare without fear. The [p. 245] occurrence of fear either manifestly, or in the form of vague apprehension lowered, when shock or strain had lowered efficiency is naturally explained if the fear has been there throughout, but in so complete a state of suppression that it never passed the threshold of consciousness.

When fear or apprehension begins to show itself in consciousness, a new process comes into action. The fear, no longer held unwittingly in check, has now to be voluntarily repressed. One who has down or fought without fear, perhaps for many months, finds himself the subject of apprehensions which he regards with shame and strives to banish from his mind. A short rest at such a time, by allowing the unwitting controlling process to regain the upper hand, will often bring about the disappearance of the apprehensions, so that danger can again be faced with equanimity and without the necessity for witting repression. Or, the lowered efficiency of the controlling forces may be temporary, and the recuperative power of the sufferer may be so great that recovery Of the normal state of suppression may come about, and witting repression again becomes unnecessary. More frequently, however, the voluntary repression of fears or apprehensions only adds to the strain and fatigue which has led to the failure of suppression. The fears become stronger and call for still stronger efforts of repression. Through the vicious circle thus set up there is produced a state of persistent anxiety in which even ordinary incidents of life, incidents wholly devoid of danger, come to be viewed with apprehension. The fears which are repressed with apparent success during the day find expression in an accentuated form at night, when the control exerted by day is removed in sleep or weakened in the state preceding or following sleep. The interference with rest so produced only serves to increase the state of strain and fatigue upon which the nightmares or disturbing night-thoughts depend, while disturbances of digestion or circulation secondary to the anxiety may react on and accentuate the state to which they are primarily due. Finally, some shock or additional strain, a slight accident which a few months before would only have raised a laugh, a misunderstanding with a superior officer, or [p. 246] some domestic trouble, will bring about a crisis and reduce the soldier to a state in which he becomes wholly unfit for any kind ;of duty. The morbid state which most frequently supervenes is that known as anxiety-neurosis, which is only an exaggeration of the morbid state of anxiety which preceded his definite breakdown. In other cases the trouble map find expression in some mimetic disability usually known as hysteria, while in those of psychopathic disposition, there may be complete mental collapse, or the unbearable situation may be solved by the occurrence of those false rationalisations we call delusions.

The special feature of practical importance in the foregoing statement of the various forms taken by the emotion of fear is that the occurrence of this emotion may be a symptom, often the earliest symptom, of a state of fatigue and strain. Owing to the way in which the society to which we belong, and especially those whose business it is to fight, look upon fear, its occurrence, especially without adequate cause, arouses other emotions, and especially that of shame, which greatly enhance the strain to which the fear is primarily due.

Treatment. -- It is evident that the state so produced is one which gives ample scope for treatment, both preventive and curative. There is no department of medicine in which a medical officer can gain results so definite as in the treatment of the early stages of the anxiety-neurosis of warfare. The earlier he can act the better, for the longer the state of anxiety is allowed to last, the greater the witting repression which becomes necessary, the longer is the period of rest which is required to enable the process of suppression to become again effective. Moreover, the occurrence of disturbances of circulation, of digestion, and of other organic functions may produce complications which greatly prolong the process of recovery. Nowhere is the adage more appropriate that "a stitch in time saves nine."

A medical officer can only hope to succeed if he is on such terms with those under his care that they are ready to give him their full confidence, for owing to the general sentiment regarding fear, it is only with the greatest reluctance that its. presence is acknowledged. It is here that the expression "wind-up" has [p. 247] its peculiar utility in that it enables one in whom strain is producing apprehensions to refer, half seriously, half humourously to his trouble. The first step in the treatment is to assure the patient that there is no cause for shame, that the fear he experiences is a well-recognised symptom of strain and is due to the temporary failure of the mechanism by which in the healthy and normal man fear is kept under adequate control. If sleep is already disturbed by dreams, a second line of treatment will be to induce the sufferer to give up the process of voluntary repression to which, in the vast majority of cases, these dreams are due. Having by this process of education put the patient on the road to recovery, a short rest followed perhaps by a period of limited duty, will usually restore him to his normal level of efficiency. To send him for a holiday without the necessary process of education and reassurauce is open to the serious risk that he will only continue during the holiday to repress or brood over his painful thoughts and feelings, with the result that the state of anxiety is accentuated and becomes a fixed habit.

In conclusion, it must be pointed out that this line of treatment only holds good for those in whom the occurrence of fear is clearly the result of shock or strain. Those who are naturally apprehensive require a different line of treatment. Their case is far more difficult and less hopeful than that in which fear is secondary to strain or shock, but much can be done with them by sympathetic encouragement in fighting their disability, and when possible, by introducing them gradually to the conditions which rouse their apprehensions. There is reason to believe that in some cases such apprehensions are the definite sequel to some emotional shock in childhood or youth which has set up faulty trends in feeling and behaviour. In such cases a thorough and sympathetic discussion of the history of their fears may be of great service, and may at least allow the medical officer to recognise how far the state is capable of amendment, whether there is a reasonable hope that the patient may acquire that state of suppression of fear which in his more fortunate comrades has come into existence in childhood.

THE END